INAPPROPRIATE
BEHAVIOUR

to Jan

Best wishes !

Brent

Published by Honeybee Books
www.honeybeebooks.co.uk

Printed in the UK using paper from sustainable sources

ISBN: 978-1-913675-06-6

INAPPROPRIATE BEHAVIOUR

A Novel

Brent Shore

Contents

Contents

And though you keep your actions hid,
Unyielding 'twixt the pull and push,
The surest sign of what you did
Is painted in betrayal's blush.

lines from *In Happier Times*
by Jonathan Steeples

CHAPTER 1

RUNAWAYS

DIMANCHE / *SUNDAY*

The woman was standing directly in front of Val in the checkout queue, ferreting in her handbag for her purse. A pair of collapsible camping chairs and an air mattress packed in a colourful cardboard box rested at the bottom of a cavernous shopping trolley by her side.

Val had looked at her twice as she approached the queue. The woman had faced her, just for an instant, looking over her shoulder, apprehensively, she thought. Then she looked away again, down at her bag, a large, sloppy, soft leather one in beige, decorated with beads and tassels of dark suede. They were standing near the exit in probably the largest shop in Saint-Benoît, even more expansive than the new Maxi-marché. It was a well-established business, Brico-Jacques, one of those places where you can buy handyman essentials, gardening equipment, camping accessories, in fact everything from roofing tar to bulk dog food. And Val was barely a metre from her, close enough to smell her perfume, a flowery Cacharel, which she recognised; perfume she had bought perhaps while waiting for the Eurostar. It was just a whimsical guess. Guessing at a little detail, on the assumption, however, that she was right about the important thing, *l'essentiel*. The woman's hair was shorter, and much darker, but the tilt of her face, the large, round, feline brown eyes, the sharp, pretty nose, the slight swelling of the lower lip – all served to convince her that she *was* the woman in the news, the fugitive from London, that she was indeed Amanda Elizabeth Ringer.

Val tried hard not to stare. Neither at her nor at her camping chairs, folded snug in long, grey canvas drawstring bags. The store was noisy, quite busy. It closed at midday on a Sunday, and there was a bustle of people anxious to choose their paint, find their strimmer cord, buy their barbecue coals in good time. A young man joined the queue behind her, carrying a large box of fertiliser. He was sweating through his tee-shirt. He offered a smile, which she returned. She was holding a multipack of batteries and for no reason felt a little self-conscious, a little stupid. *They're for our smoke alarms*, she thought to tell him, as an explanation, but decided there was absolutely no reason to. Nor did she speak to Amanda Ringer, who was now paying for her things. In cash. From a bundle of new twenty euro notes. As she fumbled with her change – the checkout girl's fault, really, all fingers and thumbs – Val spotted a set of car keys clipped to a ring sewn on the inside of her handbag: the fob had the familiar blue oval Ford emblem on it.

She heard her bring the perfunctory exchange to a conclusion in adequate French, and within seconds she was pushing the trolley away towards the wide glass doors, and it was Val's turn.

"*Bonjour, madame. Les piles, c'est tout?*"

"*Oui, c'est tout.*"

She paid, took her receipt, picked up the batteries and headed to the exit.

She lost sight of her for less than a minute. She was determined, excited even, to see where she went. She was in half a mind to stop her and speak to her. But what would she say? *Excuse me, madame. Aren't you Amanda Ringer? Aren't you the woman the police are looking for?*

She scoured the wide, sun-baked car park for her dark brown gamine hair and for a Ford with GB plates. There were several British cars, as it happened – not surprising in the town in summer – but no sign of Amanda Ringer lifting her camping chairs and airbed into the back of one. Val walked on, in the direction of her own Mégane. Vehicles were coming and going, braking and swerving to avoid customers pushing their cumbersome trolleys clumsily between the lanes. The English woman was nowhere to be seen. Then, suddenly, a squeal of brakes by the car-park exit drew her eyes in that direction: another small collision averted. A straw-haired teenage *caddie-boy*, a dopey weekend casual, had piloted a conga line of empty trolleys into the path of a 4x4 driven by a man on a short fuse. Beyond the gesticulations and soon-forgotten insults, disappearing along the road *outside* the car park, was the slim figure of the woman on foot, struggling with her cargo, but heading left, purposefully, out of town.

Val *had* to follow her.

She couldn't be going far on foot in the midday heat. Carrying a couple of folding chairs and an air mattress in a box. The campsite, of course – just a kilometre away, in the woods on the western edge of Saint-Benoît. Val threw the batteries into the car, but then decided to walk. Arriving at the campsite in a car would draw attention. On foot she could follow her in, at a distance, as if she were a fellow camper. She wanted to see exactly where she was heading. Where she was hiding. And, to be absolutely sure it was her, she needed to see her with Dean.

She kept a discreet fifty metres behind her for the ten minutes it took them to reach the shaded lane which lead directly down to the Camping des Deux Etangs. It was a large, popular camping ground, set among pine trees, whose pitches of caravans and tents reached out on a rough level to the exposed, sunlit banks of the river. Val knew that there was a bar here, frequented from time to time by locals as well as by tourists. She could follow her freely past reception, past the *mini-marché*, past the play area, right into the heart of the site. It seemed almost full of visitors and she blended in without difficulty. In her short summer dress, sandals and sunglasses she could be easily taken for a family member on holiday. In truth she had never set foot here before, but the layout was simple to navigate – even for someone with as poor a sense of direction as her – and with Amanda Ringer still in her eye line, for she was even surer than before that it was her, she sauntered in her wake, finding a picnic table to sit at just as her quarry paused ahead of her, dropping her bundle outside a pale blue tent.

She disappeared behind it, crouching, Val guessed, to unzip the door. She had pitched it to open out towards the river. From the porch she would have – *they* would have – a wide, unspoilt view of the Liselle and the fields bordering on the plantations rising on the opposite bank. The tent looked a little lost on its generous grassy pitch, flanked on either side by much larger tents with their expansive awnings and chunky cars. To the left a Dutch people-carrier. To the right a Mercedes estate, also Dutch. Further away groups of children were scampering about, a mother was folding clothes, a father peering into the open bonnet of his car, and somewhere a radio was playing pop music. But in this corner there was no sign of people. Val imagined she was unpacking the airbed, perhaps assembling the chairs in the tent's porch area.

Within moments she reappeared, wearing a black bikini top and a striped towel around her waist. Val followed her cautiously through a series of short avenues of tents towards a swimming pool. It was clearly a focal point of the site, especially on a hot day like this. She watched as Amanda Ringer pushed open the wooden gateway in the waist-high fencing that bordered the pool area, paddled through a shallow footbath, then, passing swimmers, splashers and squealers, strolled towards the random groupings of sun-loungers and multi-coloured deckchairs, mostly already occupied. Val loitered at the fence, suddenly uneasy about going any further. Absent-mindedly she read the signs by the little gate: *no smoking, no glasses, no food, no bermudas, no unsupervised children, no animals – have fun.*

Suddenly at the far side of the pool she noticed Dean Buckle emerging from a shower. He had spotted Amanda Ringer and was waving at her. What did he shout? *Mandy?* At that distance and among the laughter and the hubbub his voice was unclear. He was taller than he looked in the photos. Tall for his age: close to six feet. His damp, black hair was much shorter too, recently cut, she thought, but he had the strong features in his young face which could carry a very short style. Val watched him drying himself, his lithe young arm muscles working the towel up and over his broad shoulders, across his flat stomach, his narrow waist, along his slender brown legs. He had the body of a junior swimming champion, which, she later learned, was exactly what he was. She studied him, captivated. He moved with the naive grace of a pure bred foal. He had the base of a suntan already, flattered by the pale yellow of his tight, wet swimming trunks. Were they his own or a pair provided by the campsite management who, on hygiene grounds, frowned at the baggy knee-length shorts favoured by young British males? He turned and wandered over to where Amanda Ringer had stretched out on a lounger. Both from the front and from the back, Val had to admit that the woman's sweet man-boy filled his trunks with an effortless beauty.

Dean flicked out his towel towards her playfully, then stooped to kiss her. They smiled, then laughed together. She said something which made him laugh again. It was a natural, relaxed laugh, a laugh of young white teeth and bright, twinkling eyes. They kissed again. Then he sat down on the edge of the lounger next to hers and drank deeply from a can of cola.

Val waited a few moments longer. There was no sign of them being part of a larger family group. They were a couple, it was more than obvious. A relaxed English couple, on holiday together. Or on the run. She felt suddenly very conspicuous, uncomfortable to be mistaken for a voyeur. She turned away from the pool fence and walked briskly back through the campsite, skirting the barrier and continuing out up the lane, towards the store on the outskirts of town where she had left her car some time earlier just to call in to buy a pack of batteries.

When she arrived home there was no sign of Bobby. The gîte too was quiet; the Belgians' car had gone. She made some coffee and settled at her laptop with a packet of chocolate biscuits.

Scanning some of her favourite UK sites, the BBC and a range of other news outlets, she wanted to refresh her knowledge of the Amanda Ringer case, and add to it with any morning updates. Many reports insisted on calling it *a criminal case of child abduction*, but she couldn't quite see that. Dean Buckle was sixteen, after all. Still a minor, granted, but old enough to do most adult things. Ringer had had the good grace to wait until he'd finished his GCSEs before she'd *kidnapped* him. It was clear that the boy had fled without his parents' permission, but it was even clearer to Val that he was a willing accomplice to the crime. There was something clumsy, forced even, in the way his mother, overly made-up and tearful, had appealed to him via the television cameras to come home. *We forgive you, Dean. You're not in any trouble. Not with your dad and me. Just come back home safe, please, Dean, and we can all talk.* The father, pasty-faced with a vacant stare and a soggy half-beard, looked weak and confused and said nothing. Val could easily understand why Dean might have wanted to take an extended break.

Amanda Ringer's planning, for she was obviously the one who had done it, had been clever. A twenty-eight-year-old Modern Languages teacher, apparently responsible for several school trips abroad, she knew her way around the logistics of timetables and transport networks. It made sense to leave her car in England and access the anonymity of public transport. Val read that her black Fiesta had been discovered in a residential street in Edgware; perfect for the Underground and a direct line to St Pancras. The couple had been picked up by CCTV at passport control as they boarded the Eurostar on Thursday afternoon: hand in hand, each carrying a rucksack, the woman holding what looked like their tickets. After that, ran the official word, there had been no more confirmed sightings.

She imagined they would have spent that night in a small, unobtrusive one-star hotel in Paris, invisible among the thousands of foreign tourists in the city. Even so, the French police had been alerted, of course. A provocative angle in more than one British report was that the *gendarmerie nationale* were taking the search less than seriously. They would never concede it publicly themselves, but in the wake of last week's terrorist threat to the Métro, she could well imagine that they did in fact have different priorities. Of how much of all this background noise was Amanda Ringer aware? In her shoes Val would have stayed in Paris for twenty-four hours at a maximum. Time to buy some food, maybe a couple of inconspicuous shirts, check the internet and, presumably, to have a haircut. The several photos of

Amanda Ringer showed her almost exclusively with shoulder-length blond hair. She enlarged the clearest and studied her roots. Rather than dying her hair as a disguise, she had chosen instead the more artful option of having a cut and her natural colour restored. And for Dean, a shearing of his curls.

In her shoes Val would have left the capital on the Friday. To reach the obscurity of a provincial campsite, full of visitors, in their unremarkable town of Saint-Benoît-en-Sologne, they would have caught a train to Orléans, and perhaps spent a night there in a hotel. Somewhere they had bought a tent and some basic camping equipment. Again, two nights under the same roof were risky, so she guessed they must have arrived here, two or three buses later (and with luck not too much hanging around between connections) on Saturday, the day most of the week's campers would also arrive. And now they were here, the pursued couple, lying low, hiding in full view.

Val was rarely Valerie; she was Val to pretty much everybody who knew her, both back in England and now in France where she'd lived – *they'd* lived – for the past fifteen years. Shoulder to shoulder with Bobby, her partner, she now ran a gîte in Saint-Benoît (*delightful character property, sleeps 4, tastefully modernised interior, available April to October, please check the website*); it was the cottage adjacent to the house they bought when she inherited a modest fortune from a half-forgotten great-uncle. She had named the place *Les Genêts*, after the clumps of dazzling yellow broom growing beautifully untamed on the little ridge at the edge of the kitchen garden. Before they moved to France she had been a young lecturer in a university in the north of England – fine art and photography; it seemed a lifetime ago and, frankly, was a time and a place she would rather forget. These days she still indulged her creative side, running a little secondary business from a studio at the back of the house, photographing family groups, formal portraits, that kind of thing. As for the painting, she left that all behind in Brittany, and that was another old story.

Although not so remote as to be truly considered *la France profonde*, theirs was a quiet region, rarely seen in brochures advertising *la France touristique*. Nevertheless the discerning traveller *had* discovered it and they loved to call it their home. The land was covered by a thousand square miles of forest, a vast site of flat, marshy heathlands, countless dreamy ponds and streams and gentle rivers, mostly looping lazily in tributaries northwards to spill serenely into the Loire. Their gîte had offered a home to fishermen, hunters, ramblers and cyclists, birdwatchers and châteaux-spotters; mostly French, to tell the truth, searchers closer to understanding the essence of the place. For it was a mysterious country, often cloaked in rising mist, rich in secret shadows, which, as the sun burned off its dewy morning veil, would reveal its soul to you slowly, sensuously. Most impressive for Val was the fragile liquidity of the sunlight; there was a rare, fleeting purity even through the mist which she had seen nowhere else. She was keen to complete a collection of landscape photographs and maybe have them published one day: shafts of light cutting through the trees, rising out of moisture clouds, framing the outline of a deer drinking at a pool, or revealing a young boar foraging at the forest floor, or sharpening a distant silhouette of Meaulnes' lost manor house, all in perfect clarity, black and white, or tinted (sepia worked best, or midnight blue) ... that kind of thing. But she was not the first woman with an expensive set of lenses to try to capture the spirit of the Sologne.

Bobby, meanwhile, loveable, prosaic Bobby, had always been a jack of many trades: electrician, plumber, builder, mechanic. Strictly unqualified but, it had always seemed, highly employable.

The Belgian family – Val had forgotten their name already – were up and about early the following morning, loading their car with folding chairs, fishing rods and what looked like a heavy picnic hamper. She exchanged a few words on her way across the misty yard to feed the chickens. They were planning to drive to Theillay for the morning market, the father said, then a picnic somewhere on the way back with a little fishing perhaps.

"Il va faire beau encore, non, madame?"

"Je pense que oui, monsieur. Toute la semaine."

His wife was still inside the cottage, fastidiously checking that all of the windows were closed. They were a typical visiting family. There had been scores like them: earnest father, mild-mannered mother, a chirpy young son and a sulky teenage daughter.

Monday was a day when many of the shops in Saint-Benoît remained closed, and so for Val it was often a morning when she met Greta for coffee. Greta Barachet, née Fraser, had been a friend of hers ever since they were thrown together as a scratch doubles pairing for a tournament at the local tennis club nine or ten years ago. She had spent the first thirty years of her life in Edinburgh but had been married for the last twenty to a patient, charming French notary who was once the mayor of their commune. A series of Barachet family groupings was Val's very first portrait commission. Greta was a few years older than her, owned a dress shop in town – *specialités: robes de mariées* – and was an inexhaustible purveyor of whispers and local tittle-tattle, *tous les commérages de la commune.*

Val rang her to say that she would see her after lunch today, if that wasn't too much of a bother; she had a few tasks to see to first.

The mists had long evaporated by the time Bobby set off in his van to start some repair work on a long stretch of garden wall somewhere in one of the villages. She waited for five minutes, twisted her hair up into a tight bunch, pinned it secure, picked up an old, floppy canvas sunhat, then drove off in the direction of the campsite. She parked again at Brico-Jacques and retraced their footsteps, Amanda's and hers, from the day before. This time a little more leisurely; she had no-one to keep pace with, she knew exactly where she was going, and it was another hot, humid day.

She bought a newspaper at the campsite shop, raising not the slightest suspicion that she was not a camper. She slipped on a pair of sunglasses and sauntered through the site, vaguely in the direction of the riverbank. The camping ground was quieter today. Perhaps more people were taking day trips or had gone into town. There was no sign of life in or around Amanda's tent. She heard noises from the pool, however, and decided to find a table where she could sit, hide behind her newspaper and watch the swimmers. She considered her actions to be quite impulsive. She had no clear plan on this Monday morning, no considered motivation. No, she would insist, she was led by instinct alone. No matter the risk, she could not stop herself from *needing* to find out more about Amanda and Dean, from satisfying her burning curiosity, from confirming her suspicions. From spying.

She caught sight of Dean immediately. He was at the pool's edge, sitting on a lounger, then turning to lie on it, at full stretch, on his stomach. There was a small number of people nearby, including a trio of teenage girls sitting at the far side of the pool, their feet dangling in the sparkling water, eyeing him up, whispering and giggling obtrusively. She noticed the boy was wearing a different pair of swimming trunks today: mid-blue, a size larger than the yellow ones, a better fit, smooth over his lean buttocks – a new pair Amanda had been out to buy for him? There was no sign of her; no sign of his protector, of his guardian, his abductor, his captor, his mistress, his mother, his wife.

After a few minutes he stirred again, nimbly turning on to his back, adjusting the lounger so that he could lean at an angle. He smoothed down the front of his trunks. Val suspected he had lain on his belly to conceal an embarrassment. She smiled, and watched him stretch forward to pick up a PSP lying on the ground on top of his crumpled tee-shirt. Within seconds he was engrossed in a video game. Two of the three girls suddenly pushed the other one into the water to the sounds of exaggerated shrieking and splashing. Dean looked up briefly, then, unimpressed, returned to his console. Val folded her newspaper and walked away, back towards their tent, which sat undisturbed beneath the trees by the shimmering, grey-green Liselle.

There is an unwritten rule among campers that in spite of being fastened with nothing more than Velcro and zips, a person's tent is a most sacred place and that entry without permission is a breach, not just of canvas, but of an age-old code of honour. It may have crossed her mind that she was performing some public service, aiding the police in some haphazard way with their search for foreign fugitives, but she did feel rather grubby, ashamed even, as she ambled past the guy ropes – drooping under the weight of drying towels – then knelt down out of the sight of any passer-by and casually broke the seal on the tent, *the home*, that Amanda and Dean were sharing.

She crawled under the front flap like a scared rat. Inside there was a smell of cheese and stale clothes and sun cream. It was a three-man tent, quite light and airy, and she found herself in a small living space, partitioned from a sleeping area further back. This front section had been tidied: she saw the two folding chairs twisted together like a love seat, a pair of cardboard boxes serving as a larder of half-used food, empty cider bottles, plastic cutlery, two plates, a small gas stove, a box of matches. Tucked in a corner, almost hidden by a cluster of supermarket bags and a pair of trainers, slumped one of their rucksacks, half-empty, sagging like a neglected puppet.

She found the second rucksack once she had carefully unzipped the fabric which veiled the bedroom. Here lingered the slightly sickly scent of what she would call a young man's deodorant. Her eyes darted through the watery light. What was she looking for? What was she hoping to find here? She had very little idea. Something to identify them once and for all? But she fancied she already knew exactly who they were.

The air mattress filled the floor space. It was covered by two rumpled sleeping bags, a matching pair, and a scattering of possessions: discarded clothes, an American wrestling magazine, a packet of condoms. She picked it up: a French brand, two left. She wondered, briefly, what little ruse Ringer might employ to stop him from coming, boyishly, too early.

In the front pocket of his rucksack she discovered a chunky Swiss Army knife and Dean's passport. She opened it at his photo page: the curls of his youth, left behind on the floor of a barber's shop in Paris. Of course the police were right about his age: he had turned sixteen back in January. Out of idle curiosity she examined the knife. It looked new and inside its red casing had the usual array of blades and tools: a bottle opener, a wobbly corkscrew, even a three-inch wood-saw with tiny jagged teeth. Touching it lightly with her thumb she was startled by how easily it cut into her skin, raising blood to the surface. She kissed the nick clean; it was superficial, painless.

On what she took to be the woman's sleeping bag she saw an i-Pod, the bikini she had been wearing the day before, some tourist leaflets and a thick paperback novel. The cover art suggested a thriller, *Cliff Edge*: neither the title nor the author meant anything to Val.

She had been inside the tent for less than a minute, her heart pounding briskly throughout, when she heard fragments of French voices outside, females, advancing to what seemed a matter of metres away. She quickly backed out away from the mattress, turned and crouched behind the chairs in silence. The voices had stopped, or retreated, and soon all she could hear was Dutch being spoken perhaps two or three pitches away and the muffled background music of children playing. It was disorienting to match up outside sounds and distances from within the blindfold of the tent. Suddenly she was anxious that she would be spotted or even caught snooping. She had been foolishly bold. Had she seriously imagined that she was invisible?

She slipped out of the tent as stealthily as she could, into the glare of the full sun, softly refastening the door flap, and then dodged towards the riverbank, down a slight incline and partially out of sight. She was startled by a pair of swans taking off fractiously from behind a clump of rushes growing by the far bank. Within a few seconds she had walked away, flanking the river on a rough path for thirty metres or so, parallel to the row of pitches, and could re-remerge unnoticed between two caravans. Both were occupied by families who were too busy with children and chores to pay her any attention.

She had defiled the integrity of the tent. Nonetheless she thought she had left it exactly as she had found it. She had disturbed nothing beyond the passport and the knife, which she had slipped back into their pocket. She was sweating around the rim of the sunhat and felt cold droplets run down her spine, but she could breathe a sigh of relief. It was much later, when she stopped the car outside their house, that it occurred to her, quite brutally, that on her hasty way out of the tent she had forgotten to zip the centre partition back up.

The internet provided news of developments in England. Following a text she had received – *Don't worry, Mum, I'm OK* – Dean's mother had issued a second televised plea for him to return home. A new photograph had been released but it was already four days old: a blurry image of the couple walking side by side on a platform at the Gare du Nord. The police were putting more pressure on their French colleagues and had sent a team of detectives to Paris where there had been several unconfirmed sightings of the pair. Ringer was travelling under the assumed name of Mandy Rowntree, apparently. Her searchers believed she had emptied a sizeable savings account a week earlier, and it appeared that a series of large cash purchases of euros in several post offices had followed. Latest reports had sightings of the couple in Marseille and the thinking was that their next move would be to board a ferry to North Africa. Someone was convinced that from now on they would be travelling as mother and son. Val smiled as she read these far-fetched guesses from so-called police experts, psychologists and other self-important commentators. She knew that the pair were keeping a low profile right here in her town, unlikely to harbour a single thought between them of Tunis or Algiers or any other exotic port.

It had also been revealed that Dean had been a member of a school trip Amanda had organised the previous autumn to Normandy. One of his mates told a reporter that Dean had said to him that he *fancied her like mad*, and everybody knew that he was her favourite. Rumours that she had been previously disciplined for inappropriate behaviour at school had not been confirmed. The beleaguered head teacher was expressing very little beyond his hope that Miss Ringer would see sense and come back before more damage was done.

Meanwhile the newspaper blogs were full of sniping condemnation of Ringer the predator, the child chaser, the cradle snatcher, the cougar. There was even a website devoted to tasteless jokes about her. (Example: *For French lessons when I was at school you had to bring an exercise book, a text book, a dictionary, a pen, a pencil and a ruler. Nowadays all you need is a rubber*.) A few made Val laugh, but almost in spite of herself; she felt uncomfortable reading clumsy slights against a person that none of her critics really knew. They had no right. It went without saying – but somebody enjoyed saying it anyway – that the woman had wrecked her career. She would never be allowed to work with children again. And how could she ever imagine that the two of them would have a future together? Val unearthed another photo of Dean which had been posted overnight: head and chest, grinning, wet hair, posing in a county-logo tee-shirt with a neck full of swimming medals. Dean was pitied, the victim, the lost boy. But the woman – a teacher, for goodness sake, who had *shamelessly exploited her position of trust* – was demonised without respite.

Val didn't know whether they *would* have much of a future together – they had managed barely a week so far – but to her they seemed, for the moment at least, like a happy young couple who were very much in love. Not so very different from the way Bobby and she herself had been.

Bobby was barely nineteen when they left England together. She was thirty-one, ready to move on after five years as a junior lecturer. She had been in a relationship at the time with a book publisher which was starting to suffocate her. She met Bobby at a Christmas party in someone's flat. He was very young, blond, gorgeous, and a little drunk. And he confided in her. He admitted he felt out of his depth at university, struggling through the early months of an engineering course on the back of some mediocre A Level results purely, it seemed, to please his father. He'd come up from Dorset, bored by farmers and old people, and he'd thought that a vibrant northern city would do him good. He had hated the first term. Even the city depressed him: it was dark and cheerless, he said. And expensive. His best friend was having a gap year picking peaches in Australia and he regretted not tagging along.

By the summer they had already made plans to leave for France. Not just for a holiday together, but to stay there, at least until the money, or the love, ran out. And in spite of hostility from his parents, and censure from her family and friends too, not to mention much sarcastic vitriol from Zachary the publisher, their plans became fulfilled. Val regretted the quarrel with her closest colleague as much as anything. Claudia, a classics lecturer with whom she shared a birthday and much else in the way they viewed the world, tried vainly to persuade her that Bobby was an impulsive mistake. Harsh words fractured their friendship. Before anybody else tried to sow doubts in her mind, Val and her boy sailed to Saint Malo.

They joined a community of artists she had been in touch with on the south coast of Brittany, and lived in a one-room apartment with a shared studio for her work. She made a living selling the occasional abstract or some moody study of a shoreline, supplemented by bar work in the summers. Bobby was just happy to be free, one day repairing a car for a new friend, the next strolling along the beach, picking up a twist of driftwood tossed up by the ocean whose shape might just give her an idea for her art – yet every day he was her muse, her lover, the fuel in her fire. He learned some French and was funny and popular with it. He joined a local sports club. Val was so proud of him: proud to cook for him, to have him at her table, to have him in her bed.

When she inherited from her great-uncle they moved on, bought the house and cottage here, and she asked him to marry her. He had laughed. He had made fun of her. Without ever really meaning to be, he had been cruel in his dismissal. But she had only to catch his boyish grin, to see that sparkle in his eye or to feel his fingertips trail across her shoulder, and he was wordlessly forgiven. Indiscretion, absolution, Bobby seemed unaware of either. He had made her dance around the subject for days, conceding fleeting moments for the briefest consideration of all the angles they could think of. It was long enough for her to agree, as he had insisted, that a bourgeois convention like matrimony held no meaning for free spirits such as them. And, most of the time, they'd been happy together. *Most of the time*, that was success, she thought, wasn't it? Had the age difference been a problem? Well, her biological clock was ticking towards an eleventh hour, and he was thirty-four now, still the same boy at heart, with no interest at all in being a father. So, yes, there was a small problem. And Greta would tell you, if you allowed her the breathing space, that there was a bigger problem too.

Bobby was still in wonderful shape: tanned, healthy, strong. His sun-bleached hair was still thick and long, his teeth white and straight when he revealed them through his easy smile. Most of the year he worked outdoors in denim cut-offs and had great legs. His French was flawed, scattered with English, quirky, and, to a local female ear, terribly sexy. Greta was very jealous of Val, she would say in her jokey, teasing way, but there *had* been stories, she insisted – and here she would look at her friend squarely in the face, a hand on her arm – about her man and his roving eye. Or maybe Bobby was the victim, she might wonder mischievously. A target for the pretty housewife whose patio he had laid, or the secretary of the company where he picked up his materials. Val had confronted him with these rumours; he had laughed them all off. Well, until the incident with Béatrice, the daughter of their solicitor. She didn't hear much laughter after that. One evening last winter the girl's fiancé appeared at their door demanding to speak to Bobby. Their conversation was abruptly taken outside but Val overheard most of it. There were accusations, denials and finally threats. Bobby was visibly shaken. Afterwards she launched herself at his vulnerability and he admitted they had had sex. Just once. In the back of his van. The van he kept his tools and his grubby stepladder and his plastic buckets in. How very, very shabby. Like a little boy who had been caught stealing a neighbour's apples, he began to cry. She told him that if she ever found out that he was cheating on her again she would not hesitate to cut off his dick.

MARDI / *TUESDAY*

She woke up the following day convinced that Amanda Ringer and Dean Buckle would be gone. They would have decided that the best option was to keep on the move. Val would have disagreed: the more movement, to her mind, the greater the chance of being identified.

It was another hot, hazy start to the morning: sultry, sticky, with the promise of a fierce sun. Not a breath of wind had freshened the air for days, it seemed. There was no reason for her to go back to the campsite other than to test her intuition. However she admitted to herself that seeing them, one or both, was becoming an addiction. And she still had no idea what, if anything, she was going to do with her secret.

Their breakfasts partly overlapped in near silence. Bobby wanted to talk, she thought, but he could sense that she was preoccupied, even a little grumpy. She left him re-reading yesterday's mail with a second cup of tea and went upstairs to wash. She brushed her hair, caught sight of the lines of grey peeping through like stains of milk in a *caffè macchiato*. She chose to tie it in a loose ponytail and searched out a faded pink sun visor. And a different pair of glasses: last year's, slightly scratched.

Bobby still had several days' work on the garden wall in Cossonnette; at least until the end of the week. She discovered him round the back of the house loading sacks of cement into the back of the van – *that* van. As she left she told him that she was driving over to Blois with Greta, to keep her company on a trip she had to make to see a supplier.

Less than half an hour later she walked into the campsite, carrying a flimsy plastic bag with nothing more inside it than her phone and a small purse. Nobody paid her any attention apart from a labourer, a wiry, dusty man running a mower over a patch of grass in front of the office building. He stopped his engine and shouted across to her: *Guten Morgen!* He smiled, then resumed his work. Was it *her* he was talking to? Did he think she was German? Had he confused her with someone else on the site? She walked on, deciding to ignore him. He probably thought she was some terribly stuck-up bitch from Baden Baden.

She veered off in the direction of the swimming pool, hoping to catch a glimpse of Dean one more time. The site was fairly quiet again, many of the tents and caravans left closed up for the morning, and the pool was virtually deserted. She realised why when she saw that the only person inside the fencing was a fabulously tanned young man in baggy shorts and a baseball cap straining the glinting surface of the water with a long-handled net to catch leaves and floating insects.

She drifted towards what she imagined, she *feared*, would be an empty space where Amanda's tent had stood. A large sandy-coloured family tent seemed to have taken its place in the shadows of the pines, but as she got closer she realised that the newcomers' pitch was the neighbouring one, the one where the Dutch Mercedes had been until that day. Amanda's tent *was* still there, partially hidden, its back to her, its porch to the river, and what's more, she could hear English voices, excitable, giggling. And suddenly she was standing obliquely to them, Dean and Amanda, about ten metres away, watching them, almost a part of their intimate, domestic scene: they were sitting together on the folding chairs, facing out towards the Liselle, absorbed.

"Don't make it too strong this time!" Val heard the boy say. It was the first time she had seen him wearing a tee-shirt. The woman was leaning forward, laughing, stirring tea in a pair of mugs on the ground.

The harsh trill of a water bird echoed across the shallows. Something caught his eye and he suddenly turned in his seat and looked over his shoulder towards Val. Like a startled doe she froze.

"Mandy...," he said, and the woman looked up, first to him, then to the stranger. There was a flame of protection, almost maternal, in her bright, hazel eyes. She stood up, defensively, and addressed her:

"*Je peux vous aider?*"

"*Excusez-moi, madame...,*" Val replied, "*Je cherche mon p'tit chien. Désolée.*"

Had she recognised her from the hardware store? She made a little show of peering over towards the river's edge for an imaginary lost puppy, even calling out unconvincingly: *Milou! Viens ici, mon p'tit!* Yes, Tintin's dog, but it was the first name that came to her. She turned back and walked sharply away. She could feel her heart jumping inside her ribs. She took deep, quivery breaths. She felt genuinely sorry that she had disturbed them. Truly she had no right to intrude into their privacy.

A sense of unease troubled her during the entire drive home. She parked in the shade by the chicken run and walked slowly across the yard. She suddenly felt hungry. The Belgians' car had gone; another day out touring. She cast a cursory glance across to the gîte. There was a glare of sunlight reflecting from just below the roofline. Surprisingly, the two upstairs windows were open; despite the warm weather it was very unlike *madame* to leave them like that.

In all their years in that place they had never had any bother with intruders. Not even chicken thieves. Not even a fox. Nevertheless she wandered over to the door and found it unlocked. She tapped on it, gently pushed it open and crept inside. Unsure as to whether she should announce herself or not, she stepped further inside without a word. It took her no time at all to realise that there was nobody downstairs. It was as she reached the foot of the wooden staircase that she heard the light patter of a shower running upstairs.

"*Bonjour? Il y a quelqu'un?*" she called nervously, climbing the stairs.

Bobby had heard her voice at once but he had no time to react. She reached the open door to the bedroom just as he was frantically pulling at a crumpled sheet to cover his nakedness.

"Val!" he gasped. "What...? Oh, Christ!"

She could find no words, not even a sound to express her anger, her shame, her confusion.

"I can explain," he continued desperately, just as a skinny young woman with dripping hair emerged from the en-suite, half covered in a large white bath towel. It was the Belgians' teenage daughter.

"Qu'est-ce que tu dis, Bob?" she asked before noticing Val, or rather the back of her as she ran down the stairs and out into the yard.

"She *is* seventeen!" Bobby's pleading voice was chasing after her. "Val! Believe me! She is!"

"You're a monster!" she heard herself screaming up to the open window, panting for breath.

She stumbled across to the main house. She did not know if he was following her or whether he had even fully stirred from his post-coital stupor. Nevertheless she slipped inside the hallway and made a point of locking and bolting the front door. She was shaking. She could feel her ears burning and her heart thumping. She took a long, deep breath. She went into the kitchen, locked the patio door from the inside, picked up a half-finished bottle of Vouvray from the top shelf of the fridge, found a glass in a cupboard, poured out a large measure and drank most of it down in one. Still trembling, she refilled the glass, slightly over the brim, and spilled a little as she carried it into the sitting room. Where she then sat, sipping, sniffing, wondering what to do next. She felt the heat rising to her face, blushing her cheeks as both alcohol and shame were wont to do. But she didn't feel anger, not pure anger; rather she felt adrift, helpless and very lonely, deadened by a reality that wasn't even a shock.

She was saddened by something, someone, she should have been saddened by months and months ago. How she had deluded herself!

She thought to ring Greta, then decided against it. She lay back, rested her head on a cushion and closed her eyes. The image of the girl with the dripping hair would not go away. When it finally did, it was replaced by the bastard lying in bed with a soiled bed-sheet barely covering his groin.

She heard a knocking at the door. Bobby could get in if he wanted to; he had a key to the back door, and the studio door was probably unlocked anyway. But he would know not to force the issue. He knew he would have to face her on her terms. She ignored the knocking and after a few moments it stopped. What a fool she had been. For months, for years. Self-deception, the cruellest deceit of all. She burst into a fitful ripple of warm tears.

About a quarter of an hour later, just as the church bell of Saint-Benoît-le-pénitant struck twelve, Val picked up the house phone, dialled the number of a direct line to the *commissariat de police* in Orléans, and when finally connected to a real person's voice she stated anonymously, as calmly as she could, and in her clearest, most functional French:

"Please listen carefully. I have an important message for your chief inspector. The missing English schoolteacher Amanda Ringer and her young lover are living in a tent at the Camping des Deux Etangs, Saint-Benoît-en-Sologne, pitch number 22. Please apprehend her before she makes more of a fool of herself than she already has. Please don't hesitate. Stop her. You must stop her now."

CHAPTER 2

WIDOW MEREL

Clément Barachet, property lawyer, amateur archae-
ologist, former mayor of Saint-Benoît-en-Sologne, was
not a man naturally given to indulgent rhetoric. When it
was expected of him to talk in public he could be disarm-
ingly effective, calculating in court, persuasive in politics.
Socially, however, he was happy to take a back seat and let
his garrulous Scottish wife perform centre stage: she was
perfectly capable of providing enough entertaining repartee
for the both of them. Greta was unashamed to dominate a
dinner party with tales of local scandal, forceful opinions
on matters of state, high art and low manners, theories,
rumour, innuendo and the very last word on both good
taste and bad faith.

Nevertheless, afforded the opportunity and fuelled
by a hearty meal and several large glasses of a decent
Gevry-Chambertin, Clément would step in and relieve his
wife, especially if he was invited to deliver an insight into
local history. For, born and bred in the town and having
spent no more than a handful of student years away from
the Sologne, he had a broad and deep knowledge of the
region's past and was regarded as an expert on the subject.
Three academic studies bearing his name had been published, including one which had drawn attention from read-
ers beyond the immediate area: his *History of the French
Resistance around the Demarcation Line between Occupied
and Vichy France.*

On the occasion of their second meeting he had presented a copy to Greta's new British friend Valerie who, he had quickly surmised, possessed an adequate level of French to read much of the text without too much discomfort. He was less confident in the capacity of the woman's boyfriend, the builder who had introduced himself as Bobby. However, in regard to an interest in the subject of local war stories, it transpired over the months and years that he had come to know them both that it was Bobby who was the more engaged. He had not managed to read the book, of course, and indeed had admitted to Barachet that he found the title less than catchy, but in conversation he was fascinated by the notary's tales of suspense and adventure, many of which had occurred in the swampy forests that bordered their own land. And most engrossing of all, if Greta was of a mind not to interrupt, was Clément's unrestrained telling of the grisly story of a previous owner of Val's own property: the infamous widow known simply as la Veuve Merel.

"Many years before the German Army was of a mind to invade our country," he had begun, "when the Wehrmacht was no more than a light in Hitler's eye … You say that, Bobby, in English? A glow in his eye?"

"A twinkle in his eye," suggested Val.

She remembered the first time Barachet had told them the story. It was over at Greta's place, of course. After a few drinks at the tennis club the women had struck up an easy, sisterly friendship and Val and Bobby had been invited over for a meal in quick order. An autumn night, after a shared supper. Just the four of them. If Greta was a Highland terrier – and with her short white hair and feisty temperament, she was exactly that, Val thought – then Clément was a gentle bear of a man: ruddy of cheek and bald of head, compensated by the bushiest eyebrows in the whole of France.

Greta was tidying up in the kitchen and her husband had the stage to himself.

"A twinkle. Exactly that. La Veuve Merel was not yet a widow. Not at all. She was still known as Madame Plessis. Muriel Plessis."

"Plessis is the name on our title deeds."

"But of course. Muriel was, so it was said, quite a beauty: tall, raven-haired, slender in spite of having produced a pair of big-boned sons. With her husband Aimé she managed a small pig farm and a brood of chickens. At the back of where your gîte stands. What are you calling your place, Valérie?"

She smiled; Barachet was the only person she knew for whom *Val* seemed unsatisfyingly curt.

"*Les Genêts.*"

"*Les Genêts.* It will take the postman some time to get used to that. It was always known as *Chez Plessis*, naturally. For generations. Right up until you bought it."

The lawyer coughed lightly, dabbed the corners of his mouth with his napkin and then resumed, sharing his gaze between the fire-lit faces of his intimate audience.

"As a child," he said softly, "this *vie de paysanne,* this peasant life, was not what Muriel imagined she would have, but in truth it suited her and she was happy. No, aged ten or eleven, it is said, she was infatuated by the large turreted mansion house ten kilometres distant, sheltered in the middle of the forest, picturing a comfortable life for herself as the young bride of the owner, the handsome Comte de Cheminolles, who would buy her the finest clothes and the rarest jewellery just to see the sparkle of delight in her eyes. Her rival in these dreams was her friend Victorine, a mousy-haired girl with whom she would wander the woods in the summertime, both of them hoping for a glimpse of the count on horseback, riding over his estate like some modern *Prince Charmant*.

"It did not take long for these schoolgirl dreams to fade. Muriel's rivalry with Victorine was soon focused instead on more mundane concerns such as schoolwork, the accumulation of cheap trinkets and the attentions of the more rustic boys of the neighbourhood. It was a spirited competition, you might say, and not always benign, for both young women were as cunning as foxes, could harbour a grudge for weeks on end and reconciliation was very often a slow process of attrition. Muriel sometimes wondered whether she hated Victorine as much as she loved her. And, the … *la bascule?*"

The tipping motion of his hand made his meaning clear.

"The seesaw?" suggested Val.

"*Voilà!* The seesaw of emotions was just as familiar to the other girl."

Barachet allowed himself a brief smile before picking up his thread.

"By the age of twenty both women were married, and attention to husband and family diluted the intensity of their fragile friendship. Aimé Plessis was the more handsome of the partners. Muriel knew that Victorine had at one time had her own designs on the pig-farmer with the darting blue eyes, but he had chosen the taller girl, the more beautiful, and to his mind the more intelligent. As compensation Victorine had cast her sights on Eustache, a woodsman and lodge keeper on the Cheminolles estate. He rented a cottage in the forest with outbuildings and a carp stream, and was ten years older than Aimé. He wore a thick black

28

beard, had a stocky frame, an easy smile and a warm heart. For many years both women would consider themselves content. And yet the closer they grew to their husbands, the further apart they became from each other."

"Are you still talking about Merel in there?" called Greta from the kitchen.

"I'm just getting started," Barachet answered with a smile to his listeners.

"Tell him to stop if you're getting fed up," she went on. "Anyone want coffee?"

"Make a pot for us, *chérie*," he called back before coughing once again to clear his throat, emptying his wine glass with a long final gulp, and settling back to his narrative.

"She's right, of course. I should move the story on. Many years later, a little before the war, came the accident that killed Aimé. It was late winter, a frosty day in January, and we can imagine, perhaps, a snowfall. Aimé had been helping with the forest clearance: strategic felling which, as you may know, Bobby, is best done at that time of the year."

He was indeed a handyman, this Bobby, *un homme à toute main*, and even in the middle of his flow Barachet's eyes were drawn to the fellow's large paws, scrubbed pink and raw, the one lolling upturned on his unopened napkin, the other cupping the sides of his wine glass with a grip better suited to something more rustic, like a clay cider bowl.

"It seems," he went on, "that a couple of the estate manager's men were sick and Eustache had offered Aimé the chance to earn a few extra francs making up the numbers. Anyway, it was towards evening time, the day's work was done, darkness was falling and the two exhausted men were heading back together through the quiet woods on their way home. You can imagine their thick breath clouding in the icy air. Suddenly they heard a shriek, the unmistakable throaty rattle of a *sanglier*, an angry wild boar. And from out of the shadows the disturbed animal, a pregnant female, was on to them in a panic, crashing through the crisp undergrowth with gathering speed. The men fled in separate directions, shouting in vain to scare the beast away. It was Aimé's misfortune that the sow chose to follow him, leaving Eustache as a witness to the chase until they disappeared from his view and careered deeper into the forest.

"I can see that you are thinking, what a horrible death for poor Aimé: gouged and ripped apart by a frantic, snorting wild animal. You have seen a boar's tusks, Valérie? The female's are smaller, they bite rather than stab, but their jaws are just as powerful. But no, no, that was not the way of it. Eustache cautiously made his way towards the distant grunts of the beast and the screams of his comrade, stopping after a few hundred metres to pick up Aimé's walking stick which had been hurled into a tangle of frosted ferns. Led by a pathway of broken branches and marks in the snow, he eventually found his way to the edge of a frozen pond, whose cracked ice caught the pale light of the rising moon. He may have heard the faint, faraway crunch on frozen puddles or the shredding of bracken but there by the pond there was no sign of the sow. Following boot prints that had skidded down the bank, he knew his friend had hurtled on to the ice which had given way like a pastry crust under his weight. He called his name again and again, *Aimé! Aimé!* - louder and louder with little thought for the returning boar, turning in full circle in the blind hope of seeing his companion emerge from the dark pines with a smile of relief on his face. But no man appeared. The forest grew ever quieter. Eustache stood alone in despair, breathing hard. He was too late. With a soft, mournful creak the pond's surface was already refreezing over the black, watery gaps. He knew the man's body would be locked beneath the frozen lid until the thaw."

Val had not noticed her friend return to the table bearing a tray of coffee cups. Only then did she realise that she had also discreetly dimmed the lights. Greta knew better than to interrupt Barachet in full flow. This was his story. She had heard it before, indeed she had told bits of it herself, but no-one related it quite as artfully as her husband. He took a sip of coffee but wasted no time in resuming his tale.

"Muriel was beside herself with grief," he said, almost in a whisper. "*Folle de douleur*, we say. Crazy, mad. And it *was* the start of a madness, I am sure of it. She never recovered. She was still prone to hysterics years later. And she blamed Eustache. *How could you leave him like that?* she screamed at him. *You know those woods! You were his guide! He trusted you! I trusted you! But you ran, didn't you, Eustache? You were a coward. You let him run to his death. He spent the day helping you out with your work and you let him run to his death. You are a coward and I will never forgive you!* And she never forgave Victorine either for standing by her husband.

A second sip of coffee. The guests shuffled slightly on their seats.

"A year or two later the German army invaded. In many ways life changed very little for country folk. But Muriel had already aged ten years, so it appeared to her neighbours. She became more reclusive; her once-straight back bent with the burden of her loss, her dark hair lost its gloss and faded to a stringy, lifeless grey, her once-fresh complexion took on a desiccated pallor, skin hanging from her cheekbones like folds of dripping wax. The black clothes she had worn in mourning became a sort of uniform. She was rarely seen in any other colour. With the help of her two sons, Sylvain and the younger boy Augustin, she kept the small farmstead in business and made enough money to survive. Even her working clothes were black, so they say. It was at this time, I believe, that she was given the nickname Merel. It was never meant as a spiteful name. It was not so much of a jump for some village comedian to make from Muriel to la Veuve Merel. Merel is a girl's name in its own right, quite rare, and an Old French word for blackbird. *Le merle* in modern French. I see you nodding, Valérie."

A deep breath, then a rhetorical question addressed to both:

"You may know something about the black market during the Occupation? The Germans tried to enforce rationing, of course, and suppliers and retailers were registered with the authorities to follow strict price guidelines. Merel's farm became a registered supplier and as such she was limited to what she could ask for her meat, her eggs, and so on. It took her no time at all to realise, however, that a few independent traders, whom she might regard as her competitors, had avoided official bureaucratic scrutiny and were operating illegally, that is to say selling for cash rather than for coupons and, by the by, making more substantial profits than she ever was allowed to. She knew these people. She had known some of them since she was a child. They were French, they were not German, not the enemy, but they were cheating. *Tricheurs.* Cheating the system and cheating her. Merel had no scruples about approaching the authorities now stalking the municipal offices with their barked foreign words and their stiff grey uniforms. She became an informer. One by one she discreetly pointed her finger towards the racketeers. She took no pleasure in news of arrests but was gratified to take the generous sums the Germans were prepared to pay her for information.

"Until the end of 1942 the southern half of our country, broadly speaking, was allowed to govern itself in cooperation with the Nazis in Paris. The southern capital, for want of a better term, was Vichy. You have heard of it, yes? It's a pleasant enough town, of no significance nowadays beyond its spa. You can imagine, can you not, that from Switzerland to the western Pyrénées arced a line of one thousand kilometres that divided the occupied area from Vichy France: a line of demarcation, patrolled here and there but not everywhere. That line ran not so very far from where we are sitting. Saint-Benoît was in the northern zone but a little more than twenty kilometres south of here – a five-hour walk through the woods, yes? – beyond Romorantin, across the river, the Cher, was the open zone. The *Maquis* – *la Résistance* – were as active down here as anywhere else in the country. Romorantin was what was known as *une étape clandestine*, a staging post for the escape route from the north, from Paris, from Orléans, for hundreds of men fleeing capture by the Germans – notably British airmen, parachutists and such, and some of our own French agents, often Jews, on the run."

Barachet lifted his coffee cup and drank the residue.

"You may think I am digressing," he said with a conspiratorial smile, "but have patience, I beg you. For the widow Merel reappears in this scenario before very long. I cannot say how she was politically. She may have thought that once the war was over the Germans would leave France a better place. I dare say she was as much a *patriote* as the next woman but above all by now she was embittered, self-absorbed, avaricious – increasingly venal.

"She knew something of how the *maquisards* operated. She could easily discover more. Her son Sylvain was a sympathiser, on the margins of things. Her contact in the town hall, her so-called "cashier", had tempted her with additional money for information of illegality beyond the black market. She knew what he meant and was not of a mind to dismiss the idea. The man's work name was Bruno; it is a matter of record. It was said that Merel mistook it at first for Pruneau, the French word for prune, and due to his wrinkled, swarthy Bavarian features she thought it suited him better. Later on it might have occurred to her that *pruneau* can also be used as a slang word for a rifle bullet and in that respect the name was even more apposite.

"For many months Merel alerted her cashier to the imminent movement of fugitives. Some hid in Saint-Benoît but she never knew exactly where. Some arrived directly from Orléans and were secreted in the forest. She had known for some time that Eustache's lodge was regularly used as an *étape*. The Germans explained that a raid on the lodge would be counterproductive. And that they must be selective in their ambushes, for fear that the lodge would cease to function at all. It was a question of prioritising targets. When news of movement into the Sologne of *significant criminals* reached them, Merel was told to discover the date of their passage. Flight to the Cher was always at night. Her signal to the German patrols was a lighted candle at the shrine of the Madonna at the crossroads, les Quatre-Routes, one kilometre south of the village. Herr Bruno gave her a lantern made of pink glass to protect the flame from the elements.

"We do not know how many or how few men Widow Merel betrayed in this way, nor how much wealth she acquired for her treachery. We do know that her final act led not only to the arrest of a pair of British officers but also to the deaths, a day or two later, of Eustache and, to her horror, of her son Sylvain. They were shot by firing squad in the courtyard of the old police station in Blois.

"She was sick with anguish and guilt. I cannot imagine how much money the Germans offered her to resume her

34

collaboration, her timely positioning of the pink lantern, but she would not budge. Her other son Augustin thought she would kill herself, take off into the forest and drown herself in a lake. Well, it was not a drowning, but the miserable widow's end came soon enough.

"For Sylvain had a fiancée, a *patriote*, a young laundry woman who lived with her mother on the edge of the forest in a cottage with a view of the shrine at les Quatre-Routes. The woman had noticed a figure in a black cloak coming at dusk, at irregular intervals, to place a light in a pink lantern by the Madonna's feet. Indeed it happened on the evening of her fiancé's arrest. And, when she thought long and hard about it, on the evening earlier in the month when a Jewish father and daughter had been intercepted near the lodge by a German patrol.

"On the pretext of comforting her, she visited Merel with a posy of wild flowers, and while the widow's back was turned she poked around in the cupboards until she came across the lantern she had anticipated finding. *This is a pretty lantern, Merel,* she said as the other reappeared. *Where did you find that?* she snapped. *What are you doing rooting around in my kitchen? – I am sorry,* answered the young woman. *I was looking for a little vase for the flowers. I have seen a lantern like that one at les Quatre-Routes once or twice. Would that have been this one? It is quite unusual. – Not so unusual,* replied Merel, but there was a quiver in her voice, an averting of her eyes, signs enough for the laundry maid to sense the truth. Anger rose in her blood, and with it a seething contempt, but she would not make any wild accusations, she decided. She would gather herself, go away and consult with a friend; she would plot a studied course of revenge.

"How studied, you might wonder. How cool the heads remained as the plot was hatched. For the following evening, as darkness was falling, as Merel was closing up the chicken coops for the night, a shape emerged from the shadows carrying *une machette* – a machete – a blade of half a metre, curved and, of course, whetted – is that the word in English? We say *aiguisé*?"

"Sharpened is good, *chéri*," said Greta from the shadows, "or honed."

"Whetted," insisted Barachet, "to razor sharp."

He paused to let Val and Bobby appreciate just how lethal this weapon was, then suddenly:

"And swinging this machete with all her force, she sliced the widow's head right off her neck and swiftly disappeared into the dense cover of the woods. It was Victorine. Victorine, of course: childhood friend of Muriel, widow of Eustache. She confessed to the murder on her death bed twenty years later."

At this point Val and Bobby had gasped, as all previous listeners had gasped. Greta, unseen, rolled her eyes. Barachet laughed.

"I am sorry. I do not laugh because it is a joke. Because it most certainly is not. It is very much a true story. Perhaps the woman was stabbed to death, not decapitated. But they do say, those that have seen her ghost, that beneath the hood of that black cloak no face is ever present – just a dark, empty headless space."

"Her ghost?"

"Well, yes, naturally. You may see her one of these nights. At twilight perhaps. After all, she lived, and died, on your property."

"Clément!" shouted Greta. "Enough! Behave yourself! Stop alarming Val!"

"It's fine," said Bobby. "We don't believe in ghosts. It's a great story, though."

"If you ever see a pink light shining in the darkness…"

"Clément! That will do!"

Barachet smiled mischievously.

"Oh, *je m'excuse*. I'm simply giving our friends due warning. Another thing, Bobby. Merel is always seen in the dark, in her cloak, holding a pink lantern. And the next morning, wherever she was seen, people have spotted, or heard, a blackbird."

"A blackbird?" sighed Greta. "*Tu exagères, toi!* You're making that up. You never mentioned a blackbird before."

Barachet sat back in his chair and shrugged his shoulders. His story was told. His job was done. Take it or leave it. Val and Bobby shared an uneasy smile.

"I think you've upset our guests, Clément," Greta went on, taking Val's hand in her own. "And not for the first time. They're lost for words. Listen, get yourself out of that seat and go and find a bottle of brandy and four glasses. And, for goodness sake, let's talk about something a little more frivolous!"

Barachet was on his way to the cabinet already. A smile formed on his lips as he remembered he had a box of expensive cigars somewhere in one of the drawers.

CHAPTER 3

ROSETTE PLESSIS

Val was woken from a fitful sleep by a blur of light and the sound of a car creeping past the house: tyres crunching on the gravel, the cough of its engine, the slam of two doors, a pause, and then a third.

A dull stagnant pain hung above her eyes. It seemed the room had gone dark. She wondered what time it was. Slowly she opened her eyes once more. The afternoon had turned to evening and she found herself lying twisted on the sofa with an ache in her shoulders, staring through the gloom at the ceiling. She pulled herself up and the pain in her head throbbed like an electric bass. She took a moment. On the table by her knees was a telephone handset, an empty wine glass and a bottle, half full. Lying beneath the table she saw the outline of a second bottle, empty, its open mouth jutting forwards towards her like a reproach. She raised herself and shuffled to a reading lamp, switched it on, stood in its glare, put her fingers to her eyelids and rubbed.

She picked up the phone and carried it over to its cradle. Its battery was all but drained. The air in the room felt lifeless. Normally at this time of the day there would be cooking smells, conversation, maybe music or the television. She wandered into the kitchen, pulled at the patio door; it was locked as she had left it. There was no sign that anyone had been in the house while she had slept. Bobby's van had disappeared. Val ran herself a glass of water, poked around in a drawer for some paracetamol. Beyond his parking space, beyond the line of oleander, her eyes were drawn past the Belgians' Peugeot towards the lights in the gîte. She could see blurs of movement in the downstairs windows, the mother's silhouette flitting in and out of the kitchen's glow, images of a film on mute: the family settled in for the evening, the little tart of a daughter asking how their day had been, ramping up the affection, offering to help with dinner as though butter wouldn't melt.

Val filled the kettle, flicked on the switch, opened a box of teabags. Thoughts were ambushing her then receding just as abruptly: confusion, a residue of fury, resignation, defiance, defeat. Only the roll of the boiling water cut through the silence. She desperately needed to talk to someone, to hear somebody else's voice. Even Bobby's. No, not his. Not Bobby's. Greta's. She would call Greta.

In the fridge, behind a six-pack of his favourite dark beer, she found a leftover piece of quiche. She warmed it up in the microwave, stirred milk into her tea. Took them both into the lounge where the empty wine bottle still lay under the coffee table like a sulky cat. Suddenly she no longer felt like talking to anyone. She wouldn't call Greta after all. The quiche tasted good and she felt a little refreshed already.

The television set loomed in front of her but she couldn't face its artifice of enthusiasm. Instead her eyes settled on the wall behind it, on the framed photograph hanging in the penumbra of the lamp. It was a photograph Val was especially fond of, one she'd had expensively mounted, the one favourite she'd rescued from the blitz when the house was being emptied prior to their arrival here. They had been visiting the place, she and Bobby, to get a detailed measure of the property just as a team of removers were in the middle of sorting out what was left of the contents. The owner whom they had met before, a woman named Eliane Touzeau, had been supervising operations. Val had been unable to resist the sight of several dusty photo albums lying rejected in a skip. The only picture she had been drawn to, however, was this one: grey and white, enlarged – thankfully with little loss in resolution – and set in a blood-red frame. Rosette Plessis, aged eighteen. Rosette, who went on to own this house, to live in it for fifty years, the mother of Eliane and her brother Jean-Luc; a Rosette with shiny dark hair falling to her shoulders, a Rosette on the threshold of womanhood, staring unsmilingly at the camera lens, determined yet fragile. In a park or a garden somewhere she sits on a low wall in a cotton summer dress – Val guessed lemon or pale pink – with a dark coloured kitten on her lap. There is a little tension in the hand that caresses the animal's neck as though she doesn't trust it to sit still for a second longer. She looks to have fire in her eyes but could burst into an enchanting smile at any moment. Perhaps the cameraman had asked her to strike a serious pose. Perhaps a similar photograph, one taken of her laughing, had gone missing down the decades or had been fondly kept by the family. This one, by Val's calculations, was taken in the early postwar years, perhaps on Bastille Day, a celebration in the late 1940s.

"*Maman* rarely struck such a sad pose," Eliane Touzeau had told Val, "but there is something of her integrity in this image, I believe. She was *une femme sérieuse.*"

Did she mean serious, or responsible, Val wondered.

"Then you must keep it, *madame.*"

"*Mais non*," she had said dismissively. "We have many photos. Certainly enough. Take it, *madame*, if it appeals to you. Keep it in the house. *Maman* would be glad for something of her to remain within these walls, in this home where she lived for so many years."

From her position halfway up the wall Rosette stared back at Val through the ages. A young woman with a message of resolve for an older, confused victim of what? Bad luck? Val had noticed something about this portrait before; Bobby had told her she was *losing it*, imagining things. But here it was again in the half-light, that hint of movement: Val was not looking at a still anymore but was peering through the lens of the camera itself, into a grainy past, into the photographer's moment. She could hear the kitten purring, could glimpse a strand of the girl's hair caught by a breath of wind, could anticipate the tiniest motion of her lips to form a thin, knowing smile.

Sébastien Albiero, surveying his life from a pedestal forty years high, considered himself a success. He had married the most beautiful woman in Saint-Benoît and had the prettiest nineteen-year-old daughter in all of the Sologne. He ran the best garage in town and had recently secured the Citroën concession from a rival business on the south side of Blois. Tall, slim and arguably still handsome, he enjoyed carp fishing in the lakes on his doorstep, took his family holidays on the Ile de Ré and remained agile enough to play five-a-side football once a week at the local *salle omnisports*. Séba, as he was known, had a hammer of a left foot. Only a lack of accuracy had prevented him from becoming a professional, he was known to repeat over a beer at the end of a session. A man of generally unflappable disposition, he had been knocked off balance this evening, arriving home to find his friend Bobby, the English *bricoleur*, the handyman, his five-a-side goalkeeper, sitting at the table in his kitchen behind a tiny cup and saucer making jerky conversation with his wife.

"*Salut, Séba!*" he had said, raising his eyebrows. And to

Albiero's look of surprise, added nothing more than "That's a great coffee machine you've got there, *mon ami*."

Bobby had allowed the man time to kiss his wife, wash his hands and pour out a couple of beers before he beckoned him into the garden for a private word. The family cat darted outside ahead of them the moment the door was opened.

"Val's kicked me out, Séba."

"Kicked you out? What do you mean?"

"Thrown me out. Told me to leave."

"To leave?"

"To stay away. *Dégager!*"

"To leave for good?"

"Well, not for good. For a bit."

"For a bit?"

"For a day or two. Maybe longer."

"She is very angry?"

"Very angry. Very."

"*Et pourquoi?* Why is she very angry, Bobby?"

Bobby took a long draught of his beer.

"*Pourquoi*, Bobby? I can guess, I think."

"*Une nana.* A girl."

"A girl?"

"Well, a young woman. Not a child, obviously."

"Obviously."

"She caught us at it, didn't she?"

"At it?"

42

"In bed together."

"*Chez vous?* In your house?"

"In the gîte, actually."

Séba knows what I'm like, he thought. *He's not judging me, bless him.*

"Do I know her, Bobby, the girl?"

"No. Nobody does. She's on holiday. Just a tourist staying at the gîte. Little Belgian piece."

"Belgian?"

"Does it matter where she comes from?"

"*Non. Baisse ta voix, hein?* Keep your voice down."

"Sorry, Séba. Hey, I've been a dick, I know."

The Frenchman looked back to the scene through the kitchen window. His wife was at the sink. He was about to wave but changed his mind.

"Don't you reckon?" Bobby was waiting for an answer. Albiero faced his friend, a goalkeeper who looked like he had just let a feeble shot go straight through his legs.

"What?"

"I've been a dick. I'm a fool, aren't I?"

"You are if you love your wife."

"Val's not my wife. I told you."

"*Ouais, je m'excuse.* Sorry, I forgot. But you still love her, no?"

"Of course."

"So you'll have to ask her to forgive you."

"I know I will."

"But…"

"But I can't do it tonight. It's still too raw. She's in a state. She won't listen to me right now, Séba. You know what

43

women can get like. I've got to give her some time to cool off a bit."

"That makes sense."

"She'll come round."

Albiero drained his glass, wiped his mouth with the back of his hand.

"Another, Bobby?"

"Can I stay here tonight, Séba?"

"Here?"

"Please. I've nowhere else."

"A hotel, maybe?"

"A hotel? I don't want to be on my own, *mon ami*. I need to feel the warmth of a home. A proper family home."

"The warmth of a family home? You're talking shit again, Bobby."

Bobby smiled.

"Okay, I just don't want to stay in a hotel. You understand, don't you? I'd rather stay here if I could. If it's alright with you."

"Alright with Mireille, you mean."

"With you *and* Mireille. Just one night. I'll be no trouble. Quiet as a mouse. Gone straight after breakfast. Please."

Séba had paused, weighing up the options.

"*Entre*," he said finally, patting his friend's shoulder. "Come inside. *Je rigole, hein?* I'm kidding. Of course you can stay. *Mais il vaut mieux demander à Mireille*. Better ask Mireille first. Make her think it's her decision."

"And better not to mention the girl."

"For sure. I'll tell her you had a big dispute about money, yes?"

Three hours later Bobby had been welcomed and well fed but a long evening watching French television held no attraction. On top of that he had noticed a gradual chill in Mireille's attitude towards him. He insisted to his hosts that he was tired, emotionally drained if truth be told, and he would like to take the chance to get a good night's sleep.

The second bedroom belonged to the Albieros' daughter. Fortunately she was on holiday: a final release with her friends before starting university in a month's time. Grateful though he was, Bobby took in his surroundings with a sense of unease, finding himself surrounded by a virginal femininity. Scattered artfully at the head of the single bed were teddy bears and frilly cushions in pastel colours. The bedding was pale pink. The room had a floral smell, too sweet. On the bedside table sat a small lamp with a strawberry-coloured shade and a photograph of three teenage girls making faces at the camera. He clicked on the lamp, filling the small space with a soft rosy glow. On the walls hung posters of pretty-boy pop stars – nobody Bobby was likely to recognise. And a calendar with paintings on it. July looked like a Matisse but he was no expert. Val would know. He drew his eyes away from the names and places, the plans and appointments, neatly handwritten in the day-by-day boxes; he had no business prying. Neither did he open any of the drawers for fear of discovering something intimate: a piece of jewellery, a note from a boyfriend, a box of tampons. He cast a cursory glance at a bookcase: school textbooks, colourful books from childhood, a few novels, poetry – all in French of course, nothing he knew.

He unrolled the sleeping bag Séba had found for him in the attic. Mireille had insisted that he slept on the bed, not in it. Fair enough, Bobby thought. He'd done enough defiling for one day.

Opening the wardrobe door to find a hanger for his jacket, he spotted a row of shelves, on the middle of which sat a neat pile of knickers. Skimpy, lacy knickers, a range of colours, including crimson, the same shade as those worn and then slipped off by the Belgian girl. And on the shelf above, a tangle of flimsy bras. Bobby shut the door with a slam he immediately regretted. Had anyone heard it downstairs?

He closed the curtains. It had gone dark early tonight.

He pulled out his phone and before he had time to prevaricate rang Val's mobile number. He had little idea what he would say to her. He would rely on instinct. React to whatever she said. Bend to whatever wind she blew.

There was no answer. Finally Val's voicemail message trilled out, impossibly, incongruously cheerful. *Bonjour! Je ne suis pas là à ce moment. Pourquoi pas me laisser un petit mot?*

Pourquoi pas? A word or two? Why not? Bobby could think of a dozen reasons why not. For one he didn't know which words to use, and for two he doubted whether he could find any words at all without his tongue tripping up over them.

He switched his phone off, looked at the dark screen.

He switched it back on again.

He formed a sentence in his mind and then abbreviated it to a text message of five short words. *Sorry, Val. I really am.*

He sat on the edge of the bed, crumpling the duvet cover. He looked again at the words he had typed. He could not think of anything less or more adequate. He pressed Send.

He waited for an age with the phone clamped in his hand – actually ten minutes. He might as well have been holding a bar of soap. Val could be stubborn. There was no reply.

Darkness was falling like a heavy sigh. Silent raindrops were glancing the windowpanes. Val pulled herself away from the television and closed the curtains. She had found a dubbed American comedy show which had superficially entertained her; comfort viewing. There had been nothing on the evening news to suggest that anyone in the Orléans police department had followed up her information about Amanda Ringer. Meanwhile the pain in her head had been replaced by a sickness in her stomach. She had eaten a pot of chocolate mousse that might have passed its use-by date; she hadn't checked.

Suddenly the phone rang: her mobile. Val muted the canned laughter and picked it up with no sense of urgency. It would be him. Bobby's name duly appeared on the screen. She let it ring out until her voicemail took over. Standing in silence in the middle of the room she waited for a message, but none came. Either he was a coward or he couldn't be bothered.

She had already lost the thread of the American sitcom and was about to switch it off when there was a ping of a text and she turned back to her phone. Bobby again: *Sorry, Val. I really am.*

Bobby the wordsmith, the poet, the lyrical hero giving it his best shot. She was sorry too. She really was. She closed down her phone, deciding to have a long soak in a warm bath and an early night. Face the world tomorrow.

Ten minutes later, just as she was letting the tub fill and searching out a fresh tee-shirt to sleep in, she thought she heard a knock on the door. She turned off the taps and listened. Nothing. She liked to borrow Bobby's tees, large and sloppy, but tonight she wanted an old favourite of her own, a blue and white stripy Breton one that hung halfway down her thighs. Then it started again. An urgent knocking, first on the wood, then on the windowpane of the patio door.

Val descended into the darkness downstairs and saw the reflection of a torchlight dancing against the kitchen surfaces. There was another series of knocks as she approached the door, unlocking it and switching on the light that illuminated the patio. On the doorstep was a figure in a dark hood, its back to her, its torch now aimed through the drizzle at the shapes looming in the garden.

The figure spun round to face her. It was a woman in a baggy kagoul whose face, damp and jaundiced by the artificial light, Val tried to recognise.

"*Madame,*" came a shrill voice. "I am sorry to disturb you."

Val picked up an edge to the woman's French and she suddenly realised she was listening to the Belgian, the wife, the mother of the family renting the gîte.

"*Qu'est-ce qu'il y a, madame?*" she asked. "What's the matter? *Entrez.* Come inside, it's raining."

"I won't, thank you," replied the woman, fiddling with her torch. "I simply came to tell you of the disturbance."

"Disturbance?"

"We heard noises outside the gîte. My husband saw movements in your garden." She turned again to wave a hand across the black expanse. "It's the chickens, we think. Maybe a fox. There are dead birds, I am sure. I am sorry, *madame*. We thought you should know."

Val stepped outside in spite of the rain. The Belgian

woman followed her towards the middle of the lawn where the outline of the chicken run, a wooden frame covered with wire mesh, was lit by her torch. The door was open and inside the shadowy, muddy space was littered with the broken bodies of half a dozen chickens and scraps of feathers scattered as if by a storm. There was no sign of life, not a trace of the remaining birds who had either managed to escape into the woods or had been carried off by a predator.

"I am sorry, *madame*," repeated the woman. "It is a terrible sight for you."

Val closed the door of the frame and fastened the catch. A fox-proof catch. Had she left it open that morning when collecting the eggs? Bobby was meant to feed them earlier. He was meticulous about the chickens. They both were. It was a mystery, but not one that could be solved in the dark.

"Thank you for letting me know," said Val, her hair already dripping. "Go back inside, please. We'll have a proper look around in the morning."

MERCREDI / *WEDNESDAY*

Val had deliberately left her phone downstairs, buried under a cushion. Downstairs, buried *and* powered off. At seven o'clock she woke up feeling refreshed but was immediately confronted with a seesaw of concerns from Bobby to dead chickens and back again.

She pulled back the curtains. The rain had stopped but the low sun was hidden by a white rag of a sky and the air looked cold. It seemed to her that summer was already well past its zenith. The window of her bedroom – *their* bedroom – gave on to the lane skirting the front of the house. She decided she would eat breakfast before inspecting the grisly scene at the rear.

While waiting for the coffee to brew she could not prevent herself from digging out the phone. There was a text from Bobby, sent in the early hours, followed swiftly by a voice-mail which said pretty much the same thing: *Val, it's me. Please forgive me. I've been a shit, I know. It must have looked bad! You can't imagine how sorry I am.* His voice seemed to mock her. It was too cheerful; he was putting on a brave face, encouraging a perception that it had actually just been an unfortunate misunderstanding after all. Another text, sent ten minutes later and smothered with self-importance, offered details to put her mind at rest: *I'm staying at Seba's. A bit cramped in their spare room!* She hated the excla-mation mark. He was channelling the jokey exasperation of an uncomfortable camping trip. Was she supposed to come over and rescue him? She texted back, jabbing at the keypad: *Leave me alone. If I ever forgive you it'll take longer than 24 hours.*

She was annoyed with herself for making the coffee too weak but couldn't be bothered to pour it away and start again. She made some toast and took everything into the lounge. She flicked on the television just as another text message landed in her phone:

B.   *I need some fresh clothes, Val.*

She responded without delay: *You have your key, don't you?*

A pause. Bobby was a slower texter than she was; his fin-gers were too big.

B.   *I'll come home later this morning. OK?*

V.   *Home? It's not your home anymore.*

B.   *What do you mean?*

This time Val paused.

B. *I'll come round later this morning.*

V. *I'll make sure I'm out.*

B. *What's the matter? Can't you bear to see me now?*

Pause.

B. *I said I was SORRY!*

V. *Get what you need and then leave me alone.*

B. *For how long?*

Pause.

B. *For how long?*

Val closed down the dialogue.

Images on the television screen prompted her to turn up the sound. A police detective was making a statement about the arrest of the English schoolteacher Amanda Ringer. He struck Val as an earnest man with a chubby, pleasant face; a man for whom police work would probably throw up too much nastiness for him to ever stay in the job for very long. He was addressing an invisible bank of nodding reporters, eloquently furnishing details of an operation to apprehend the fugitives: the lady – he called her *la dame* not *la femme* – and her young friend – he did actually refer to Dean Buckle as her *ami* and neither *captif* nor *complice*.

Yes, there had been many tip-offs from the general public.

No, the town of Saint-Benoît had not previously been on the police radar.

Yes, the British authorities had already interviewed Mademoiselle Ringer.

No, the young man was neither injured nor harmed in any

way.

A reporter appeared, filmed live, standing outside the entrance to the Camping des Deux Etangs. She was interviewing a man whom Val recognised as the fellow with the lawnmower who had shouted at her in German yesterday; he was introduced as the campsite manager. Pictures then followed showing a scene within the site, possibly recorded after the arrests had been made: the fugitives' abandoned tent on the pitch by the river, one of the folding chairs on the back of which a pair of yellow swimming trunks appeared to be drying. At the end of her report the show moved on to something else: a story about striking air traffic controllers. The French had done with Amanda Ringer and Dean Buckle. They had resolved the case and from now on it was a British affair.

Val swallowed the last of her toast and took her coffee mug outside. There was nobody stirring in the gîte. The chicken coop was a scene of carnage; in front of her eyes, imposing itself in the morning light, lay the discarded evidence of a frenzied, feral attack. She examined the ground both inside the cage and around it for prints in the mud but found nothing distinct and gave up. She had been expecting, even hoping, to see boot prints: not the paw markings of a fox but the imprint of soles beneath human feet.

Something that Clément Barachet had once said about the chicken run as a scene of death suddenly came back to her: something from the tale of the murder of Widow Merel during the war. Of course this was not the same rickety poultry cage, but Val had a memory that the later one, this one she was staring at with a sickness rising to her throat, this one stood on pretty much the same spot on the land behind the house.

Slowly she withdrew into the kitchen, closed the door, set

about tidying up. But wherever she looked, whatever she did, her gaze kept returning to the window and the view of the plot. She remembered what Eliane Touzeau had told her about the property, years back when she was considering buying it. And the details that Barachet, local historian of repute, had added when she had asked.

She imagined that after the gruesome slaughter of Merel the chicken coop would have been demolished, for the birds were the widow's preoccupation and nobody else's. Her remaining son, Augustin, maintained the pig farm for many years, during which time he married Rosette, she of the red-framed photograph. The couple had two children: a son, Jean-Luc, according to certain accounts a lazy, dishonest boy, and a younger daughter, Eliane, who was devoted to her father. Although their home stood within the limits of the commune, the family lived a somewhat isolated, peasant existence. Augustin Plessis inherited the property but was not a wealthy man. And Rosette remained loyal to him, yet knowing all the while that her hopes for a more fulfilled life were drifting away with each passing summer. Sometime in the 1960s, suffering from fits of depression and anxiety, Augustin made the decision to sell the pigs. He levelled the sties and had a large glasshouse built on the site in which he grew tomatoes to sell to local businesses. He followed this course for several years. The growing season is long but in this somewhat damp corner of France, endless days of summer heat are not so guaranteed. He had good crops and bad crops, made a small profit one year and went into debt the next. Around the start of the 1970s, encouraged by a few friends of dubious character, Augustin took the fateful step to diversify. Initially infiltrating them in small numbers between the tomatoes, he gradually became less and less coy until he had whole rows of thrusting, undisguised marijuana plants sharing the soil. Soon the operation was producing a healthier family income. Rosette received unexpected gifts from her husband – a silk scarf, an extravagant necklace – and didn't think to ask where he had found the wherewithal to pay for them. Jean-Luc, by now a twenty-two-year-old working as a railway conductor, had been involved in the distribution of the cannabis buds for a couple of years. Even Eliane, a feckless schoolgirl but a schoolgirl nonetheless, had been under her father's instructions to develop and cater for a student market since she was a fifteen-year-old in the *troisième*. One summer Rosette wandered into the glasshouse and noticed the musky smell and the tangles of hairy plants on which there was not a trace of ripening red fruit. She could not believe how blind she had been. Barachet insisted she was not a stupid woman but this had indeed been an aberration.

"Keep your mouth shut," insisted her husband when she confronted him. "What I'm doing is paying for your wine. Filling your larder."

"It's illegal, Augustin," she complained.

"Then you'll understand why we must keep it a secret, yes?"

"I don't want Jean-Luc to be a part of it."

"He isn't."

"He isn't?"

"Believe me, *chérie*, he isn't."

Rosette did not believe him, even when her son himself denied it. Meanwhile it never crossed her mind that Eliane too was involved.

She lived with the dilemma for months, her obedience as a wife grinding against a contempt for criminality that had been a part of her character since childhood. In the end her decision to betray her husband's trust came from a concern for his health, a desire to save him from himself, and so not at all what she would ever call a betrayal. Augustin had begun to smoke the weed himself, medicinally, he would say, to help him relax, to drown out the images that continued to torment him. For he maintained, and Rosette believed him in this, that the ghost of his mother haunted him. He saw the widow's faceless figure in the evening mists and it petrified him; he shivered each time he saw a blackbird or heard its shrill, fluted warble. Firing squads plagued his nightmares, he saw his brother Sylvain lying bleeding from a hundred and one bullet wounds. There were moments, however, when it was clear to her that the marijuana was making him worse, making him even more anxious, more prone to outbursts of anger and self-harm. One evening when she found packets of compressed buds in the coat pockets of her son, she resolved to act. Augustin was arrested the next day, the illicit crop along with the burgeoning tomato harvest was destroyed and it took little formality for him to be locked up. Rosette Plessis was beside herself with guilt and her children turned against her. When his father died in prison less than a year later, Jean-Luc left Saint-Benoît for Paris and never spoke to his mother again. According to Barachet, the pig farmer turned horticulturalist was strangled in his cell by a fellow inmate.

With the help of a mortgage and astonishing resilience, Rosette had a small cottage built on the site of the glasshouse – with a view to starting a new business renting accommodation to tourists. A few renovations down the years produced the present-day gîte, now named *Les Petits Genêts*, currently home to a family of Belgians with a promiscuous teenage daughter. It seemed that Eliane was eventually reconciled with her mother and together they managed the business successfully for many years, even after the daughter married, became Mme Touzeau, moved to Blois and could contribute only from a distance. Greta knew Eliane Touzeau. She still ran a tourist hotel on the banks of the Loire with her husband, apparently. Greta knew everybody.

In more recent times, as Rosette's health deteriorated and she was obliged to move into a nursing home, letting agents took over. In 2003 Rosette passed on. Two years later the Plessis family sold the property to a foreigner, to English Val. For her and for Bobby it was a blank canvas: the start of a long and exciting chapter in their life together.

Val was placing the last of the wretched carcasses into an old sack when she heard a high-pitched voice from her neighbour's field. She recognised it by its shrill spike of anxiety as that of Madame Motta, who since the death of her husband the previous winter had lived alone in her leaky, neglected house. Val remembered him as a kind man, as generous with advice for new neighbours as he was with the fruit from his cherry trees.

"Madame Bobby!" she was shouting over the laurel hedge. "Madame Bobby!"

A misunderstanding when they had introduced themselves to the couple years ago, never corrected, had led to both of them addressing Val in this way ever since.

"*Regardez-moi ça!* I have a dead hen in my potato patch. *C'est à vous?* Is it one of yours?"

Val approached the woman, saw the blood in her glaring eyes, the stains on her teeth. Wrapped around her head was a grey towel, twisted like a turban.

"*Probablement oui, Madame Motta, je m'excuse.* I'm sorry. A fox got into the coop last night. *Un renard.*"

"*Un renard?*" She looked so alarmed the culprit might

have been a tiger.

"They're all dead. Either dead or disappeared."

"Well, I don't want it. Not in my potatoes. Shall I fling it over?"

"Just pass it to me, please, Madame Motta. I'll deal with her."

The woman had already turned to shuffle towards the far corner of her land.

"And another thing, Madame Bobby," she shouted. "*Votre générateur*. It is too loud. It woke me up last night. It is too loud for this neighbourhood. This is a quiet neighbourhood."

Val was puzzled. The generator hadn't been turned on for months.

"We haven't used the generator since last winter, Madame Motta."

"*Trop fort*. Too loud," she was muttering, still on her way to the potato bed, one hand on her towel which appeared to be coming loose.

"Not since the storm. Since the power cut."

"Much too loud."

Val had suspicions that the poor woman, however physically robust she remained, was slowly losing her mind.

"I'm sorry, Madame Motta," she called.

"Sorry? So you should be. Sorry for what?"

"I'm sorry about the chicken, Madame Motta. Sorry about the fox."

CHAPTER 4

GRETA BARACHET

Repairing the chicken coop was one of a long list of jobs that needed attention at *Les Genêts* once the holiday season had dribbled to a close. Visitors were still booked into the gîte for weekends and the odd day or two here and there until the end of October, but there were times in between when superficial improvements could be made, not that Val had much motivation for making a start. Maintenance of the property was Bobby's department and Bobby had been absent for weeks. She turned her attention to painting the downstairs walls in the gîte but her heart wasn't in it. She made a mess of it – she wasn't that kind of painter, for Christ's sake – and left the job half-finished. She began work in the garden but couldn't fathom how to operate the lawnmower. She had forgotten how exhausting a day, or even just an afternoon, clipping hedges, weeding flower beds or digging over empty vegetable patches could be. She would soak in a bubble bath, take herself off to bed for an early night and expect to sleep off the aches, but lately she had lost the knack of untroubled sleep. Often she would awake unrefreshed, with a headache that might take beyond midday to clear. The main task they had given themselves – rather the one Bobby had resolved to do before the winter set in – was to build a brick patio and barbecue area behind the gîte: an upgrade on the cracked concrete floor that had seen better days. Nothing would be done until Bobby came home. Came back.

A reluctance on both their parts to make the next move had led to a pause in any communication between them. More a breakdown than a pause, in fact, due to the inertia of a phoney war looming over the dwindling weeks of summer. Pride, obstinacy and cowardice had all played a part in littering the path with stumbling blocks, and their avoidance had been going on for so long now that it no longer really mattered who blinked first. Obstinacy was her problem; she knew that. Cowardice was Bobby's, she would say. Cowardice or apathy. He had stopped texting. It crossed her mind that he had given up on her, had actually moved on. And some days she found it hard to convince herself that she did actually want him back. Was it already too late? Had it all stagnated in front of her eyes? Their relationship was turning to dust and she couldn't find the energy to save it. They were better apart. She was coping without him, wasn't she?

"Still no word? That man's making you suffer, Val. Or else it's you that's making him suffer."

Greta Barachet stooped to place a heavy tray on the low table between their seats. The rich smell of coffee filled her spacious lounge. Val offered her friend the emptiest of smiles.

"You fancy a wee dram in that?" asked the older woman, pouring the coffee into china cups. "Make it an Irish?"

"That'd be nice," Val nodded. "It's a bit early but that'd be very nice, thanks."

"So, are you going to be the one to make the first move?"

"I wasn't planning to."

"Well, if you want my advice, dearie, and I've told you this before, I'd let him stew for as long as it takes for him to come back on your terms."

"You said."

"That's if you have any terms. Any Ts and Cs."

Val sighed.

"You're missing him, aren't you? Aren't you?"

Greta was unscrewing the top off a bottle of her husband's finest malt.

"Bits of him," said Val, looking up to her friend. The instant their eyes met they shared a short, smutty laugh.

"Well, who wouldn't, dearie?" asked Greta, raising an eyebrow and expecting no reply. "And I'm sure he's missing you," she went on, splashing a glug of whisky into the cups.

"That's the problem, Gret. I'm not."

"Not what?"

"Not sure he's missing me."

"Of course he will be."

Val declined to agree.

"I'm still buying too much food," she said. "You know, forgetting that I'm just catering for one. And I am missing him around the place, I suppose. As a contributor to the business. I feel a bit lost on the maintenance front, you know. There's loads to do."

"Give it a break, Val," insisted the Scotswoman. "The place looked fine the last time I saw it. You had any complaints this year?"

"No."

"Of course you haven't. There you go. You're worrying too

much about the house when you should be looking after yourself. You've looked better, you know, if you don't mind me saying."

"I've felt better."

"Look at your fingernails, for a start. And believe me, you desperately need to see your stylist."

Val smiled at her friend's cheek, tugged at her hair, long since grown out.

"As a matter of fact, what you need," Greta went on, "apart from a decent haircut, is a break. Get away from here for a week. Relax a bit."

"I can't afford the time, Gret."

"Why ever not?"

"And he might come back while I'm gone."

"And what if he does? He'd ring you first, wouldn't he? And if he did rock up here and find your place empty, well, he'd ring you then."

Val had already finished her coffee. Greta's was untouched.

"I tell you what," she was saying, "I'll ask my cleaner if she'd spend a day at yours while you're away. Straighten everything up. Félicité. She's a lovely young lassie. You've met her, of course. I'll get her to pop in. I'd love to go away with you myself but I've got so much on at the moment. I told you about the wedding in Romorantin, didn't I? The banker's daughter?"

"You're right," said Val, cutting her off.

"I am?"

"There's nothing to stop me getting away. Have a break, a change. Recharge my batteries."

"That's the spirit! Where'd you go? England, I suppose. Spend some time with your father?"

"That would be the exact opposite of relaxation."

"Scotland, then. I know you've never been, to your shame."

"I'll go to Brittany. Visit a few old friends. Find a little hotel on some windswept clifftop."

"That sounds about right for you. And what about Félic-ité?"

"Who?"

"My cleaner. Shall I have a word? Book her in?"

Val's eight days on the south Breton coast were dominated by one missing man. The friends who knew them as a couple were puzzled by her sudden appearance in their midst without him, and a few – both men and women who long ago had fallen for his coltish English charm – remained quietly unconvinced by her brittle explanation. She had overreacted, she had been inflexible, even cruel. She had been misguided, irrational, mean-spirited. Nobody said these words to her, of course, but she read them in their eyes. Or at least she thought she did. For their part her friends were warm and welcoming and sympathetic. She went on a long beach walk with one couple, drank calvados into the early hours with another, was invited to a family birthday party by another. That they were all couples now – these members of such an amorphous grouping of artists and poets and associated bohemians back at the turn of the millennium – was not lost on her.

Even the once fiercely self-contained Rosée, *collagiste*, confidante and new mum, had a husband now. Val had never known the woman's real name. She had chosen Rosée as a *nom de guerre*, she had once told her: *you say 'dew' in English. La rosée, c'est la pureté. The dew, it's purity, Val. La vie, life itself!* The dear friend made her week by asking her, in a quiet moment under the pines on a long stretch of sand, if she would be godmother to the six-month-old baby Valentin. She took the bus into Quimper and bought the cutest pair of navy blue designer dungarees as a gift for the child the very next morning.

Finally she made her excuses and, as she promised to Greta she would, took a coach west to Audierne, to the very fingertip of the land, booked into a garret in a comfortable hotel for three nights and indulged her desire to withdraw into herself. In a narrow backstreet running down to the harbour she found a hairdresser's whose manager was willing to give her a cut at short notice. She was a youngish woman whose own hair was cropped and spiky and dyed a shade of lavender. She had a tongue as sharp as her scissors and an intrusive curiosity that Val, with a hidden smile, found herself having to deflect. She reminded her of one of the gulls at the quayside, circling and squawking and strutting about waiting for scraps, only, for want of patience or in pure greed, suddenly to help themselves from the decks uninvited.

The days drifted agreeably, one into the next. She read, she walked, she breathed in the fresh, briny air, took photographs of the wide Atlantic rainclouds, of the rolling waves pounding the edge of the continent. Even she couldn't lose her bearings tramping along the coastal trails; if the ocean was on her right, she was heading east. She wandered alone, ate and drank alone, slept long hours and woke alone, but he was with her at all times, that one missing man.

The spirit of Bobby had followed her from the Sologne

to Finistère and back home again. Once re-established at *Les Genêts* she started noticing, more than his absence, the things he had left behind. Already she was hearing his voice, anticipating the sort of comments he would make out of habit to express surprise or delight, exasperation or disappointment. It was a funny thing about the ironing: even after all these weeks she still missed smoothing a pile of his freshly washed tee-shirts. Now she kept coming across the forgotten clothes he had left at the bottom of her drawers, the objects scattered around the place that they had bought together, the wine rack that not only had he chosen, he had also assembled. His music CDs were still in the house, littering her shelves, as were his football trophies and most of his books, not that Bobby was ever a great reader. She even rediscovered his Aston Martin mug, at one time his favourite until she had relegated it to the recesses of the most inaccessible cupboard, peevishly insisting at the time that it didn't go with the new kitchen colour scheme. She left every one of his belongings where she found them. There were still times when she believed that one day soon he would be back to take his place among them. Yet another explanation haunted her: that every article of his that remained had been left behind for a reason. That they were no more than relics of a cosy domesticity that he had chosen to abandon. That as Val had slipped snugly into middle age, he had realised he was neither ready nor willing to join her. That the twelve years between them suddenly meant more to him than to her.

"I'm sorry if the place isn't as spick and span as you'd have liked it, dearie, but in spite of my best efforts I couldn't persuade Félicité to go over to yours. She was busy with family things. Not sure what. She looks after her mother, poor woman's in a wheelchair. It's not really my business to ask."

Val pressed speakerphone and sat back on the sofa with a glass of Vouvray in hand and the mobile resting on her knee.

"It's not important, Gret, but I was wondering if you called round here yourself for anything?"

"Well, you gave me a key, didn't you?"

It was a rhetorical question.

"I popped a bit of post on your kitchen table."

"I saw that. That was you, was it? Thanks."

"So I just cast my eye over the place for you. No sign of visitors. You know, male, blond, English, tail between legs."

"I noticed the big pots at the back had been moved to one side."

"Had they?"

"Might have been the neighbour, moved them out of the way for a bit of shelter. Did you have any storms last week?"

"There were high winds on, where are we now? ... Friday. Friday night. That'd be after I was over. I came by on the Thursday afternoon."

"Probably Madame Motta then. She does show an interest if she's in the mood."

"There was a car parked outside the gîte. A jeep type thing. Val de Marne plates."

"That'd be the Parisians. My regulars. Four blokes down for a few days fishing. They know the ropes."

"I didn't see them. Just the car."

"No, they'd be at a lake all day. They usually drive down in two cars."

"You sound well, Val. The break did you good, I bet."

"One other thing, Gret," she said, cutting her off. "Did you move anything else?"

"Anything else?"

"Inside, apart from the mail."

"I don't think so. No. I'd no reason to."

"Not a photograph?"

There was no reply.

"A photograph," Val repeated. "On the wall in the lounge? You know which one. You've seen it often enough. The girl with the kitten. In a red frame."

"It's been moved?"

"Well, obviously. That's why I'm asking. I found it on the floor, leaning face in against the wall."

"Damaged?"

"No, it's not damaged. Just moved. Taken off its hook and placed against the wall. A bit weird. I don't understand why."

"Maybe Félicité took it down to dust it."

"Félicité? You said she didn't come."

"No. No, of course she didn't. No, sorry, I'm getting mixed up. Piles of mail, potted plants, Madame Motta, fishermen in two cars down from Paris. I don't know, my head's all over the place some days. Must be the change, finally come to claim me. Sorry, Val, I haven't a clue about your old photo."

Val swiftly buried all thoughts of the menopause as far to the back of her mind as was possible.

"Then it's a mystery. Never mind."

"You didn't take it down yourself, did you, dearie? Did

you?"

"No. Was that a genuine question?"

"You know you weren't yourself the last time I saw you. You had a lot on your mind. More than a wee bit distracted, I'd say."

"I think I'd remember if I'd moved it."

"But you're feeling better now? Re-energised by the Breton breezes?"

The broad puffy-clouded seascapes of Brittany already felt like a distant memory. A full day's journey on a succession of stopping trains had brought her back to the autumnal shadows cast by the forests of the Sologne, the steaming mists, the smell of rotting leaves and sodden grass.

"I had a nice time," Val said after a moment.

"I told you it'd be a great idea. If ever Clément looks like he's getting into a rut, I'll suggest a holiday. Well, you know what I'm like, Val."

"Anyway, it's back to work for me. So many jobs to do."

"You said you'd wait for you-know-who to put in an appearance before you got the paintbrushes out again."

"Bobby's gone, Gret."

"Oh, he'll be back soon."

"I'm not so sure."

"You could always call him. Make the first move."

"Swallow my pride?"

"Exactly."

"I'm not quite at that point yet."

"You know what," said Greta with a sudden enthusiasm in her voice. "I've been thinking. Thinking about your predicament."

"Really?"

"No, not about your marriage."

"I'm not his wife, Gret."

"Of course. No, I know that. It's just, well, you know what I mean. Anyway, no, it's not about Bobby."

"So thinking about what?"

"That you need someone. Someone able, willing and cheap to do a few jobs for you."

"I could hire a brickie, at least. I've thought about that myself."

"Well, you could, Val, but I've got a better idea. A much cheaper option for you. His name is Florian."

"Florian?"

"Florian. He's a lovely young laddie. I've met him. He's Félicité's brother. In fact he did a job for Clément a few weeks ago. He put a bit of flooring down in our attic. Quite a neat job, he did. Clément was happy with it. Told him he'd write him a reference if he ever needed one. He can look a bit surly but that's not what he's like. Félicité thinks the world of him, her kid brother and all. "

"So, what, he's a professional *bricoleur*?"

"He'd probably like to be. He wants to make a name for himself. He's a handy sort but he's, well, he's some kind of special needs. He's a bit slow on the uptake but when he knows what you want from him he's very obliging. He has a job at Brico-Jacques at present. Part-time, as far as I know. Stacking shelves, keeping the trolleys tidy in the car park. A big strapping laddie, hair like spaghetti. You might have seen him."

Val knew Sébastien Albiero better than she knew his pretty wife, but it was Mireille she was drawn to when she spotted her alone in the town's Maxi-marché one day towards the end of October. The younger woman, thinking too hard about the choice of breakfast cereal, did not recognise her at first.

"Madame Albiero?" Val prodded.

"Oui?"

"*C'est Val. Votre mari*, your husband, he is a friend of Bobby's. *Le football?*"

"Bobby? Sorry, yes, of course. Val. I have met you before, I think. Perhaps only briefly."

Val wasted no time on small talk.

"You must know that Bobby and I had issues. *Problèmes, oui?* He walked out three months ago. Rather I encouraged him to walk out."

Mireille Albiero dropped a box of muesli into her trolley without taking her eyes off Val.

"He fucked a teenager in your house," she said abruptly in fluent Anglo-Saxon.

"Not in our house exactly."

"He stayed with Séba and me that night. And for nearly a week after that. Have you been in touch with him? Where is he?"

"No, I've had no contact. I was wondering if *you* knew where he was."

"*Aucune idée.* No idea, *chérie.*"

"Did he say where he was going after he left yours?"

"He had some work to finish around here. He went back to yours for clothes and tools and things, no?"

"Yes, but I didn't see him. I kept out of his way."

"I see."

"And so, after the work?"

"He talked to Séba about going to England."

"England?"

"Yes. He would be missing from the five-a-sides for a few weeks, he said. I only remember this because Séba has been complaining about having to take his place as goalkeeper ever since."

"For how long in England?"

"Hey, I have no idea. I said already. I really cannot help you. We haven't seen him since the summer. Sorry, Val, I must be getting on."

Val had imagined Bobby flitting from one friend's spare room to another's sofa-bed, maybe a cheap hotel for a while, never too far away from Saint-Benoît. None of their mutual friends in Brittany had heard a word from him. He didn't know anyone in the rest of France, as far as she knew. Nevertheless she had never considered that he might actually leave the country without telling her.

She had shed a tear of self-pity more than once since he left, but the moment she opened the desk drawer where they kept most of their valuable documents – she had never thought to look before – and saw her own passport, still bound by an elastic band but without its partner, the emotions rose up inside her and she cried and cried until her chest ached.

Later that evening, having closed the curtains and lit the first open fire of the autumn, she curled up on the sofa with a bottle of Beaujolais and let the dancing light of the orange flames and the glow of the alcohol guide her fitful thoughts. She came as close as she ever had to calling the missing man on her phone. For an age her finger hovered over the handset symbol by his name before she preferred to pick up her glass instead for a mouthful more of wine. And then the moment had already passed and rather than emboldening herself to call, she had steeled herself not to.

She tossed the mobile to the far end of the sofa, beyond her toes. Why should she make the first move now, after so long? It would be read as an admission of defeat. An admission that she had overreacted, that she had been irrational and that she was as much in the wrong as he was. What *would* be wrong was to stop reminding herself of what he had done. The Belgian girl was not the first. He had humiliated her and he needed to understand that. She had this conversation with herself many times and it always made her feel ill, yet it was at moments like this that she missed him the most. The tasks of the day were done, and the promise of an evening together with thoughts, eyes, ears, lips and fingers only for each other flickered in the firelight.

Where on earth was he? Still in England? Where would he go? To his parents' place in Dorset? Not necessarily. Relations were still frosty even after all these years. What was he doing for money? He had his private account but there was never much in it. The business account was in her name only. Unless he had found work he would be running short of funds by now, for sure. She decided he must be in Dorset; in spite of everything his mother and father would never see him on the streets. She swallowed the last of the wine, the logs crackled softly, the shadows swayed around her like a gentle caress. *Come home, Bobby,* an inner voice whispered. *Come back to me, get down on your knees and give me a reason to forgive you.*

Florian was as good a worker as Greta had promised. He

claimed to be self-taught and seemed to have an instinctive understanding of basic building principles, not to mention a certain dexterity with a paintbrush and even the confidence to attempt rudimentary plumbing.

Val had plenty to occupy his talents and after a confirmatory telephone conversation with Barachet she had invited the boy over to explain her needs. Even now, after a week or two of daily visits, she thought of him as a boy – and Greta always referred to him as a laddie – but it was clear, on watching his muscles straining to lift a stack of bricks or stretching to reach a ceiling with a brush, that he had the well-developed body of a man. No matter the weather, he preferred to work, both inside and out, in a sleeveless tee-shirt and a pair of cut-off jeans.

She interrupted his labours with a mug of coffee or, on warmer afternoons, a *panaché*, and sat chatting with him, marvelling at his lack of affectation, his artlessness. He told Val he was eighteen, adding the date of his birthday for good measure. He told her about his sister Félicité, about how she had fallen in love with Kamal, the skinny *beur* in the phone shop, how he had fixed her phone for free, how they were planning to move to Orléans and live with his cousins in some Arab district of the city. He told her about their poor mother, injured three years ago in a car accident, confined to a wheelchair and, since the absence of her husband, dependent on her two children for support.

"*Vous savez*, you know, if she knew Félicité was talking about going to the city she would be very angry, I am sure," he told Val. "She's never heard of Kamal. Me, I keep out of it."

He had a broad smile and was generous with it. He spoke slowly but in an uncomplicated French and she understood him perfectly. She envied him his sense of certainty, of simplicity.

"I don't like your coffee, in fact," he told her once, open-faced, running a hand through his straggly hair. "But I will drink it if you want me to."

Meanwhile she had to keep an eye on the clock for him. He struggled to tell the time and asked her to warn him when he needed to start tidying up. Most evenings he had a shift at the hardware store.

One day when he had swept the last of the dust from the new patio he called over to Val, who was pruning rose bushes at the far side of the garden. She saw his puffed out chest, his grin of pride in the completed job. She walked across and patted him on the shoulder. She could see a few lines that were a little short of perpendicular – Bobby would have noticed them too – but she admitted that the overall effect was sound and, moreover, he had finished two days ahead of schedule.

"*Très bien, Florian,*" she said. "That's really wonderful!"

"*Merci.* Hey, you're bleeding," he said with a look of genuine concern.

"It's just a scratch," she replied. "I caught my hand on the thorns. I do it all the time."

"You should wear gloves, Madame Val."

"Probably I should."

"They sell them at Brico-Jacques."

"They sell everything at Brico-Jacques!"

"No, they don't, Madame Val. They don't sell everything."

She wiped her hand on the sleeve of her old fleece and smiled.

"I do this every year," she said, "scratch up my fingers. But I can't have a garden without roses. And you can't have roses without thorns. So I just prune away."

"When will the flowers come out?"

"They'll be out in June."

"Then I look forward to seeing them out. That's if I'm still coming here to do jobs for you in June."

The forecast of a run of cooler, bright mornings inspired Val to dig out her best Canon and reactivate her ambitions for her book of images of the Sologne. It was a project she knew was by no means unique and so her photos had to be exceptional, every one of them worthy of a prize. To capture the purity of the light, the sharpness of the shadows, she had to be in her car before dawn. A certain composition of trees, a lake, earth, mist and sky was often enough to frame the essence of the place, but wildlife of some sort – a bird in flight, a jumping fish, a pair of deer, better still a sounder of wild pigs – could elevate a photograph to near iconic status. One of her favourite walks was through the forest to the edge of a small, secluded lake known as the Etang de Broussaille. It was less than a dozen kilometres south of Saint-Benoît but seemed little visited by humans.

On her chosen morning she left the Mégane at the end of a forest track and hiked up a slight incline, following the semblance of a trail between rows of dewy oak and beech. For once she was confident in her directions; this was a path she had trodden before, more than once hand in hand with Bobby, her guide, pathfinder, protector. Today the air was damp and musty, the ground was soft and muddy where it wasn't covered by the slick debris of decaying leaves and fallen pine cones. The sun was peeping over the rim of the treetops, its rays sifting through the low branches like silvery breath, scattering shadows, glinting like star-drops on the puddles and ponds in the middle distance. For this was the land of a thousand and one pools, some green with algae, some dark and deep and edged with reeds where in the summer dragonflies flitted and danced, but whose chill surfaces were today unruffled. Cautiously Val stepped over the forest floor, avoiding clumps of spotted mushrooms. Her eyes peeled for signs of fauna, she heard the throaty call of a heron, the muffled bark of a fox, but saw nothing. In the distance a shiver of mist, theatrical dry ice, diffusing the sunlight like a blessing, indicated the edge of a body of water – she was approaching the Etang de Broussaille.

Arriving at the shore, she found a fallen branch to sit on and immersed herself in the silence. She held her camera on her knee, loaded like a rifle, pulled the zip of her parka up to her chin, and waited. Here and there ripples were popping up, signs of invisible life beneath the dark surface of the water. Presently, whispers of wind parted the mist and the hazy silhouette of high pines appeared on the far shoreline a kilometre away. A little closer, the strengthening sunlight picked out the ochre-yellows of the sycamores and turned them into a cascade of golden flames, and cast beech leaves in a blaze of copper. Jewels sparkled shyly on the water and high above it the pines soared into a sky of dazzling blue. The lake-scape was as stunning and as mystical as Val had ever seen it. She stood and found the best position for a run of shots.

And then suddenly her prayers were answered. Several metres away to her right she heard splashes and, turning her gaze, spotted a young deer paddling in the shallows, dipping its head to drink. Rooted to her spot she took half a dozen shots through the willows. A moment later the animal lifted its head, cocked it and fixed Val with a frozen stare, at once both curious and defiant. She had the animal in profile: it was a beautiful image, the sunlight burnishing its sandy hide, but the composition was not ideal. Should she creep back and find a wider angle? Or should she wait a moment? For she was sure that where a fawn might wander, its mother would be bound to follow. Risking spooking the animal, she looked for a route through the bracken and fallen branches and made tentative steps away from the shore. No sooner had she retreated ten metres she was rewarded by the sight of the adult doe, darker in tone and standing in half-shadow, her head held to meet Val's eyes, locked in silent confrontation.

The beast was too close for the kind of tableau she wanted but she slowly raised her camera, knowing that the deer would hold her ground so long as she made no brusque movement. Before she had time to frame the image, however, the crack of a gunshot echoed through the trees and the animal darted away from the clearing. A second shot followed and Val watched in dismay as the pair of snowy backsides, doe and fawn, sprang away through the undergrowth and disappeared into the shadows.

Val followed their escape path as far as she could but had little hope of finding them again. She heard a third rifle shot and the flutter in the treetops as a small flock of birds took flight. She retraced her steps and to her surprise, a moment or two later, she found herself no more than a dozen paces from a man with a gun. He had stepped out from a line of birch trees, rifle in hand and pointed to the ground. He was dressed in full hunter's garb, down to a thick checked shirt with a fleecy collar, three-quarter woollen breeches and muddied black gumboots.

"*Et que faites-vous, madame?*" he shouted. "What are you doing in these woods?"

Val had never seen him before. Above his stocky frame sat a head surrounded by gingery fur: a low hair line and a whiskery beard.

"What are you doing here?" he repeated. "Can you understand me?"

"Of course I can understand you," said Val as calmly as she could.

"These woods are private," declared the hunter, stepping closer to her.

"Private? They're not private. I've been walking these woods for years."

"*Dans ce cas-là, madame, c'est une violation.* Then you've been trespassing."

"*Monsieur*, these woods are not private!"

"Better not to argue with us," said the man, looking over his shoulder, Val imagined, for a colleague or two.

"*Vaut mieux partir*," he went on. "Better to leave. *Tout de suite*. Right now. Before you get into trouble."

"Into trouble? Is that a threat?" She held up her camera. "All I'm doing is taking photos."

Val's heart was pounding. For all her brave words this man was frightening her.

"We saw your car back on the track," he was saying. "*Votre bagnole*. You'd better go and find it before it gets stolen."

She had more to say but kept her words to herself. She walked away from the hunter, felt his stare on her back as she rejoined the path, and the steamy lake came back into view. She thought to plod on for a kilometre or two, find a different prospect, but the man had unnerved her, she was concerned about her car and she felt alone, vulnerable, unprotected. The sight of a second stranger ahead of her on the track unsettled her even more. Taller, younger, clean-shaven and carrying nothing more lethal than a hazel walking stick, he was dressed in similar fashion to his associate and had the same menacing scowl. He held his ground and gave her a hard, silent stare as she was forced off the path to pass him. She was determined not to look back, knowing that his eyes would still be on her; she could feel them penetrating her collar at a distance of twenty metres. Once she was beyond his sight she broke into a run and scolded herself for showing fear. She tripped on a fallen bough, slick with moss, stumbled and almost lost her balance. Her breathing was shallow. She came to a halt, tried to steady herself. Her brow felt clammy, her camera case hung around her neck like a millstone. Several minutes later she came across a low wire fence and realised that in her haste she had taken a wrong turn. There was a dampness at the base of her spine. She realised she was trembling.

She had not strayed far from her route but it took her thirty minutes to find the place where she had left her car. She wondered if it had been moved. Of course it had not; neither had it been tampered with as far as she could tell. No angry note had been stuck on the windscreen, no paintwork had been scratched, no tyres had been deflated. The car was still shaded by the trees and inside it felt as cold as death. She drove home directly, fast along the forest roads, anxious to see a friendly face.

It was market day in Saint-Benoît. Out of season half the traders were missing and the few groups of customers were drifting from one stall to the next like schoolchildren traipsing around a stale museum. The sun shone on the town today but as Val steered slowly through the detour she sensed little joy in its colourless streets. A couple of people she knew from yoga class waved at her through her windscreen as she edged across the *place de l'église*.

As she finally approached *Les Genêts* she noticed a figure on a moped pulling out from her drive. She recognised Florian and pipped her horn. He was wearing a new pair of skinny black jeans, one size too small, she thought. It was the first time she had ever seen him out of his ripped denims. She was not expecting him today. She lowered the window as he swung back to steer level to her car.

"*Bonjour, Madame Val*," he called, a little breathlessly.

"*Bonjour, Florian*," she said, perplexed. "What are you doing here?"

"I came round to drop off a little gift."

"A gift?"

"Yes, just a little gift."

"Really?"

"It's not wrapped up fancy." He was mumbling, blushing, avoiding her eyes. "You mustn't pay me or anything. You weren't at home so I left them on the step."

"That's very kind. I'm intrigued."

The boy was already pointing his bike down the lane, moving away.

"*A vendredi*," he called. "I'll see you on Friday."

"Friday?"

"For the hedges."

"Oh, yes. Of course."

The hedges. The laurel, the oleander. And tidying the broom. *A vendredi, Florian.* She looked to shout after him but he was already accelerating out of sight.

A minute later when she stepped out of the car she saw the small parcel, wrapped in a plain plastic bag, lying by the back door just as the boy had said. Inside was a brand new pair of pink rubber-lined gardening gloves. She smiled, sat down in the sunlight and tried them on. They fitted her perfectly.

"They sound like a couple of poachers to me," said Greta, eyes fixed on Val's computer screen, the oversized one she had set up in her studio.

"That's what I thought," Val agreed. "When I got my mind straight."

"I'm not surprised they shook you up, dearie," added the Scot. "There *are* great tracts of private land around here, but if you can walk over to the lakes without seeing signs stopping you or barbed-wire fences in your way then you are in your rights to roam as far as I'm concerned. Are these the files you want opening?"

Val looked over her shoulder at the monitor.

"Let me check those dates first, Gret."

Val was generally assured on her computer and considered herself to be digitally savvy, up to a point, but there were times like this – without warning, her machine had undertaken a major self-update and the settings had reverted to a status she didn't recognise – when she needed someone not so tech lazy, someone with a surer touch to help her out.

Florian had over-confidently offered his expertise and Val had given him ten minutes before he admitted defeat. He suggested calling his sister's boyfriend Kamal but all things considered, Val knew that Greta was a better bet if she were available.

"I want the photos I uploaded last week. God knows where they are now."

"How are you finding Florian?" Greta asked out of the blue.

"He's great. Not the tidiest worker but he gets the jobs done. No complaints."

"He's sweet, isn't he?"

"Sweet?"

"Don't tell me you haven't noticed."

"He's sweet-natured."

"Yes he is, and he's a bit of a dish too."

"I *haven't* noticed."

"You liar! I've observed him stacking shelves. On more than one occasion, I don't mind admitting. He's got the sweetest pair of buttocks this side of the Loire."

"Greta!"

"What? Don't give me 'Greta!' As if you haven't watched him hopping around in his shorts from your kitchen window!"

"We have a purely professional relationship," Val insisted, knowing full well that her friend didn't believe a word of it.

"Put some coffee on, dearie, and give me ten minutes to get to the bottom of your files."

"They're all re-ordered for some reason. I can't make sense of it."

"Put some coffee on, girl. Relax. Let me take over. And when I've finished you must reset all your passwords."

The computer was fixed. Repaired, recalibrated, reformatted, whatever Greta had done to it. It was working fine. And her passwords could stay put; she had no trouble remembering them and couldn't be bothered thinking up others and trudging through the tedious setting-up procedures. Anyway, thanks, Greta. Now she could add to her album of images for the Sologne collection. She could begin to redesign the gîte website for next spring, she could deal with her backlog of emails, she could read the online British press.

A few days later, in between a reminder of insurance renewal and a brief note from Rosée with an attached photo of little Valentin in his blue dungarees, it appeared on her screen: the email, the message, the signal, the flare she had for weeks been hoping for, wishing for. Contact she had almost given up on. Contact from Bobby.

As excited as she was to click it open, she was just as quickly deflated. He was asking for money, nothing more, nothing less. There was neither remorse nor regret. No warmth ran through his words. He wanted half of last season's profits from the business; what he said he was owed. It wasn't a begging letter, more an unvarnished demand. Nevertheless it gave her a reason to write to him, something she had been itching to do for so long.

It was hard to find the right tone. Instinctively she wrote a paragraph and agonised over whether to sign it off with a kiss.

Dear Bobby,

In spite of the disappointing thrust of your email I was pleased to hear from you. It's been too long, don't you think? I don't know where you are but I'm guessing England. That was the last word from people I've met in town who know you. Please tell me. I do care about you even though I am still angry about what you did. I think it's probably time that you came back to Saint-Benoît and we can have a grown-up conversation about where we go from here. I don't think an argument about money is going to be helpful at all. Surely there is more to save in our relationship than numbers in a bank account.

Call me or write back. Please don't leave it too long.

Val X (?)

Letting it simmer, she took half an hour to clear her head. Of all things she decided to fill a bucket of hot, soapy water and wash the Mégane. By the time she sat down and re-read what she had written she had changed her mind. His email did not deserve such a conciliatory reply; it was a submission, a sign of weakness. She deleted the draft and started again:

Bobby,

Thank you for writing to me. At least I know you're still alive. Your request for money from the business is out of order. You know the arrangement. Perhaps you'd have more of a shout if we were married. And then you'd have been less likely to betray me. Maybe, maybe not. I'm sorry our relationship has become so monetised. Will you be considerate enough to write back to tell me that there is still more to it than numbers in a bank account?

Val

Without reading through what she had typed she pressed Send and suddenly felt quite serene.

A week later an envelope arrived in the post from the office of a company of solicitors in Dorchester, Dorset. Inside there was a polite covering letter explaining that the notary, a woman, whose signature looked like that of a five-year-old, was writing on behalf of her client with regard to a validated claim for financial settlement as outlined in the enclosed duplicated documents. She would be grateful if Val could sign, date and return one copy of the documents to indicate acceptance of the terms stated therein.

Val unfolded the sheets of pale grey paper and found, in concise form, an expectation that the client, the missing man, would be entitled to fifty per cent of the equity of any future sale of the property known as *Les Genêts,* including grounds and adjacent cottage in the town of Saint-Benoît-en-Sologne, Loir-et-Cher, France.

Even by the time she had driven to the Barachets' place and placed the pages flat on their dining-room table, her heart was still thumping.

"He can't have it," said Greta, hugging her friend to her chest. "He can't just make demands like that."

Clément picked up the papers. He scanned them for a moment or two before letting out a hearty laugh.

"You've nothing to worry about in this, Valérie," he declared, flicking the sheets dismissively. "Really, it's just a heavy-handed threat wrapped up in polite legalese. Unless he marries you he has no claim. I think you can safely ignore it."

Already she felt a little relief, trusting in the wisdom and substance of the *notaire* and former mayor of the commune standing before her. Suddenly Greta spoke again, with more of a flourish than Val thought necessary, words that took the wind from her sails:

"Well, Val," she said. "I reckon one thing we can safely say is that your Bobby doesn't much love you anymore."

The following afternoon Val descended into a lull. She had endured a minimally fulfilling morning, achieving little and postponing plenty. It was one of those vapid days when even the weather couldn't be bothered to turn up. The garden was drab and lifeless, there was no energy in the air, the daylight was in power-saving mode. The effect of two glasses of white with lunch added to her listlessness. Deciding against picking up a book but refusing to give in to the urge to nap, she turned to her mobile to break the boredom and it occurred to her to ring Rosée, her friend in Quimper.

Rosée was quite a different character from most other people she knew, particularly Greta. Whereas her chatterbox of a tennis partner was a fizzing bundle of sarcasm and teasing, the artist was gentle and sweet-natured and invariably optimistic. Val had once thought of them as a pair of insects flying around her head: Greta was the wasp and Rosée the butterfly. Bobby aside, they were the best friends she had ever had, both with hearts of gold, but she did admit to herself that they were both acquired tastes. To truly appreciate their qualities she had to be in the right frame of mind: Greta could be wearing at times, Rosée could be a little too intense. But seeing her smiling, sun-tanned face on the icon in her contacts list, Val decided a new voice was what she wanted to hear, a cheerful voice from another place.

She learned that the weather in Brittany had been foul for two days. Rosée had plenty of work to be doing inside so she was keeping dry. Little Valentin was growing, he would soon be one! Val had seen a little knitted cardigan in a shop in town that she thought would be a perfect birthday gift. The way Rosée was talking she imagined he had already grown out of his blue dungarees and maybe the cardigan would be too small as well.

"We call him Val, rarely Valentin," the proud mother said. "There's only really my father, his *pépé*, who insists on Valentin. He has thick, curly black hair like his daddy. And talking? Well, it's more sounds than words but he never stops, Val! We think he's going to end up a politician. Or a comedian."

"Is there much difference?" Val asked and they both laughed.

Loïc was still working at the restaurant in Concarneau but was looking out for a small business to buy nearer home where he could start up his own place.

"It's wonderful to see him so enthused, Val, so ambitious."

Without prompting, Val brought up the subject of Bobby. Rosée was predictably sympathetic and at the same time surprised.

"I was sure he would have come back by now. You two always seemed so together, you know, united, like a favourite pair of shoes."

"That was fifteen years ago, when you knew us like that."

"Everybody loved you both when you first came to Brittany together. Val and Bobby, Bobby and Val. Everybody thought you'd be solid."

"It's the age difference, Rosée. It's finally caught up with us. Well, with him."

"Men can be very selfish."

"Even Loïc?"

"He has his moments."

"This is more than a moment. It's been five months."

"I'm sorry, *chérie*. But don't give up hope. I'm sure he has his reasons, but he will be back."

He has his reasons? Rosée always was willing to see both points of view in any argument. Too willing. Too balanced.

"Anyway, how are you otherwise? How's the business? How's the book of photos coming on?"

"The photos are good, thanks. I've taken loads. I've probably got too many."

It was nice to chat, of course it was. But the kindness of Rosée, her charitable nature, was founded – and Val thought this to be truer than ever today – on the good fortune of her happy life. Even as a young woman she had rarely been struck by life's arrows. Her parents were not wealthy but they were loving and supportive. She was talented and in her modest way had become successful. Now she was married to a gifted chef with plans to open his own restaurant and she had her sweet little son to warm her heart for the rest of her days. In spite of everything Val could count many of her own blessings, and by nature she was not an envious person, but when the conversation was over, when she had switched off her phone and drifted over to the fridge to find the half-empty bottle of wine, she felt utterly bereft.

It was several weeks later, when winter was beginning to bite, that Val happened upon a paragraph in the online edition of a British newspaper under the headline: *ABDUCTION TEACHER SENTENCED IN TEARFUL COURTROOM DRAMA*. Surely that was misleading; some weeks ago she had read somewhere that as Dean Buckle was sixteen years old at the time, the offence of child abduction did not apply. In addition, the boy had admitted that he had accompanied her to France voluntarily.

"In a dramatic session of crown court," she read on, *"for the abuse of her position of trust and related sexual activity with a minor, Amanda Ringer, 29, was given a jail sentence of eighteen months."*

There was a photograph of the woman in a loose grey trouser suit, handcuffed, being led towards a police van by two female officers of the law. A curtain of dark hair, caught by the wind, covered part of her face, solemn and much paler than when Val had last seen her, smiling, sitting in a camping chair and taking in the summer sun by the languid Liselle.

CHAPTER 5

FLORIAN (I)

Val's resolve to stonewall Bobby's demands wavered through the dreary months of winter but she did not capitulate. Her father had once called her the most stubborn mule he had ever known. Their battles during her teenage years seemed titanic at the time: wilful adolescent meets bully of a man whose attitude towards women was fossilized in the 1970s. He liked to say to his friends that his daughter was born with a fully formed set of fingers, toes and opinions. Her fragile mother, until she was taken from them in a freak accident, tried in vain to keep a flimsy peace between them.

The poor woman had died from injuries sustained when she fell fifty feet from a faulty ski lift on to a sheet of ice in the Italian Alps. Val had imagined her mother to be a timid skier, a reluctant companion cajoled on to the slopes by her overbearing husband. She had been at boarding school at the time and remembered being pulled out of class by her housemistress quietly to be told that her mother had been transported to a hospital in Bolzano where she was in a critical condition. For a moment she had imagined that she was bandaged up in a bed making disparaging remarks about the nursing staff. It had been a short winter holiday during her father's posting in Rome. Even in his middle age he had remained a so-called junior official in the diplomatic service: a clerk, a statistician, a facilitator, a translator, a glorified secretary. After his wife's death he requested an immediate move, suddenly believing that all Italians were slapdash and irresponsible. His last job was in Lisbon, if Val remembered correctly, the one he was fired from for subordination. She could easily imagine what he had said to his superiors, and how he had said it – and probably on more than one occasion too.

Val had never clipped on a pair of skis and had never wanted to. Her obstinacy, she reckoned, had stood her in good stead through her life so far. She was nobody's pushover. She was a force to be reckoned with. She would bend for no-one. This was a projection she would encourage, yet at the same time she would privately admit that it was far too simplistic. She had her weaknesses just like everybody else. She wanted to be liked, to be loved. A hard exterior hid a knot of insecurities and often gave a false picture. And friends had often grown tired of her caustic refusal to go with the flow, of her recourse – especially as a child – to tantrums, of her inability to compromise. Boyfriends and lovers had mostly been wary of the impression of strength she exuded. Only two had stuck around long enough to see the real Val, to witness a softer, more vulnerable side to her, to come to know a woman who was far from supremely self-possessed, whose sheen of confidence was questionable after all.

She thought rarely of Zachary these days, but when she did, when a memory might be jolted by an image on television or by a photograph online – something tender they had shared – she thought of him warmly. Sure, he was over-possessive, he was pompous, he called a collection of grotesque snobs his friends, but there was little doubt that he had loved her. Actually, he had been devoted to her. When she left for France she broke his heart. Had she been too hasty to discard him?

At the time she had felt just as sorry to lose his mother as a friend. Sometimes she seemed to get on better with Margaret than with her son. A surrogate mother? Well, of course she was. No need to psychoanalyze that particular combination, but wasn't it a bit weird to miss her lover less than his mother? Val remembered the day she had taken her to Wimbledon: Margaret's treat, everything paid for including a splendid lunch for the two of them at the Café Pergola. Tickets for Centre Court where they had even seen Navratilova – not in a final or even in a match at all. They saw her in the royal box, semi-retired by then but no less charismatic than she had been when Val had idolised her as a child, watching her on television as she roared to one championship after another. In so many ways Martina had been a role model, an inspiration. And not simply because of the tennis. She was determined and uncompromising, she was intuitive, courageous and inventive. She had everything Val wanted to copy and take with her into her own life. And she also remembered the day she saw her in London, the Selfridges end of Oxford Street, it was: for a moment she was sure it was Martina, then as the vision was lost in a crowd, she was less sure. Had it been her or just someone who looked a bit like her? It was funny how your mind could play such tricks; how your perception, just like your memory, could betray you.

Bobby had stuck around too, of course. And with the best of intentions. He knew her better than anyone in the world. He knew her strengths and what she was capable of, and he also knew her needs and the ways in which she was inse-cure. With the passing years, from once being in her thrall he had gradually, imperceptibly gained the upper hand. She hated to admit it but suddenly she needed him more than he needed her. But all that was over, those days of Val and Bobby, Bobby and Val. She had to reassert herself and the best thing to do was to give his delusional solicitor short shrift. And then to stick to her guns.

"So, how's Florian?"

"Florian?"

"Florian. Your handyman. Handy-boy, whatever you call him. How's he getting on?"

"I haven't seen so much of him since Christmas."

"No?"

Greta Barachet looked up at her friend for a reaction to her provocatively raised eyebrows.

"There's not so much to be done this time of the year."

"I suppose not. No inside jobs, perhaps?"

"Another madeleine, Gret?"

"Another? Well, I shouldn't, but they *are* very good."

Val was catching up with the Scotswoman who had spent a week over Hogmanay with her elderly parents in Edinburgh. Apparently there had been talk of them moving into a nursing home. Some soft-voiced suit had all but persuaded them to sell up and sign in at Golden Leaves. The way she told it, Greta had arrived just in time to expose more than a few empty promises. Showed the pair of them the folly of the move. Spelled out the facts to her old man, who should have known better. Five years ago he *would* have known better. Then she'd set in motion an application for an enhanced care package. Her parents would remain in their home after all, with neighbours either side whom they could trust, who had been good to them for years.

Val had nodded along, made coffee, served cakes. And suddenly they were talking about Florian. It wasn't strictly true that she had seen little of him lately. He had spent a week replacing some of the fencing that separated her land from the woods. He had repainted most of the interior of the gîte. Only last week he had helped her tidy out the store-room at the back of her studio. He had spotted a loose collection of her landscape photography and his eyes lit up; he told her how he felt he could walk right into the pictures, smell the forest, get his boots muddy. On a high shelf they came across a sample of her early abstracts, various oils and acrylics she had experimented with in Brittany. Straight away she could tell by his face that he hated them. She didn't mind, of course – she wasn't so sure about them herself in hindsight. He simply told her that he didn't like them, thought they were just shapes, not pictures at all, which she took to mean that he didn't understand them. She had deferred an explanation of the principles of symbolism and expressionism. Was the concept of representation too much for the boy to grasp? How those smears of mauve could portray the pain of loss or loneliness, what these bold, spiky blocks of fiery orange said about passion or anger or lust. She had let it go. Her art wasn't for everybody. It was just an accident that Florian had glimpsed some of it.

"I'm glad you like the photos at least," she had said with a comforting smile, packing the offending artwork back inside its case.

There was something about Florian that she wanted to keep to herself. Greta was a dear friend but she was also a world-class gossip. She admitted to herself that she liked watching the boy at work. He was a little cack-handed at times, he had a habit of scratching the back of his neck if he hit against a snag and he often laughed at himself, unaware that she was listening.

Greta had launched into another tale of her days in Scotland. It was New Year's Eve. Some party. She had too much to drink. *Thank Christ Clément had stayed in France! Never seen so many whisky bottles, dearie.* Something like that. Val had stopped paying attention.

It was last Friday when Florian had dropped the large frame and shattered the glass. It was a photograph she had taken, had enlarged and mounted years ago: ocean spray on the rocks near the Pointe du Raz. Twilight, rind of a moon. One of Bobby's favourites too.

"*Désolé! Désolé, désolé!*" he had repeated, angry and ashamed of his clumsiness.

"Hey, Florian, *ne t'inquiète pas!*" she had said. She had dropped formality, hadn't called him *vous* for weeks. "Never mind! Don't beat yourself up. *Et fais gaffe*, watch what you're doing in all that glass."

The boy was already on his hands and knees, picking up shards and slicing open his fingertips. Val insisted he stop at once. Raising his hand to slow the bleeding she led him into the kitchen and let the cold water flow over his cuts. His hand, his bare arm, his shoulder – all were warm to her touch. She stood behind him, watching the water run through his fingers; she stayed close to him, unnecessarily and for longer than she ought, smelling his scent, hearing his every breath.

"*Merci*," he said at length, taking a bunch of paper towel from her with an embarrassed smile. "*Que je suis bête*. I am such a fool."

"Of course you're not," Val had said, moving away to hide the blush that she knew had appeared on her cheeks, at her throat.

She was the fool. She was the one who imagined what it would be like to hold his body close, to kiss his face, to run her fingers through his scruffy, flaxen hair. He would not resist her, she knew that. More than once he had told her that he loved coming to the house. The garden gloves were the first of several little gifts he had brought her over the weeks. He had offered her a small box of coloured macaroons for Christmas. And she had insisted that he took from her a case of expensive Belgian beer. And she did look forward to him coming to the house. Made him stay long after the jobs were done. She wondered if he undressed her with his eyes in the same way she did him. She even wondered if he were a virgin.

"You're not actually listening, are you, dearie?"

"What? Yes. Yes, I am."

Greta set her plate on the coffee table with more force than she needed to.

"Sorry, Gret," said Val with a sigh. "I'm having trouble concentrating."

"Mm. And you're looking a bit flushed too. You alright?"

"I do feel a bit lightheaded."

"Not starting on the menopause too, are you?"

"Oh my God!" exclaimed Val. "I bloody hope not!"

Greta had left quite abruptly. Sometimes they did rub each other up the wrong way. And today Val was glad she'd gone early. She opened a bottle of wine and put on a little music.

It was already going dark and the house was filling with shadows. Having loaded the dishwasher she now found herself drifting aimlessly from room to room with a second glass of Vouvray in her hand. She opened the door to the studio, switched on the central light and saw the creased photograph in its large split frame still standing up against the wall. The broken glass had been swept up days ago. The memory of the mortified look on Florian's face brought a smile to her lips. She finished the wine in a long, unsatisfying draught. Of course it was she who was the fool. Hot flushes, cold sweats and a libido she could no longer predict. One minute she was a bundle of electric sparks, her skin prickled by the thought of Florian, Bobby, even Zachary, and the next she felt flat, cold, as dull and as lifeless as a stagnant pool.

She stood in the doorway for a minute, breathing erratically, debating her next move, quite uncertain about why she was standing there at all. The moment she switched off the light she noticed a faint glow beyond the wide studio windows, a small circle of pinkish light hovering in the darkness of the garden. Her instinct was to close the door and retreat into the lounge but she could not. The light was feeble yet hypnotic. Slowly she made her way across the room in the dark, careful to avoid the furniture, the tripod, the boxes cast across the floor. As she approached the French windows, the pink glow floated towards her at chest height. Suddenly she could make out a figure: what appeared to be a human form cloaked in black, holding a torch, directing it into Val's squinty eyes. The figure's head was blurred by a dark shadow and its face, if there was one to see, was invisible.

Val stopped in her tracks, her heart was thumping, she raised a hand to touch the glass door. She was curious and at the same time terrified. There was a sudden shattering of glass and she realised she had dropped the wine glass on to the floor; it had ceased to be a part of her. She looked up from the tiles as the pink light flickered and retreated into the depths of the garden. With her face pressed against the window she watched as the human shape dissolved into the darkness and the light disappeared.

It took a moment for her breathing to recover something close to its normal rhythm. Beyond her was the night. Finally she unlocked the doors and stepped outside. The winter air enveloped her and she wrapped her arms around her shoulders, peering into the garden. There was no sign of movement. There was nothing to see. She glanced over towards the gîte. Its bulky silhouette stood heavy and still beneath the deepening blue sky. There were few clouds and the first stars were alight.

Val took a deep breath, turned to regain the warmth of the house and then something in the air made her stop to listen. It was the strident whistle of a bird establishing its territory for the night. And then her mind was racing, knocking over obstacles like a crazed hurdler. There it was again. She could only think of one bird. She slammed the doors shut and immersed herself in the comforting silence of the house, still clasping her arms around her body to stop herself from shivering.

Was it a blackbird perched in the treetops? Do blackbirds even sing at night?

There was nobody else to hold her. Nobody else to rub her shoulders, to comfort her with a smile or words of reassurance. She locked up, turned off all the ground floor lights and took the wine bottle upstairs. From the window in one of the back rooms she looked out over the studio roof to survey the familiar dark shapes of the garden: all appeared peaceful. She ran a hot bath and let herself soak in the soapy, steamy warmth of it until she felt slightly dizzy. She dried herself slowly, lay a clean bath towel on her bed and lit half a dozen scented candles in the room. If nobody else would love her then she would have to love herself.

In the flickering light she spent a moment warming a

small bowl of lemongrass oil over one of the candles. Then she sat down on the bed, and dipping her fingers again and again into the bowl, ran them gently around every part of her forty-six-year-old body she could comfortably reach. And when the bowl was empty she heated up a little more oil and slowly she massaged herself once again from temples to toes, once again from nape to knees until the candles began to go out one by one, flaring with a brief intensity before their dying flames shifted into tiny strings of smoke. As a velvety blackness filled the room she slipped into her bed and in no time at all had drifted into the deepest of sleeps.

There was no reason to mention the torchlight incident to anybody else. Certainly not to Greta who would ridicule her in some dismissive, flippant way and then Clément would be told and he in turn would want to rehash all that gruesome nonsense about Widow Merel. And in any case, by the following morning Val had put her own mind at rest. Back in the studio to sweep up the broken wine glass, she had noticed the photocopier sitting on the cabinet on the far side of the room. Its little red standby light was on. That was the light she had seen reflected in the plate glass of the French window. The human figure? Well, that would have been her own reflection tottering towards the pane. She had been drinking, had even admitted to Greta that she had been feeling a little fragile. It had been a trick of the light, an illusion that her imagination had run away with. And the birdsong? She could not in all honesty say that what she had heard was the eventide call of a blackbird. It could have been one of a hundred other species. A night owl? A warbler? A robin? Did they have winter robins this far south?

*

The short days of early spring brought a cool dampness to the Sologne. Mostly the breezes were light but when the winds picked up Val liked to sit in her studio and watch the treetops in the woods sway and bend beneath the scurrying banks of cloud.

She had arranged a couple of portrait sittings – photographs of young families who turned up to *Les Genêts* wearing new clothes and practised smiles – but she saw nothing of Florian during these empty weeks. She convinced herself that this was a good thing. Meanwhile from Bobby, from the missing man: nothing. Neither from his solicitor.

On crisp, dry days when a watery sun might make the hoarfrost sparkle, she took herself off into the forest with her camera to photograph aspects of the landscape that caught her eye. Since her meeting with the poachers she had deliberately avoided the Etang de Broussaille; there were plenty of other pools to tramp around.

One day, quite by chance, on a shady bank by a sandy path between two small, secret ponds, she came across a carpet of green tips promising a crowd of early snowdrops before very long. She made a note to return to this spot. Gauging her bearings from the white disk of the sun, she decided that the late afternoon glow, if she were lucky, would best catch the flowers' purity. Soon there would be wild crocuses in these woods too, and the buds on the deciduous trees which were already forming would open into a timid flush of green.

And so it was, one afternoon in late February, that Val retraced her steps through the straggly hawthorn, between the dark pine trees, over the musty drifts of decaying leaves to this very same place. The little white flowers, *des perce-neige*, hundreds of them in tight bunches like sprays of confetti, strained to reach the day's last rays of light. She took dozens of photos, from this angle and that, with and without her tripod, as a clamour of rooks circling the trees punctuated the silence. She figured she couldn't be far from the Château de Cheminolles. It was a place that was notoriously hard to find but she would swear that the woodsmoke she could see above the distant pines was rising wispily from the chimney of one of the estate lodges. In her imagination it was always the mysterious domain of Frantz de Galais' engagement party in *Le Grand Meaulnes*, her favourite French book of all. Many more of the forest tracks had been closed off in recent years, had become overgrown and hidden, and many more signs marked *Propriété Privée* had appeared among the avenues of trees. According to Barachet, the château and its grounds were now in the hands of an American, a dollar billionaire who had made his fortune in data technology.

Suddenly feeling a chill, she packed away her camera, her macro-filter, the compact Manfrotto. Her spirits lifted by the coppery glow on the horizon, by her success with the photographs, she decided to extend the moment by driving the longer way back, skirting the edge of the forest on the south side of Saint-Benoît and forking left at the Quatre-Routes.

Val could never pass the crossroads without thinking of the story of Merel, of Sylvain's fiancée, of the lantern of betrayal. She saw the familiar outline of the stone shrine to the Madonna as she slowed the Mégane to take the corner. On the opposite side of the road, as ever, stood the isolated cottage, in its flat brick and render style, typical in this region with its paucity of local stone. Set back a little beyond a beech hedge and with the sun dropping out of sight behind its roof, it looked dark and abandoned. Meanwhile, just a few metres to the side of the shrine another shaped block of limestone caught her eye, a rectangular slab set on a plinth. She hadn't noticed it before. She stopped the car and got out to take a look. It was by no means new. Dotted with lichen, it held in place a weathered bronze plaque, a memorial to those lost in the war years, local men executed by the occupier:

A NOS FILS GLORIEUX

COMBATTANTS DE LA RÉSISTANCE

FUSILLÉS DANS CETTE COMMUNE 1941-45

MORTS POUR LA PATRIE

She read the inscription again. She thought of Eustache and Sylvain and what years ago Barachet had told her about the demarcation line. She thought of desperate men fleeing south, hiding out in these forests and tracing serpentine routes towards the Cher on moonlit nights. She thought of Merel, of Victorine, her rival, and even of a young Rosette who without maybe ever knowing them would surely have known their stories.

A faint mechanical buzzing disturbed her. She looked up for a motorbike but there were no vehicles on any of the roads converging on the junction. The sound drew her towards the cottage, where, by peeping over the hedge, she spotted a moped leaning against the side of the building. From its grubby canvas panier she recognised it straight away as Florian's. There was no reason for her to set foot on the property but at the same time there was nothing to stop her.

At the rear of the cottage she discovered Florian the handy-boy with his back to her, pushing an old lawn-mower across a square patch of grass. He was wearing a cheap-looking tracksuit top, pale grey jeans, trainers and a pair of headphones. Not until he turned the machine around did he notice her standing there watching him with a smile on her face. His hair was much shorter than it had been in December. He'd had a severe cut, but it was neat, she thought: it showed the pretty curve of his ears, brought out the blue of his eyes. He brought the mower to a halt by her feet and switched off its motor.

"*Val! Que fais-tu ici?*" he said, unable to hide his alarm. "What are you doing here? Is something wrong?"

"*Je te surveille, Florian,*" she replied. "I'm keeping my eye on you. I've caught you working for the enemy."

"The enemy?"

"Not really the enemy. *Je rigole.* It's a joke, Florian. I know I don't have you exclusively to myself."

"*Je fais du jardinage pour le vieux monsieur,*" he said hurriedly as a matter of explanation. "This is the first cut of the year. The old man is back this week."

"The house is empty?"

"Yes, completely. He is on holiday. He takes a cruise, I think, every year at this moment."

Val took in the long expanse of land, hidden from the road, its bushes reawakening after the winter, its paths still strewn with dead leaves.

"*Je viens de finir.* I've just finished the lawn."

"I can see that, Florian. You've done a good job."

Finally he smiled at her.

"Let me put this machine back in the shed," he said, "before it gets too dark."

She watched as the boy rolled the mower away and disappeared behind a row of apple trees, their bare limbs scratching at the air.

Attached to the back of the cottage was a glass-panelled extension, a kind of garden room with closed blinds. A side door, just a few metres from where she stood, was ajar. She wandered over and pushed it open. Inside the room she made out a large sofa, upholstered in corduroy, a low table on which sat a small lamp, and a matching bookcase. Placed among the furniture were tall potted plants: a yucca, a palmetto, a family of cacti. A heavy wooden door leading into the main house was firmly locked. She fingered the top row of books which were mostly biographies of old French film stars: Jeanne Moreau, Belmondo, Fernandel, many others she had never heard of. She took one off the shelf and flicked through its pages at random with eyes for the photography: black and white mainly, of course, beautifully lit, with a few stills garishly colourised.

"You've found the way in!" said Florian, suddenly reappearing and startling her. He was wiping his hands on a rag.

"I'm allowed in here to water the plants." He held up a key to show her. "And I like to have a little rest in here when I'm done."

She closed the book and put it back in its place.

"He does have a lot of books, the old guy," said Florian.

He unzipped his tracksuit top and let it fall to the floor. Then he pushed past her and plonked himself down on the sofa, legs akimbo, hands behind his head.

"Come and join me," he said, patting the space next to him. His tee shirt had the Playboy Bunny design on it. "You fancy a smoke, Val?"

There was something quite different about the boy's attitude. She had seldom seen him beyond her place before. Here he seemed more confident, as if she had discovered him on his own home turf.

"A smoke?"

In the fading light Florian was already leaning forward and rolling out a rough cigarette on the coffee table. Into the paper he was fingering the stringy fibres of a pinch of cannabis. He licked its edge, carefully rolled up the joint and lifted his head to face her.

"*Val, assieds-toi, s'il te plaît,*" he said softly. "Sit down, Val. You look *stressée*. Come and have a smoke with me."

She could have smiled and politely refused. She could have walked away and left him alone. But she did none of those things. Closing the door behind her, she joined him on the sofa, watched as he lit the spliff and, such a gentleman, offered her the first drag. She took it, smiled at him and sucked in the harsh smoke. Her eyes watered but she took it deep into her lungs without coughing and slowly exhaled. It was strong weed, as strong as she had had. She took a second drag before handing it back to the boy.

"*C'est bon?*" he asked fatuously. "It's dark in here. Shall I put on the lamp?"

"No, don't," she answered. "Don't, Florian. It's nicer to sit here in the dark. Don't you think?"

"It's nice," he agreed, taking the cigarette to his lips. "Very nice."

Whether or not he had sensed an opportunity in his cross-wired way, had taken a blindfolded kind of initiative in inviting her to sit by him, and whether or not he had offered to share the joint with some half-baked ulterior motive, it was Val who made the first move towards intimacy. It was Val who took his free hand in hers, who ran her fingers over his thigh, across his cheek. It was Val who leaned in, smelt his skin and kissed him, softly at first then, as he squirmed in his uncertainty and timidly kissed her back, with an erupting violence. And so on she led him, encouraging him with her whispers, persuading him that, yes, he was her guide, he was her light in the darkness, it was he who was leading her along the path, leading her all the way there.

There were very few words left as the evening finally closed in on them. In their own silent, separate ways both Val and Florian contemplated what had just happened between them on the corduroy sofa in the garden room in a fug of weed smoke. Slowly the boy pulled his jeans back on and tidied up the contents of the cigarette box. Val was the first to stand up. She switched on the lamp to find her bra which had fallen to the floor. She handed Florian the key which somehow had also landed under the sofa.

"I'll lock up," he said, looking up at her. "Don't worry about that."

"I'd better go," she answered a moment or two later, talking to the door.

"Me too."

She pulled on her boots, fastened the laces loosely and brushed down her clothes with both hands as if to make herself presentable.

"I'll see you again, Florian."

"Of course."

She ran her fingers through her hair.

"We must keep this our secret, you understand."

"Of course."

"It's important."

"Of course it is. I understand. I'm not a child."

"No. No, you're not. You're not a child, Florian."

"*Notre secret,*" he repeated, catching her look.

"*Oui, notre secret.*"

"And you'll telephone me?"

"Telephone you?"

"For the spring. If you want me for jobs in the spring."

"Yes. Yes, of course, Florian. There will be jobs in the spring. I'm sure of it."

CHAPTER 6

FLORIAN (II)

Did Florian have any regrets? Val couldn't tell. She couldn't read him. He was complicated, unorthodox. As she left him quietly rearranging the sofa cushions his face had given nothing away. It was a face simply reflecting the rearrangement of sofa cushions. But inside, how did he feel?

Was he excited, elated, disappointed, even ashamed, or just confused?

Val most certainly had her regrets. From the moment her head cleared of the mild dizziness brought on by the dope and the rushes of blood. Regrets which had begun to surface as soon as she walked out beyond the beech hedge and across the lanes to regain her car. All thoughts of snowdrops and war memorials and biographies of old French film stars were forgotten for the next twenty-four hours. That she was old enough to be the boy's mother wasn't the half of it. In her mind it had to be considered no more than a moment's lapse, an unrepeatable mistake, an incident as isolated as the cottage at the Quatre-Routes where it had taken place.

It was news of a spate of vandalism that intruded into her brooding. Recent events – a forced entry and damage to a pharmacy in Saint-Benoît, a minibus burned out in the small hours in the Brico-Jacques car park – had left little impression, but two further stories rather closer to home stayed with her long after she had finished watching the reports on the local television news. There had been a night-time break-in at a house less than a kilometre away where expensive electrical items had been damaged beyond repair rather than stolen. A garaged sports car had been defaced with spray paint. The house owners, a family Val knew at least by sight, spoke to a reporter on camera: they were more baffled than angry, it seemed, by what they considered to be gratuitous actions. And immediately after that, Val watched in disbelief as a trembling lady with a towel wrapped around her head spoke in furious tones about a dustbin full of old cardboard and newspaper which had been set alight outside her back door: Madame Motta – yes, Madame Motta, her neighbour – was railing against some unknown vandals who, she insisted, had all but burned her house down. She pointed at the fire damage to her door and window frame. *Luckily I was lying awake at the time*, she said. *I saw the light from the flames. No, I didn't see the culprits.* And with that she spat on the ground at the reporter's feet and stamped away.

Val tried to concentrate her mind on her business. She had done very little to encourage the new season's visitors to the gîte. It was true that by now the place was well established, represented on several holiday company websites, but she had planned, with Bobby's help, to refresh their own site with new photos and copy. *Les Petits Genêts* was available to rent from the end of March or whenever the Easter weekend was this year. She hadn't checked. They rarely had many visitors until after May Day, *la Fête du Travail*.

Suddenly the business seemed unimportant. It was *their* business, not just hers. Without him, without the missing man, she would never have the energy to cope. Today she had all but lost her enthusiasm for it. She lifted the glass to her lips and took a long gulp of the Beaujolais she had carried into the office from the kitchen. Distractedly she fingered the smooth surface of the desk calendar, its familiar cherrywood frame home to the interchangeable marble tablets as big as her thumb which displayed the date in Roman numerals. Sometimes she forgot to change the tablets but today they were correct: XVIII and III. The eighteenth of March. The calendar had been a gift from her friend Claudia the classicist, at a time when they had briefly shared a house: six months of domestic anarchy, of impromptu parties, of demented, girly fun. Claudia the classicist, acolyte of those ancient Greek deities of indulgent pleasure whose names Val could no longer confidently recall: Dionysus? Bacchus? And whose favoured school of thought in those days was unbridled Hedonism. But clever old Claudia had been right about Bobby all along, hadn't she? That he was immature, selfish and an intellectual pygmy. *You'll regret it in the end, Val, love.* And so how was Claudia's love life right now, she wondered. What success had she had in finding her perfect partner? She had no idea. The women had not been in contact with each other since their very last slanging match.

The glow of the computer screen pulled her back to the moment. She scrolled down the list of bookings and discovered that the weeks were already filling up. July and August completely reserved: English, Dutch, Germans, the usual suspects. She would need an extra pair of hands to help with the cleaning and the laundry for sure. She had used a woman in town before but it had ended badly. Val had accused her of stealing a camera from her studio. Without evidence her harsh words were lashed back even more ferociously before the inevitable, explosive walkout. And as for repairs, maintenance, gardening, she wasn't entirely hopeless but there were certain jobs that Bobby had insisted she should never attempt. She would telephone Florian, of course. As she had said she would. As he hoped she would. But the fact was that she had delayed the call, wary of seeming needy, reluctant to appear to be encouraging him in any misguided ambition he might have. So, she would phone him soon, and then force herself to keep her distance.

The police maintained that the damage to *Les Petits Genêts* was part of a pattern of malicious incidents. There was a fortnight between Madame Motta's blazing bin and the more serious attack on Val's property but the consensus was that the escalation was, if not inevitable, then at least sadly predictable.

As before, the vandalism was inflicted in the dead of night. Shivering, gasping through short, jerky breaths, and with her friend Greta Barachet pulling a coat over her shoulders, Val explained to the police officer that she'd heard nothing during the night; nothing beyond the rain pattering against the bedroom window which had sent her to sleep. In the middle of the morning, getting into her car, she had noticed the door to the gîte was not fully closed. The lock, not the sturdiest, had been forced open. Inside she'd come across a scene of devastation: furniture broken and overturned, the television screen shattered, kitchenware scattered over the floor, crockery in fragments. Upstairs she found untouched: a consolation. She'd surveyed the wreckage on the ground floor once more, tried to make some sense of it, collapsed on the one chair left standing and had broken down in a flood of tears. It was not until after she'd phoned the *commissariat* and then made a second, more emotional plea to Greta, that she wandered outside and noticed the coup de grâce: in the middle of the long empty chicken coop, lying in the muddy earth where grass had failed to grow, was the damp corpse of a small bird. It was a blackbird – she spotted its orange beak – whose tiny head had been part sliced away and was hanging obliquely like that of a broken doll.

Later that day an investigating officer appeared at her door. She was relieved to see a man with an altogether more empathetic expression than the juvenile *flic* who had arrived on the scene in the morning with a list of rudimentary questions, a hard, pasty-faced scowl and a dozy-looking assistant in a uniform two sizes too large. He had treated her with disdain, she thought, repeating questions slowly, presupposing her French was lacking. And yet this man, this older inspector – early forties, she would say, looking at his round, ruddy, lived-in face – not only greeted her with a courteous smile and a word or two of consolation, he actually seemed familiar to her: someone she had met before, someone she felt to be competent, a proper problem-solver. He wore a neat blue tie and a pleasant aftershave. His short dark hair was showing grey at the temples, matching his eyes. He was not much taller than Val and was a little tubby around the midriff, she thought, but not alarmingly so.

She invited him to sit with her in the lounge, which he duly did, unbuttoning his jacket and making himself comfortable. Still on edge, Val had missed the man's name when he had introduced himself on the doorstep and she had to ask again.

"Ledru," he replied. "Inspecteur Marius Ledru. From the headquarters in Blois."

He spoke in English. Val couldn't be bothered to correct his assumption that she was unable to participate in a conversation in French. She offered to make him a cup of coffee. As she went about the operation he continued to talk to her from the lounge, placing the break-in at the gîte into context with other recent incidents, reassuring her that all cases were being assiduously addressed. It was at that moment that she recognized his voice. A glance back into the room to catch his features confirmed the memory: Ledru was the detective she had seen on her television screen eight months ago at the Camping des Deux Etangs, talking to journalists about the arrest of the schoolteacher Amanda Ringer.

"You must have given some thought as to why the gîte was targeted, *madame*?" he said as she reappeared with a tray.

"I've thought of little else," she said.

"And, so, anything you'd like to share with me?"

"I've no idea. Really, I haven't. I have no enemies. Apart from…"

"Apart from?"

"Well, he's not an enemy. Not an enemy at all. If your team have been doing their jobs properly you'll know why I've been living here alone since last summer."

"I am aware of your husband… Bobby is his name?"

"He's not my husband."

"I'm sorry. My error. Boyfriend? Partner?"

"Ex-partner."

"Yes, of course."

"But he wouldn't go in for anything like this. He might resent me, bear me an eternal grudge, but he would never smash up the gîte. He did most of the work on it himself in the first place."

"When did you last hear from him, *madame*?"

"Back in the autumn."

"Is he still in France?"

111

"No. He's in England now. Has been for months, I imagine."

"Do you have an address?"

"I can give you the details of his lawyer."

"That might be helpful."

Val headed into the office to find the solicitor's letter.

"At least to eliminate him," he called.

"Yes, I understand."

Presently she reappeared, handed the letter with its Dorchester address over to Ledru and watched him photograph it on his mobile.

"Your colleague took my DNA this morning," she went on.

"Yes, it's procedure, of course. I apologise if you felt it was an intrusion. And the fingerprints. It's to eliminate you too, of course. The officers examined the ground floor of the cottage, I assume?"

"Yes. They were here for over an hour."

"They need to look for any presence of DNA, prints and so on from somebody other than you. You understand?"

"Yes, I know how it works, Inspector."

"And you told them all you know about your neighbour, Madame Motta?"

Val was impressed that the man had no recourse to a notebook; he was working from memory, he was a man who could keep all the plates spinning.

"Yes, Madame Motta."

"Anything to add?"

"I have little to do with her, really. I told the officer that I find her eccentric. Eccentric but harmless."

"And you said 'unpredictable' too?"

"Did I? I might have said 'unpredictable'. She is."

"Fine. And you answered all their questions this morning."

Val nodded.

Ledru drained his coffee, stood up, refastened his jacket buttons.

"Thanks for that," he smiled. "Best coffee I've had all day. And I've had plenty! Do you mind if I look around the downstairs rooms here in the house? Check the locks, the windows?"

"Not at all. Be my guest."

"And then I'll have a snoop around the gîte myself if I may. And your land. The place is locked, I imagine?"

"Yes, they did lock up. I'll fetch you the keys."

He followed her into the kitchen. The day was almost done, the light starting to fade. But peering into the garden, the inspector was surprised to see the figure of a young man dismantling what was left of the chicken run.

"Who is that?" he asked.

"That's Florian. He does jobs for me. Gardening, maintenance and such. Since Bobby left."

"Does he normally come on a Tuesday?"

"No. He doesn't have a regular day. Especially at this time of the year."

"So you called him up today. Asked him round to help with the tidy-up?"

"Not in the gîte, obviously."

"Obviously."

She nodded. Of course she had called him up. When Greta had left, when the police had finished in the gîte, had taped it off and had driven away, she'd suddenly felt horribly alone. Exposed, vulnerable. She needed a presence around her, for an hour or two at least. To bring back some normality to her bedevilled home. That was all. No ulterior motive. For a start he could get rid of the dead bird for her. Then he could set about breaking up the sad old coop. Throughout the winter months it had stood empty and forlorn like a shipwreck run aground.

"I'll have a word with him," Ledru said. "If you don't mind."

"You know him?"

"Florian? Yes, I know him. Don't worry, *madame*. Just a word. Thanks again for the coffee. I'll be back with your keys in a short while and say my goodbyes."

Val watched him as he stepped out on to the patio and, rather than heading directly to the gîte, took several strides towards Florian, distracting him from his labours with a rough greeting. She failed to hear what they were saying but the conversation soon became heated, Ledru barking at the younger man and jabbing at his chest with a forefinger. Florian was on the defensive, that much was plain to see, answering back then lowering his head in a sulky retreat. He started picking up his tools as the policeman marched away towards the gîte and disappeared from her view.

Florian left without saying goodbye. By the time Ledru knocked on the kitchen door it was almost dark outside.

"Here are your keys, *madame*," he said. "Please stay out of there until the team has finished. They'll be back tomorrow morning."

"Yes, they said."

"An hour at the most, I imagine."

"Did you find anything in there just now?"

"Nothing unexpected. I took some photos."

"I see."

Val put the keys in a drawer.

"Any theories about the blackbird?"

"Ah, the dead bird."

"That spooked me more than the damage."

"It is unique to this case."

"No blackbirds at the other incidents. Nothing next door?"

"No. No, it is an interesting aspect to this particular case."

"But no theories?"

"No, not yet. Give me time."

His pause was an invitation for Val to offer her own thoughts but none came. He straightened his tie and spoke again to bring the conversation to a close.

"So, I'll leave you in peace. I'll be in touch, *madame*."

"What did you say to Florian?" she asked abruptly. "He disappeared without even a goodbye."

"I'm sorry. It was just something I needed to remind him of. There is no need for you to worry."

"I hope you haven't scared him off coming here. I'll need him for all sorts of jobs in the next few weeks."

Ledru cast her an apologetic smile.

"No, no. That's not my style. But you might be better off taking on somebody else. I'd let him go if I were you. If you have to have him, please be careful."

"Be careful?"

"I don't want to say anymore, *madame*. Really, there is no need to worry. You've got enough to concern yourself with. You said all the downstairs windows are lockable?"

"Yes."

"Keep them locked then, that's my advice. It was a pleasure to meet you, *madame*."

Before turning to go he pulled open his wallet.

"Here, let me give you my number," he said, fishing out a small card. "Direct to me if you feel you need it. Please try to relax. You should feel perfectly safe tonight."

"Marius Ledru," said Val, reading from the card, then spelling out the man's surname. "Do you know him, Gret?"

"Ledru? No, I've never heard the name before. Maybe he's moved to Blois just recently. I'll ask Clément. You okay now?"

"I'm fine. Really, I am."

"You don't want me to come over again? It's no trouble."

"No, really. No need."

"I could stay over."

"There's no need, Gret. I'm okay, honestly. The place is locked up. I've just cooked myself a nice bit of chicken. Halfway through a bottle of red."

"Glad to hear it."

"Yeah."

There was a short pause. Val could sense some apprehension at the other end of the line.

"I don't want to upset you all over again, dearie," Greta said presently.

"Upset me?"

"Well, actually, you might consider it good news."

"What? What are you talking about?"

"Try and stay calm, Val. It might not even be true. A good friend of mine mentioned to me this evening that Bobby has been seen in town."

"Bobby?"

"Bobby. Your Bobby. He's back, Val. Back in the area."

CHAPTER 7

AMANDA RINGER

As an avid reader of one or two of the more esteemed Sunday newspapers, Val was aware that she generally feasted on a more restricted diet via a computer screen on her French kitchen table when compared to the readership of breakfast Britain. The online editions of British titles, though providing the majority of their print content, sometimes fail to include articles from their weekend magazines. It was a genuine surprise, therefore, to discover that a certain feature interview, written up by a journalist she had never heard of, had made its way on to a favourite website. Scanning the newspaper's headlines, her eyes were drawn to the name of Amanda Ringer in a panel next to the title: Putting The Past Behind Her.

With a single click she found herself staring at a contemporary photograph of the woman – striking, almost glamorous – and below it paragraph after paragraph of text which she read quickly, gobbling it up like a plate of rapidly cooling food. She could feel her heartbeat accelerating. She stopped, took a deep breath, a gulp of coffee and started to read it all over again:

"Let's meet outside," she had suggested. "Make the most of the unseasonal warmth." She had even made a joke of having spent too much time lately cooped up inside. And when I arrive the woman is already sitting in the pub's beer garden, shaded by a sturdy pair of apple trees in heavy bud. She stands to greet me, one hand outstretched towards mine as the other lifts her sunglasses on to the top of her head, sweeping up the fringe of jet black hair. Her eyes are piercing, fizzing with life. I could almost be looking at Audrey Hepburn, circa 1962. Her clothes appear new, well chosen: understated early summer wear of salmon pink tee and white denim jeans. A cashmere cardigan in navy hangs over her slender shoulders. She smiles confidently. She radiates good health. She has been out of prison for less than a week and it is clear that she has already moved on.

Mandy Roundtree, formerly Amanda Ringer, is a forward-looking woman, not one for dwelling on the past, and who can blame her? She has agreed to speak to me, not to put the record straight, not to give her side of a well-documented story, but to invite me to share her enthusiasm for the most important chapter in her life: the next one.

Val studied the main image. Audrey Hepburn indeed. What nonsense. The journalist was too deferential, in awe of her cashmere cardigan in navy and her designer shades; she would give her an easy ride. And Roundtree? Not Rowntree? Why had she insisted on such an affected spelling? She could call herself what she liked but to Val she would always be Amanda Ringer.

A teacher of some seven years' experience, Roundtree concedes that she will not be returning to the classroom. Whether she still might have the right to do so at some point in the future is moot.

"I don't think any head in their right mind would employ me," she says. "Not that I'm not a perfectly employable teacher. You have to imagine the reaction of the parents. I must say, though, that Dean's parents have forgiven me, totally. They have been amazingly charitable."

Dean Buckle was the sixteen-year-old boy at the centre

of Roundtree's aberration. Last summer photographs of the pair were to be seen on the front pages of all the newspapers and across the internet. They were the targets of a Europe-wide search for missing persons.

A slight exaggeration, Val thought, scanning the photos. There was the infamous one: the couple with their rucksacks, the grainy still from the security camera at St Pancras. And below it Ringer's police arrest photo, complete with unbrushed hair and dark shadows around her eyes. And then, in colour, a picture of the pale blue tent at the Camping des Deux Etangs where she was apprehended.

Roundtree's own parents have been less forgiving of their daughter, she tells me, especially her mother, herself a teacher.

"My mother is a primary school head. She sees teaching not only as a vocation but as a spiritual calling. She believes I have somehow brought the whole profession into disrepute."

As for her own subject, she has a political point to make.

"In any case it seems like language learning is in terminal decline in this country. It's terribly sad. Every child deserves the chance to have their minds opened, to have their horizons broadened, and learning foreign languages does that. I believe that having two languages helps you to see the world twice as clearly.

"No, I'm going to retrain," she goes on. "I have transferable skills. For example the two most important attributes for a teacher, in my opinion: organisational ability and a sense of humour. That's the skill to organise so that absolutely nothing can go wrong, and a sense of humour for when it does."

She smiles at the elegance of her aphorism.

"I'm going to retrain as a nurse. I want to help people. Not just here, but abroad. I'd like to travel, maybe with MSF (Médecins Sans Frontières) or some other agency. I have fluent French, pretty good Spanish. When I see people's lives in Haiti, for example, I think that I could do some good there. Or West Africa. Or the Middle East. I've got my whole life ahead of me."

She looks five years younger but Roundtree is in fact not so far off her thirtieth birthday. A short prison regime has done her no harm at all, it would appear. Released halfway through an eighteen-month sentence for abuse of trust and sexual activity with a minor, Roundtree was a model prisoner. This, according not just to her own account but that of the prison governor who attested to her remorse and her willingness to contribute inside, to play a positive role in the life of the inmates.

"Yes, it's true that I was allowed to do a bit of teaching inside – once they had the measure of me, once they knew I was genuine. I gave some basic French lessons to any women who wanted to come and take part. And I helped with gym classes, yoga and stuff like that. I needed to keep myself active, involved in something useful."

I ask if she has left Amanda Ringer behind because that identity had in itself become toxic.

"It's true that Amanda was the target of a lot of vitriol," she says, as if talking about an absent third person. "Especially anonymous stuff, online abuse. I quit social media months ago. There's too much hate, it's like a sewer. It's no place for reason or common sense. Of course it was all very predictable and I'm not so stupid that I don't get it. I do understand people's anger, all the outrage, but I have taken my punishment and have earned the right to move on.

"I'm not a paedophile, for example. I spoke at great length with a psychiatrist in prison. I've studied the sociology, the psychology. That profile isn't me. It simply isn't."

She flashes a smile of such defiance that I have to return it lest I make myself an enemy for life.

"Leaving Amanda behind is my way of dealing with the shitstorm. The public will soon find someone else to demonise in any case. Amanda will soon be forgotten, she'll become just another ghost from the past. A lot of it was because she's female, I'm sure of it. Imagine if she'd been black. We don't live in a kind society - that's a great myth."

Val turned away from the screen to rest her eyes. She found the woman's self-pity breath-taking. She took a sip of coffee, rubbed the back of her neck and resumed her reading.

I ask her about her escapade with the schoolboy, not expecting much of a response. For a moment, however, staring off into the middle distance, she lets down her guard.

"I realise it was a mistake, of course I do. A massive mistake, obviously. But at the same time, in that moment, well, we were in love. It's the truth. People might baulk at that, even be offended, disgusted, whatever, but I don't think you can use the same rulebook when it's a matter of falling in love. Love can spark between people who are [and here she makes speech marks with her fingers] 'wrong for each other'. Be it socially, religiously... Sometimes it fails, sometimes it might lead to a lifetime of happiness in spite of everything. But yes, I suppose we had a match that was destined to fail. We just wanted to make it last for as long as we could. And I keep saying 'we' because it was the both of us, it was a proper partnership."

Was there a plan, something more than a few days on the run?

"Not really. I suppose I knew it couldn't last. But we were so very happy, living in that intense moment together. I was blind to the future."

A future without ever teaching again?

"Yeah, I do regret that, of course. I was pretty good at it. But it's not the end for me."

Mandy pauses, looks up at a vapour trail slowly furrowing the sky, then re-engages, smiling.

"Living for the present is the secret. Carpe diem and all that. The past is over, gone. People have memories, regrets. They train themselves to remember the good times just as they train themselves to forget the bad. But you can't go back there, can you? The past is set, unchangeable.

"And the future? Well, you can make plans, have dreams, ambitions, aspirations, but nothing in the future is ever secure, nothing is reliable. I've told you I have plans of my own, to retrain, work abroad, but who knows if any of it will happen? The future is just a curtain of mist.

"And so I live for the moment. In the moment. This is what it was like for Dean and me: relishing the present, grasping it with both hands, embracing it. Minute by minute. That's the most important lesson I ever taught him."

As if to underline her message she takes a mouthful of fruit juice, savouring the taste, swallows it slowly, deliberately, as it refreshes her throat. Her eyes are closed.

My God, thought Val. Why was this woman letting her ramble on like a third-rate philosopher? Mind you, she had a point. The present was the only place Val could come right now and feel safe. Her past was poisoned, the future felt like a trap.

"And Dean?

"Dean has moved on, and good luck to him. I defy anyone to say that he was scarred, that he was psychologically damaged in any way by the experience. Dean's a wonderful young man. He never said a bad word against me. He has a girlfriend his own age, I'm told, so good luck to them. We were never so far apart, you know, in age. Twelve years between us, that's all."

And with an eyebrow raised, she poses a final thought:

"Twelve years. What's that later in life? We'd have both been bobbing along in middle age together, wouldn't we?'"

Val scrolled back to the top. She finished her coffee but it had gone cold and she spat it back into the cup. The main photo was a clever shot: outdoors, natural light, not too much make-up. The photographer would have taken a rapid series – each portrait the same but subtly different – and he or she or the editor had chosen what was probably the last of the run, the one where the smile of Saint Mandy the Misunderstood had begun to curdle into something slightly more forced: a smile, Val thought, betrayed by the faintest trace of something unpleasant.

Sébastien Albiero was in a sour mood. Perhaps he'd had a difficult day. Perhaps she'd interrupted a domestic row. Val realised that she was not going to be invited inside the house; the man stood behind the half-opened door with his arms folded and a look of impatience on his unshaven face. The smell of fried onions drifted over the threshold and a ginger cat took the chance to slip past his ankles and out into the road.

"I thought you might know where Bobby was staying," she repeated.

Albiero coughed to clear his throat. For a moment she thought he was about to spit at her. He said nothing, casting a glance back into the house from where there was a faint radio conversation.

"As he did stay here before," she added.

"*Ecoute-moi bien, Val*, listen," said the mechanic, turning back to face her. "*Je ne l'ai pas vu*. I haven't seen Bobby since last summer. Yes, he stayed here for a day or two. But since then, *rien*, nothing."

"No messages?"

"*Non, rien du tout*."

"He's been seen in Saint-Benoît recently."

"That's news to me."

"If he were back here he would contact you, I'm sure. Even if he wouldn't contact me."

"I've told you, *je te répète*, he hasn't."

A voice from inside the house called Séba's name. It sounded like his wife's.

"I have to go and help Mireille," he said, hooking a thumb over his shoulder.

"Nobody has mentioned him at the garage, Séba?"

"Val, you're not listening. I didn't even know he had come back. I don't even know if that is the truth in any case."

She gave him a moment to change his story but the man's eyes were unblinking, as hard as ice.

"Okay, I'm sorry for troubling you."

"That's okay."

"But if you do see him…"

"What?"

"Well, please tell him I want to speak to him. Tell him that."

"*Bonne soirée, Val,*" said Albiero, closing the door.

Val turned into the street, where evening shadows were already forming. It had been a warm day. She was on foot, she would take the long, slow way back, maybe cross the bridge, walk by the Liselle, clear her head.

In the kitchen Sébastien Albiero found his wife in a cloud of steam, draining pasta in boiling water. A meal for two tonight, but there had been meals for three very recently. And that did not include his daughter visiting from *la fac.* Bobby had turned up out of the blue, then disappeared again, and it was true that his friend did not know where he was tonight. Another spare room, a motel somewhere? It was better he didn't know. But as for his van, his old white work van, well, he knew exactly where that was. Surrounded by large plastic panels advertising *Concessionnaire de Citroën 2020* and under a dusty sheet for good measure, it was hidden in one of the ramshackle outbuildings at the back of the best garage in the Sologne.

Val concluded that even if Bobby were no longer in the area, even if his appearance had been no more than an illusion, the inspector, Ledru, should know about it. The missing man needed to be placed at the centre of anything unexplained that was happening to her. Yet in spite of this she was reluctant to believe that he had been on her property while she had been sleeping. She wondered if Ledru knew about the local legend of Widow Merel. And whether he was a man who believed in ghosts. Because the moment she put what she knew about blackbirds into the policeman's head then she was implicating quite a cast of characters, not the least significant of whom was Bobby himself. She was surprised yet rather gratified that the policeman insisted that, rather than continue on the phone, he come over and speak to her in person. Would she mind? Was she likely to be in all morning? Well, no, not at all, and, yes, yes, she had a few jobs to do at home. One of which was to make herself more presentable.

The bathroom mirror was turning into an enemy: at the corners of her eyes, even before she smiled, fine lines were etched a little deeper into her skin, as if traced by the sharp nib of an ink-pen. And below them, crescents of mauve, fragile and dry like rice paper, rested on cheekbones, once pink and glowing and noble, which now appeared ever more skeletal. And not only was her hair untidy it was also home to a growing infiltration of frost. She remembered her mother's hair being snowy grey, always neatly cut but entirely grey, at the time of her death in the hospital; she was forty-two at the time, younger than Val was now. She brushed it through, screwed it into a knot and tied it up. She put on a touch of make-up, eyes and cheeks, brushed her teeth and chose a newish top from her wardrobe. She had made an effort.

When his car appeared she had watched through the window as he tucked it carefully by the wall, stepped out, straightened his tie, fastened a button on his jacket. He was wearing a different suit, she noticed: charcoal, a lighter twill for the summer, a neat, fashionable cut.

"We will keep our eyes open for your partner," he was reassuring her. "That goes without saying."

Val couldn't be bothered to correct him – *ex*-partner – again. Actually it wasn't a case of being bothered; she didn't want to seem petty, didn't want him to think of her as pedantic.

"But there have been no sightings to our knowledge. And of course, even if he were living down the road we cannot make accusations without evidence."

They were standing in the kitchen, nursing coffee cups and sharing a plate of English biscuits.

"And you, yourself, Val, you are well? I would say, recovered, since the incident?"

From the moment she had offered to refill the cafetière, he had insisted that she call him Marius, that they dispense with *vous*, that he allow him to call her Val. It seemed as natural as the sunlight that was filling the room.

"I'm fine," she said. "I'm really busy, in fact. Too much else to think about. The weeks are rattling along and I've got my hands full."

"Yes, I can see you have guests."

Almost on cue a middle-aged couple walked past the oleander, heading down the path towards their Mercedes.

"Germans, I'm guessing," said Ledru. "I did notice the plates."

"Our first – *my* first – Germans of the season. Two couples, actually. Staying for five nights."

"I'm very fond of Germany," Ledru took over, reminiscing about a family holiday in Bavaria he had enjoyed as a boy. He remembered a campsite by a blue lake where he was taught to paddle a kayak, games of football with dozens of German children that ran on well past sunset, hikes with his parents through forests and up mountain slopes, sunshine and ice cream, damson cake and smoked cheese and lots of barbecued sausages. She let him talk. She liked the sound of his voice: it was enthusiastic yet calm, confident, reassuring. And his accented English gave his words a sensual shading.

"You had the damages repaired without too much trouble, I hope?"

She realised he had changed the subject, had asked her a question, was waiting good-humouredly for an answer.

"Sorry?"

"The repairs?"

"Yes, the insurance company were helpful. The damage was quite superficial, to be honest."

"And Florian helped?"

"He was here a couple of times for me. He did a bit of repainting, that kind of thing."

"I see."

"You seem to have a problem with him, Marius."

"I just want to protect you."

"Protect me? He's harmless, I would say."

"Perhaps."

She gave him the chance to elaborate. He hesitated, taking a deep breath before addressing her again:

"He was in a lot of bother a year ago."

"Bother?"

She was already thinking of drug use.

He coughed discreetly to clear his throat, fixed her with his oyster grey eyes.

"There were accusations of incest. His sister made a complaint against him. You know, sexual advances, intercourse against her will. Actually multiple complaints, well-founded, apparently. But which he denied, so, who knows? None of the allegations could be proved, as far as I know. They were both living at home at the time. Together with an incapacitated mother, I believe. The police were involved, plus the social services. It was recommended to the sister,

I've forgotten her name, that she move out, which she did. It wasn't a case I was involved with at all personally but certain colleagues still refer to him as 'the deviant.'"

Val did not know what to think.

"As I said before, Val, I believe the best thing would be for you to find someone else to do your paintwork."

He approached her and put a hand softly on her shoulder.

"Hey, I'm sorry. I'm sorry if I've upset you."

"It's alright," she said with a shallow smile. "Just a bit of a shock."

"Shall I speak to him for you?"

"No. No, let me deal with it."

"If you're sure. Say, let me cheer you up. Let me take you into Blois at the weekend. Do you like Chinese food? There's a new restaurant opened up around the corner from my apartment. Everyone who's been says they loved it. I really don't want to go and try it on my own. Would you come and keep me company?"

It was an invitation right out of the blue. One minute he was discussing police procedure, the next he was asking her out on a date. She smiled, almost laughed. Ledru was polite, presentable and had a lovely, warm demeanour. There was absolutely no reason for her to refuse.

The opportunity to speak to Florian arose quickly. He was due the following day to tend to the vegetable beds. Having spent time the previous month planting out with Val, that corner of the garden had become a joint project in his mind: something he could share with her, and the thought of it gave him a cosy feeling.

She was waiting for him as he carefully wheeled his moped through the narrow gap between the two large German cars. Rather than welcoming him with her usual fondness, rather than letting him get settled into his routine of ferreting out the tools from the outhouse, she beckoned him into the kitchen and sat him down on a breakfast stool. He thought nothing of her sullen expression, expecting to be offered a drink and maybe a biscuit, five minutes for a chat before he set about his weeding. Val remained standing and, with no little unease, suggested to him that his work on her property should cease. She remembered him blinking; he was not understanding her, she needed to repeat her message. The second time it sounded blunt, harsh, dismissive. She remembered trying to answer his question why. She had rehearsed the lines but she found herself stumbling with stage fright. *There is less to do these days. I can manage on my own. I cannot afford to pay you anymore. You should look for better work somewhere else. You need something more regular, something substantial.*

"This is because we fucked, isn't it?" he said, bringing a sudden silence to the room.

"Isn't it?" he demanded.

"No. No, it's not that, Florian."

"I'm an embarrassment to you."

"No, not at all."

"You want to forget all about the fucking. To forget all about me."

"You know that could never happen again, Florian."

For an instant he looked hard into her eyes, willing her to take back her words.

"Couldn't it? Really?"

131

"Be sensible."

"Sensible?"

Suddenly the boy – he seemed even more of a boy that morning – was wiping his eyes.

"Hey, please don't cry."

"I'm not crying," he sniffed, rubbing his face with his open palms. "I'm not."

"I still like you, Florian. We can still be friends, can't we?"

He looked up at her, his wide, bloodshot eyes searching for her lies. Getting down from the stool he made to leave, turning back as he reached the door.

"I know what all this is about," he said, scratching the back of his neck.

Val watched his face contort into a snarl.

"*C'est le flic*. It's the cop. The cop who saw me here. He's your new boyfriend, isn't he? You're dumping me for him, aren't you? Aren't you, Val? Dumping me for a cop."

She felt ensnared by his words. And she had no words of her own to answer the boy, either to defend herself or to comfort him.

"I don't blame you," he said solemnly. "I knew you'd dump me soon enough. But for a cop?"

She remembered how he had shaken his head and left her alone in the kitchen, gently closing the door behind him.

Val had second thoughts about going to Brico-Jacques later that week. She needed a hosepipe extension and it was the obvious destination. But it would be stupid, cowardly even, to head instead into Blois or to visit some distant garden centre she'd once driven past near Romorantin. If she bumped into Florian, well, it needn't be awkward. She tried to convince herself that she would not avoid him, that she would not walk down a different aisle if she caught sight of him stacking shelves or talking to a customer.

As it often will, fate threw them together almost immediately. She passed the service desk and saw him just twenty metres away in his bright green dungarees with a mop and bucket wiping up some spillage. He looked up and saw her. She had no choice but to say *bonjour* and offer a few words of neutral small talk. But why she chose to ask him how his sister was, how Félicité was – she actually mentioned by her name – was beyond her. It was impulsive, born of nervousness.

"She's okay," he said dismissively. "I guess. I don't see her much." He might have added: "Why you asking about *her*, Val?"

But he didn't. He just carried on wiping the floor. Just as well, she thought afterwards. Short of ripping the lid off a can of worms, she would have had no idea what to say.

An hour later she received a text message from Florian. In the time it took for her to buy the hose, drive home and make herself a sandwich, in the time it took for him to clean up the aisle, take a coffee break and think again about what she had said, he had reshaped his anger into words he was determined she should read:

It was Félice who raped me! Over and over. Made me do it. Forced me. Then blamed me. The cops believed her. Can you believe me?

Florian wasn't a saint but he was no rapist. And it was important for him to tell her. In his clumsy way and for the sake of his fragile self-esteem, the boy was demanding her validation. She might be the only person in the world to believe him, and for that reason above any other she texted him back:

I believe you, Florian.

And it was true. His simplicity allowed no space for pretence. She found it was easy to believe him. Oh, how wrong they were: Marius, with his unconfirmed reports and his well-founded rumours, and Greta, too, in her rose-tinted way. Half a truth was much worse than no truth at all.

Brico-Jacques, that oversized hardware store – she had forgotten its name, if ever she knew it – had flashed one or twice across Amanda Ringer's thoughts. Incarcerated, with empty hours on her hands, she had had plenty of time to reflect on the recent past.

She had thought with affection about her short relationship with Dean, their ill-advised adventure, the unrestrained joy she had experienced with him during those crazy days, cruelly curtailed, running ahead of the chasing pack. She had considered the discomfort and embarrassment their capture had put him through. She regretting hurting him, hurting his parents, the school, everyone. And she felt sorry for herself, had long days of self-pity, of self-flagellation.

She had thought deeply about the very end of it all, the final hours of their escape. The abrupt and indiscreet arrival of the police cars. The very weird atmosphere that suddenly descended on the campsite. Somebody had betrayed her, somebody had given the game away. The more she thought, the harder she forced her memory to spin through a thousand and one images, the more certain she felt that she knew who.

Inside the police car or at the *commissariat* in Orléans, or somewhere else in between, she had overheard snippets of unguarded conversation: police in uniform, detectives, grumbling, mumbling, whispering about her case. Generally beyond her earshot but now and then within it. In French, naturally. So no harm done, she was English, she wouldn't pick it up. But, of course, she had. Bilingual, quick-witted and brimming with nervous energy, Amanda Ringer had convinced herself she had heard someone say that a breakthrough phone call had come in from a female.

She had crossed paths with many women since she and Dean had boarded the Eurostar, but the woman whose face, whose voice faded in and out of her consciousness with ever-increasing focus was the woman with the pink sun visor who had hovered just a couple of yards from them as they sat in front of their tent making tea on their very last morning. The woman with the dog. Milou. Tintin's dog. A dog that neither she nor Dean actually saw. *Excusez-moi, madame. Je cherche mon p'tit chien.* She remembered the tremble in her voice. The breathlessness. And the slight but unmistakable English accent.

Dean had made a disparaging comment when she'd gone. He'd called her batty or spooky or something. Neither of them believed she was camping there. She must have been a local, someone who knew the site and its river walks. And there was something else about the alarm in her expression – something that made her think of Brico-Jacques, that shop, the queue at the till, the dry heat of the car park. Had she seen the same face there? Was it one of the customers or the woman at the checkout who had taken her money for, what was it, the camping chairs? No, she was just a Sunday girl.

Something vaguely superstitious prevented Amanda Ringer from journeying to Saint-Benoît-en-Sologne by the same tortuous route along which she had led Dean Buckle almost twelve months earlier. She had deliberately avoided St Pancras, the Gare du Nord and all that waiting around at railway stations and bus stops. She had decided instead to fly from Southampton to Paris Charles de Gaulle and hire a car. And there was no reason to skulk around this time, at least not until she got much closer to her quarry. Wearing a blond wig, she'd arrived at the tourist hotel she'd chosen in Blois just as the streetlights were coming on.

The next morning after breakfast she drove directly south-east, following forest roads until she arrived, with a flutter of apprehension in her chest, on the outskirts of the familiar town of Saint-Benoît. The campsite was quiet: mid-morning, early season, less than a third full. She drove in and parked by the reception office, nonchalantly wandered in and asked for a brochure of local attractions. She was hoping to find someone she might recognize, someone to throw out an innocent question to. And suddenly there he was, outside in the sunshine, the gardener who had kicked a ball around with Dean for half an hour, the mower of the grass, the cleaner of the *bloc sanitaire*, the self-styled manager of the campground. He was ferrying rubbish bins from one side of the building to the other and seemed grateful for the interruption. She told him she was in the town looking for a long-lost school friend, an Englishwoman in her forties who may or may not walk a dog by the river over there from time to time. She gave him as much detail as she could recall about her appearance: not much at all, really, but enough to elicit a reaction. Scratching at his whiskers for a moment, the man was apologetic. He could think of several dog-walkers, none English as far as he knew. Saint-Benoît wasn't a big place, he said, foreign residents were rare, but he knew of a German lady who more or less fitted the description. German? The man might be mistaken. Ringer improvised: yes, her friend had married a German, maybe he had seen them together? *Non, jamais ensemble. Never together here on the site.* She was a lady who had a big house on the edge of town. She ran a gîte next door. *Come to think of it, there is a man lives there too. Son mari. Her husband, I suppose. Drives a van about, does a bit of building work. The only reason I know this is from doing the bins. I used to work for the council on the bin lorries.*

It took him a moment to remember the lane, to direct Ringer into town and then back out the other side. To finesse her search she googled local gîtes and found a spot called *Les Petits Genêts* that seemed to fit the bill. The website was rudimentary but the accommodation looked very presentable, nicely photographed. Not that she would ever be staying there.

And so, ten minutes later, here she was at the far end of the lane, sitting in her hire car with her sunglasses reflecting the glare of the sun, having already driven by the property – the main house *Les Genêts* – three or four times. She was hoping for a sight of Milou's mistress. The driveway was cluttered with vehicles, presumably guests at the holiday home. The woman had appeared quite suddenly: caught in profile between a pair of cars, talking to someone out of sight. Even from a distance it looked right: her nose, her cheekbones, her jaw. Her height, her mannerisms, the way she leaned forward a little to engage. Ringer opened up the website again. A rather twee introduction ran through the clichés of comfort and location and value for money. And everywhere it was Val's place. *Val's friendly welcome. Val's tasteful touches. Val's helpful suggestions for visitors.* And there, even a photograph of the conceited Madame Val. Yes, she was the woman who had stood over their tent, the woman who had lied about her dog, she who must have betrayed them.

Ringer scrolled up and down. Milou was nowhere to be seen. And there was no mention of a husband. No mention of Val and Vinny's tasteful touches. The builder man with a van was absent, out of the picture. Suddenly she had an idea. She called the number on the website contact page and found herself almost immediately in conversation with a person she had to assume was Val. She realised she hadn't quite thought it through. Speak in English or French? Val answered the call in French. So she followed suit.

"*Excusez-moi, madame. Je voudrais parler avec votre mari, s'il vous plaît.* I'd like to speak to your husband. It's about a little job to be done up in my attic."

"*Désolée, madame,*" came the reply. "I'm sorry but I cannot help you. Bobby no longer lives at this address."

"*C'est bien dommage.* That's a shame. I had heard he was very *assidu.*"

"And he's not my husband."

"Oh. But you may have a phone number? He still lives in the region?"

"He lives in England now. At least I believe so. I don't have a phone number. I can give you the address of his website, such as it is. Contact him that way."

"*C'est gentil, madame.* That would be kind. Even if he is no longer in the country, perhaps he could recommend somebody else."

Moments later she had scribbled down an address, thanked Madame Val and rung off. German? She would bet against it.

As for Val, she too recognised an English accent, a certain hesitancy in dealing with the more complex sentences. But no alarm bells rang, and why should they? It was not so strange to hear such a voice in the Sologne. British expats were not so uncommon here. Greta Barachet might know every single one of them but for her part, well, Val would never quite have that social reach.

Marius Ledru had taken her by surprise when he turned up unannounced one morning, tapping on the French windows with an inquisitive look on his face. Val was not the only one to be disturbed: she was in the middle of a portrait shoot, composing a series of informal photographs of a young couple and their first child, a babe just three weeks old. She had drawn back the curtains and there he was.

"*Désolé, Val,*" he had said. "I had no idea you'd be working. I can come back."

"No, it's fine," she had insisted, pleased to see him. "I've nearly done. You can sit outside or come in and find a discreet corner."

And nodding politely to the young couple, he had chosen to creep in and watch her at work. He admired the professional manner she had with her clients, the ease with which she guided them, suggested a pose, rearranged a composition. And when they had gone and she was packing away the spotlights and the screens, he told her so.

"I love the way you work, the way you manipulated those two. Well, the three of them. The child was so well-behaved for you, wasn't he?"

"It was a little girl, Marius! And she was fast asleep."

"Was she?" he laughed. "I know nothing about babies."

"Neither do I, really. I can tell when they're asleep, though!"

He had got up from his seat and was helping her tidy up.

"So, no children in your past?" he asked airily. "No children of your own?"

He caught a sigh as she began to reply.

"No. Motherhood has passed me by."

"It's not too late."

"Marius? Don't flatter me!"

He smiled at her, took her hands in his and asked her to help him celebrate his birthday at the weekend with a meal together:

"No, not the Chinese place. A nice hotel-restaurant in the countryside."

The Chinese place had turned out to be a Vietnamese restaurant where they'd both struggled with their chopsticks and had made a jokey competition of it until an observant waiter had provided a sympathetic smile and some knives and forks.

A nice country hotel. A village halfway to Orléans. Somewhere special.

And here they were, sitting with a view over an ornamental lake, the sun setting tangerine over the distant treetops, each with an empty dessert bowl before them, sharing the last drops of a fine Sauternes recommended by the unsettlingly youthful sommelier.

It had taken Val a little while to make her mind up about this gentle, engaging policeman. Well, policeman was irrelevant. He was a gentle, engaging man. She enjoyed his company. He was talkative but preferred to contribute to a conversation rather than to dominate it; he had plenty of entertaining anecdotes, amusing observations and interesting opinions. Nothing directly related to his work, she noticed, and she was not inclined to pressurize him. If he ever spoke of his job it was only in the broadest of terms. She gleaned that they had him working on multiple cases

Marius was not so presumptuous.

Instead he drove her home along the dark forest roads, listening to a playlist of English rock ballads. Here and there he would absent-mindedly contribute to the chorus. He admitted he didn't understand all the words so Val had to help him out, teasing him in the process.

"What are you singing, Marius?"

"Hm?"

"Carry the what? Carry the *noose*?"

"Carry the noose, yes."

"What do you think they are," she laughed, "a gang of hangmen?"

"Hangmen?"

"He's singing carry the news! *All the young dudes, carry the news*."

"Really? I always thought …"

By the time they arrived in Saint-Benoît he had put his inhibitions to one side. She invited him inside and he accepted without missing a beat. She found a white Saumur in the fridge and had him pick up a couple of glasses. With the bottle in one hand and his wrist in the other, she led him up the stairs and suddenly she had a man in her bedroom, in her bed, for the first time in almost a year.

She was awoken by the grating sound of a moped engine revving in the lane. It was a little before six o'clock. The half-light in the room told her the morning had not yet broken. Marius was sound asleep. She watched his chest rise and fall, saw the serenity in his face. She couldn't believe her luck. She dozed for another hour or so, then went downstairs to prepare some coffee in a pair of matching cups.

A tap on the door surprised her. It was one of the week-enders, one of the group down from Normandy with their VTTs, their off-road bikes.

"*Madame,*" said the young man breathlessly. "*Votre voiture.* Your car."

Pointing towards the end of the drive where Ledru had left his Audi, tucked in behind a pair of SUVs, he repeated:

"Your car." It was almost an apology. "Someone has vandalised it."

Val followed him down the driveway. The car looked to be perfectly intact, paintwork gleaming in the early morning sunlight, but on closer inspection she could see that the man was correct. The vehicle had sunk lower to the ground, each of its four tyres was flat, and not just deflated: the valves themselves had been snapped off with bolt cutters.

She swept back into the house and prepared to tell Marius the unwelcome news. And in spite of everything she would keep Florian's name out of it. It was up to the inspector to come to that conclusion himself, without any prompting from her.

Nobody in France could say for sure where Bobby was at this time, but after a little research and a couple of telephone calls his whereabouts were ascertained by a recently released female prisoner with teaching qualifications.

Amanda Ringer had viewed Bobby's website with nothing short of contempt. The limited selection of photos were of low resolution – what was Val thinking, letting him get away with that? – the copy was brief, unimaginative and included at least three spelling mistakes – *extentions?* – and half the hyperlinks failed to work. She called the mobile number advertised, let it go to voicemail and decided against leaving a message. Instead she chose to ring the number of a business quoted in one of the reviews of Bobby's work. It was a supplier of his, full of praise for his reliability, whose premises she discovered were in Dorset. The man she spoke to seemed to know Bobby well; at least well enough to know that he was out of the trade, at least temporarily, and was spending the summer managing a campsite.

"Which site would that be? I wasn't after a building job. It's a family matter I need to see him about. We've kind of lost touch."

"Sorry, my love. Don't rightly know. One on the coast, I reckon. He did say he liked the sea air."

"In Dorset?"

"Oh, yeah. He ain't gone far."

There weren't too many more websites to trawl through. The undulating Dorset coastline is dotted with campsites and caravan parks but only one had a manager answering to the name of Bobby. She was enquiring about a decking job in her garden. Yes, near Maiden Newton. Could he come round and give her an estimate? She heard his voice for the first time: clear, confident, polite. He was taking a break from all that, he apologised. Maybe she could call him again in the autumn? Really she was hoping to have the work done before that. Never mind, she would try someone else.

Smugglers Top was primarily a caravan park. There was a field designated for tents, mainly used by overnighters pausing between walking stages of the South West Coast Path which fringed the southern edge of the property. It was a popular site, especially in summer, and even in late May Amanda Ringer discovered that several of the caravans were occupied.

It was just after six in the evening when she arrived. She left her car by a gate at the foot of a sloping drive which curved up into the site through a wood. She stopped to get her bearings on a map printed on a noticeboard. The park occupied a strip of land running high along the cliff top for about two hundred yards. Two parallel lines of static caravans covered most of the upper space, those on the front row enjoying a spectacular view of the Channel and, hooked round the west, the misty outline of the Isle of Portland slicing the horizon like the blade of a carving knife. A sprawling jumble of brick buildings, comprising the reception, a shop and what looked like a bar was planted at the near end of the caravans. Least impressive of all was a lodge whose façade was clad in rough-cut timber to attempt the effect of a forest cabin. A note on the door of the office advised new guests to check in at the bar, indicated by a hand-drawn arrow. Ringer followed the instruction, came to a pair of swing doors and poked her head inside. It was a dimly lit space, filled with cheap furniture, vaguely maritime bric-a-brac, the smell of beer and the sound of a jukebox balladeer.

Bobby needed no introduction. The place was filling up with visitors but sitting at a corner table in a black tee-shirt and denim shorts, in conversation with two young women who appeared to be hanging on his every word, laughing at his every remark, was the manager, the handyman, smug Madame Val's one-time lover who for God knows how long had shared her home in Saint-Benoît-en-Sologne.

She took a stool at the bar where a teenage girl was serving, and for five minutes sat reading her phone with a cola and ice, her back to Bobby, just enough leg in profile for his wandering eyes. She guessed his interest in the other women would soon wane. For a start, they were foreign and their English sounded ropey. She'd heard their accents: Dutch or maybe Scandinavian. Sure enough, before too long she sensed him crossing the floor towards her and she turned to him with a hesitant smile.

"Hello," he said. "You new to Smugglers?"

"I'm here to meet a friend," she lied.

"Right. Thought I'd not seen you before. I'm Bobby, by the way. Site manager."

"Bobby? Nice to meet you."

Which was not a lie; the man was a dish. Youthful but worn-in. Lucky old Val.

"Do you mind if I talk to you until my friend turns up?" she asked.

"No problem."

"I feel a bit self-conscious alone at the bar like this. You know, single woman…"

"I'll keep you company with pleasure. Another drink? Sorry, what did you say your name was?"

"I didn't," she smiled again. "But it's Mandy."

"Mandy? That's nice."

"Yeah, Mandy, that's me," she said, offering a dainty hand to shake. "Mandy Roundtree."

CHAPTER 8

MARIUS LEDRU

The set of family portraits that Val had produced for the new parents was well received and as good, she believed, as she had ever done. Nevertheless it was the last commission she'd had and was now several weeks ago. A camera business in the town had recently expanded from simply selling and servicing equipment into event photography. It was normal, she told herself, that she should lose some trade.

The gîte, meanwhile, more or less ran itself, but it was turning into a disappointing summer. There was nothing Val could do about the rainfall but several of the published reviews from visitors to *Les Petits Genêts* were less generous than usual. She wondered if consumer expectations had suddenly got higher. Complaints had begun to appear online: the electrical equipment was outdated and unreliable, the second bedroom was cramped and gloomy, the internet access was unstable. *Not enough space to sit out in the sunshine*, one ungrateful boor had written. Val recognised the author: the wife of an English couple whose week in the area had been blessed with seven days of grey skies and drizzle. Had she really let things slide or was this just a sign of the times? When guests who once would have bitten their tongues, or at worst might have had a quiet word with her, now felt entitled to rant at their keyboards and then post their poison for all the world to read. A local electrician was employed to check the integrity of the wiring. He asked Val if anyone had tampered with the fuse box: he had found examples of loose wiring in the circuit breaker which could be the reason for interruptions to the electricity supply.

It occurred to her that she was enjoying her activities away from the house more than the time she spent there. She picked up her tennis racquet and took to the sport with Greta Barachet once again. Her game had deteriorated to such an extent – and so had her friend's, it must be said – that they could do little more than ridicule each other's efforts. It was even harder to hit a shot when you were laughing.

And although Marius Ledru was occupied with a "work-load from hell" – his words – the couple generally found time at weekends to relax together. He took her to corners of Blois she had never visited, to the theatre, to a strange contemporary art exhibition entitled *la Fondation du Doute (Doubt Foundation)* where every installation provoked a clash of hotly disputed interpretations, and even to watch the horse racing at the hippodrome in Orléans. They egged each other on to place a bet or two on the afternoon gallops and Val excitedly lost twenty-five euros in less than an hour. She could afford to smile about it though, as Marius, cursing his bad luck, was taken for fifty.

For her part, she led him into favourite stretches of the forests, they sunbathed together in a secret clearing, paddled in the waters of a limpid pool. She couldn't help but laugh out loud when he mistook a shy speckled salamander for a common frog. Pulling a comedian's *how am I supposed to know?* face, he explained he was more at home on the pavements of a city than out there in the bogs. Accepting his defence – okay, he was a cop not a biologist – she surprised him by pulling him close and, as the insects hummed and buzzed over the shallows, she laid her head on his shoulder and held him for several seconds. It gave her a warming glow to realise that once again, after a year of pain and emptiness, she had a proper boyfriend to cling to.

They were walking back to her car on one such excursion, on an evening whose glorious pink sunset gave the illusion of a forest bathed in fairy lights, when Marius spoke of money.

"I hope you know me well enough to say that you can trust me," he began.

"Trust you?" she laughed. "I was taught to always trust a policeman."

"It's just that I have a proposition. A request, really."

"Oh?"

"Your business, the gîte, it ticks along quietly, yes? The accounts are steady, no alarms?"

"Alarms? No, it's a decent income. Seasonal, of course. Reap the rewards in summer and live off the fat in winter, that sort of thing."

"I thought so. I was hoping so." Ledru coughed to clear his throat, holding back a low branch for her to pass ahead of him. "Mind that puddle."

"To be honest, Marius, it has crossed my mind lately to sell up. It's hard to run it alone. It was always a joint venture. You know, something that Bobby and I could do together."

"Sell up? Surely not. I get the impression it's a fine little business."

Val stopped without replying and knelt to touch the smoky blue petals of a clump of wild violets that had caught her eye.

"It's just that I have some money," she heard him say. "Quite an amount. It's a bonus from my last promotion, plus a tax rebate. Money my wife knows nothing about. And I'd like to keep it that way. She has a very clever accountant. She's forever making demands of me."

Val let him speak. She could not guess where he was heading with this.

"Basically," he went on, offering a hand to help her up, "I'd like to park it. Park it somewhere temporarily where neither she nor her accountant will get to notice it."

"Park it?" repeated Val. "You mean hide it?"

"Park it, hide it, disguise it, whatever term you like. It's not illegal, Val, don't think that."

"So, what, you want to put it into my account?"

"Into your business account, yes. For the short term. If you are agreeable, of course."

"That's why you ask about trust?"

"Well, yes. It's just a lump sum. It'll just sit there. It's not like a virus or anything, it's not going to infect your account."

"I suppose not."

"And *I'd* have to trust *you*. Not to spend the money yourself! I do trust you, of course I do."

He took her hand as the path widened. Up ahead they could see the car poking out from the tree cover, the last rays of the sun glinting off its windscreen.

"How much money?" she asked.

"Around thirty-five thousand euros."

"That's quite a sum."

"It is, I know. You'd keep the interest on it, that goes without saying. You'd be doing me a great favour. You've no idea how venal Clarisse can be. Like a vulture, she is."

Behind them the cumulus clouds were curdling purple into a violent bruise. Val felt in her pocket for her keys.

"Let me think about it, Marius. I'm sure it'd be fine, but please let me think about it, okay?"

"You do realise you've still got a photo of Bob the builder in your downstairs loo, don't you, dearie?"

"Is there?"

"In that collage on the wall. I think it's an old one. Must be, your hair's still dark! One of you two together by the sea somewhere."

Val knew exactly the picture Greta was kidding her about: Concarneau, 2004. Okay, it was an oversight but she wasn't going to start unpicking collages. Everything else about him had been erased from the house months ago. Most of what he hadn't been back to collect had been binned. Sometime before Christmas she'd given Florian the few tools he'd left behind. Admittedly there were exceptions, mainly photographs. She might have wished to airbrush Bobby from her life but she had no desire to forget her own part in the time they had spent together. One day, she hoped, she would be able to look at those few photos and smile fondly at happy moments in her life. She had gathered them in a folder and had hidden it in the attic in case that day ever arrived.

"Just that I thought you'd made a decision to treat him as a non-person."

Greta was in a mischievous mood. Earlier she had beaten Val in a single set of tennis that had taken them over an hour and a half to complete.

"Especially now you've got yourself a tidy replacement!"

Val indulged her with a wry smile. Greta was more or less up to speed with Marius Ledru: his likes, his dislikes, and how many times he had shared a bed with her best friend. But a line was drawn when it came to the money transfer, Val had decided. Greta did not need to know all her business.

"A tidy replacement? You make him sound like a garden gnome."

"Or a teddy bear…"

"Or a Labrador pup…"

"Or an inflatable man-doll…"

"Hey, girl, that's my boyfriend you're sexually objectifying!"

"You're out of paper in the downstairs loo, by the way," added the Scot with as straight a face as she could muster.

For the first time Val had witnessed a less savoury side of Marius Ledru. Impatience was a natural reaction, she conceded, but there had been a testiness about him, a sudden chill in the air around them. One moment he loved her, the next he had seemed to resent her.

Her crime was to ask for more time to consider allowing him to conceal – there was no better word – forty-six thousand euros in her *compte d'entreprise*. The amount had mysteriously increased. She had decided not to ask her bank for advice. There was no branch in Saint-Benoît and she had always found the staff in Blois to be arrogant. Meanwhile she could think of little worse than speaking to an unknown office clerk on the end of a phone line in Paris or Guadeloupe. Her best bet would be Clément Barachet – in confidence – but he was often away and as yet it had been hard to engineer a meeting with him that did not involve his wife. More time, that was all.

Happily, Marius' sulk did not last for long. They strolled around her garden – a little neglected this summer, she would admit – and whispered sarcastic comments about the current occupants of the gîte: like a military commander, the father was directing his children in an over-complicated operation to wash the family car. He was an officious man, Val explained sotto voce, a professional politician of some renown, apparently, in his native Denmark. Earlier that morning he had complained about the lack of air-conditioning and a dripping tap in the bathroom. Suddenly a shrill voice cut through the air from the opposite direction. Madame Motta was standing by the laurel, a knitted hat pulled over her ears, hurling pieces of gravel and colourful expletives at an invisible pack of wolves. Val and Marius looked at each other and laughed aloud.

Back inside the house Val opened a bottle of chilled Vouvray, handed him a very large glassful and earned herself both a long hug and a gratifying apology for his selfishness.

Summer had passed its zenith but a residual heat in the still air made for a muggy few weeks in August. Even beneath a single cotton sheet Val found sleeping difficult. Meanwhile Ledru was obliged to spend too much of his time in Blois. A week might pass when all they shared was a snatched phone conversation and a dozen text messages.

The evening mists never failed to enchant her. Sometimes they filtered through the boggy woods and dangled wispy fingertips over the ridge at the back of her land, curling around the feet of the broom, drifting across the straggly lawn. In the light of a full moon the vapours took on a sheen of silver and in her mind she was transported to a distant, ethereal place lit only by starlight where she might wander alone in glass slippers and a white wedding dress.

It was a night of humidity and mists when Merel reappeared.

There was no moonlight, the dark skies were covered with a veil of cloud, trapping the stagnant heat, hiding the stars from view. It was a night during which she had no contact with a soul: not Ledru, not Greta, nobody. The gîte sat empty for the week, an English family having cancelled late in the day. She had gone to bed early and had fallen asleep before ten o'clock.

Whatever dream she was having, whichever cloud she was floating on, she was brusquely awoken from it by the crash of broken glass. She sat up in her bed, her heart was racing – from slumber to a state of anxiety in five seconds. She noticed the bedside clock read 01:55. There was another brittle sound, a tinkle, then a crunch, all coming from downstairs, the back of the house, the studio.

She turned on the bedroom lamp, found her dressing gown and slid on a pair of sandals. She made a commotion, enough for two people, stamping on the floor, thinking she might alarm an intruder, panic them to backtrack. She opened the door and peered into the landing, down the staircase, partly lit by the light from the bedroom.

"Hello!" she called out, but her throat was dry, her voice was wobbling and the sound she made was all but inaudible. She coughed and coughed and then she couldn't stop.

"*Qui est là?*" she shouted finally. "Who's there? *J'ai mon portable. Je téléphone à la police!*" She had the wit to lie. Her phone was downstairs somewhere. At that moment she didn't know exactly where she'd left it.

It didn't actually matter; there was no reply, the house had gone quiet. Then suddenly another crash, a splintering of glass, followed by the sound of cupboards being slammed shut, the scudding of furniture being shifted, the clattering of objects falling to the ground.

"*Qui est là?*" she repeated, swallowing her fear and taking to the stairs. She descended into the gloom of the lounge where an armchair had been disturbed. Meanwhile the sounds coming from the studio had stopped, save for the crackle of escaping shoes over shards of glass.

Val paused, tried to catch her breath which was all but running away from her. She looked around for a weapon. There was nothing in that room; she thought of a kitchen knife. A moment later, armed with her heaviest frying pan, she stepped into the studio, finding only the outline of dark shapes suggesting a scene of devastation, a chaotic stage set, a railway carriage flipped on to its side. She stared into the space, her eyes at once blinded by the flickering beams of light which flitted from one object to the next, creating silhouettes of disorder: it was a dazzling pink light and it was coming from beyond the smashed French windows, from the pitch dark, from the middle of the garden.

She cried out, in vain. Once again her voice had betrayed her. Splinters of glass littering the floor barred her way. She stood rigid, in disbelief. For not only had her studio been ransacked, she was now staring at a figure in the night, front-lit by the dancing glow of a rosy phosphorescence, the black-caped shoulders of a human frame, a heavy sack of a hood toppling over a face of no features, an impenetrable shadow, no face at all. For a moment time stood still, as still as the two antagonists: Val trapped in her horror, the devilish vision staring at her with unseen eyes, with frozen defiance.

And then, just as suddenly, the light went out, the scene turned black, she heard the sounds of scurrying, of broken twigs, of bushes whipped and twisted: the vanishing, the escape, the nocturnal beast retreating to its lair deep in the woods. And when Val had breathed again, regained a hold on her trembling limbs and turned on the studio lights, she wandered through the debris of upturned cabinets and contents spewed from dislocated drawers. Like a sleepwalker she drifted through the fractured doors and stood on the step, sweating in the damp air, peering uneasily into the garden for vestiges of something she couldn't really believe she had just witnessed.

She had a torch in the kitchen; it took her a moment to think where it was. A minute later she was outside again, examining the illuminated patch of earth – that barren spot where once the chickens pecked – anticipating a sign, a harbinger. She pointed her light this way and that, believing, *knowing* it would fall on another bird, a dead blackbird, another mutilation. And there *was* something: what looked like a bundle of straw, flattened, teased into a circle. It was a tiny nest, and prising it open with her fingertips, she saw its fragile contents: bright turquoise in the torchlight, three little eggshells, each one broken, each one leaking its viscous fluid into the earth.

Val did not call the police emergency number first. Instead she phoned Ledru directly. Without success, as it happened: he was unavailable and she left a hysterical message. Then she called Greta, begging her to come over and sit with her until the police arrived. Until daylight. Until she could begin to feel like herself again.

She changed into some day clothes and sat in the kitchen, all the lights aglow, cursing the English family for cancelling their holiday. The gîte was as dark and quiet as a mausoleum. She couldn't face the mess in the studio. She started trembling again. She cried and cried until the tears ran out; got it over and done with before Greta arrived.

A quarter of an hour later her friend appeared with her husband, Clément, who hugged Val – *ma pauvre chère Valérie* – as warmly as any doting father.

"Of course you must mention the story of Widow Merel," insisted the lawyer once she had composed herself sufficiently to describe not only what she had heard but also what she had seen.

A pair of police officers were already examining the bird's nest, searching for footprints in the earth and fibres in the bushes.

"I'm not suggesting that your intruder was a ghost, Valérie," Barachet went on, "But he or she…"

"Or they," offered his wife.

"Or they, indeed," he conceded. "Whoever it was knew about the history of this house, of the Plessis family story. The police must follow that line of enquiry."

"I say 'they', dearie," added Greta, "because there's evidence of disturbance in the lounge as well. You've seen it?"

Val had not. She had stayed put in the well-lit safety of her kitchen. She followed Greta through to the front of the house. Her friend had drawn back the curtains and the timid light of dawn crept across the space. She saw how an armchair had been dragged across the room, but that appeared to be the sum of it.

"Look at the wall," said Greta.

An empty space. A blank. A flagrant gap. The red-framed photograph of Rosette and the kitten had disappeared. It was not on the carpet, leaning against the skirting board. It was not on the coffee table, not placed conspicuously on a shelf. It had simply gone.

Marius Ledru arrived as Greta was frying mushrooms and grilling toast. He held Val in a long, tight embrace – rather ostentatiously, the Scotswoman thought – and then confidently introduced himself to the Barachets, who, after an abbreviated breakfast, left her, reassuring her that she was now in the capable hands of the officers of the law.

The story of Muriel Plessis' betrayal of the Resistance network and her subsequent murder was much less widely known than Val had thought. Barachet dined out on the grisly drama of the tale but it had all happened such a very long time ago. Almost eighty years had passed since Victorine had hacked the widow's head from her neck.

"The chances that a random intruder would have the historical baggage to wear a black cloak and carry a pink flashlight are non-existent," insisted Ledru, back at *Les Genêts* the following day.

"None of your team believes in ghosts?" asked Val, surprised that this even sounded like a serious question.

"No-one," Marius smiled. "Ghosts don't break down doors, Val. They don't run off with framed photographs. Clearly we are looking at your friend Bobby as our prime suspect. You say he knows the history of the house, he has a motive, of sorts. It's true?"

"I still can't believe he could hate me so much as to break up what we created together."

"But let's not forget that it was a targeted attack. Only the studio was damaged. That was your space."

"He built it. He built the extension."

"Maybe. But it was for you, Val. And now he's destroying it. He's doing that for you too."

"What about the damage to the gîte a few months ago?"

"That was not necessarily the same perpetrator."

"There was a dead blackbird left behind."

"That is true. But in itself that is not conclusive. And there was no so-called ghost reported in that incident."

He was right. Ledru stepped into the lounge.

"It is puzzling why the picture has been removed," he said, almost to himself. "Was it a favourite of Bobby's?"

"No, not at all," she replied, following him into the centre of the room. "It was my photo. I rescued it. It spoke to me."

"Well, then, I would guess it was a theft born out of spite."

He had all but made a case against Bobby. It was one that she could still not fully accept, but little else made sense.

"Did he leave anything behind here?" he asked after a moment. "I mean, since he left, what was it, a year ago?"

"Nothing I haven't already thrown out or given away."

"Anything you shared? Something we could pick up clear prints from?"

She thought of their music, their collection of old CDs. She found the boxes in a spare bedroom. Bobby had not pillaged it; there were still a hundred or so flat plastic cases containing discs representing both his and her musical voyages through the 1990s. She picked out half a dozen of his favourites.

"You'll find his fingerprints all over these," she said, handing them over to Marius.

"Thanks. And his DNA?"

That was harder. Sweat, blood, saliva, semen. Not anymore.

"Did he leave a hairbrush behind? A toothbrush?"

"No. He cleaned up. There's nothing like that. He left here almost without a trace."

Several days passed. Even though Val felt sure that he was in England, the police circulated Bobby's photograph locally. Meanwhile she had guests to prepare the gîte for at the weekend. She had her studio to set right, insurance claims to file, new equipment to order. Greta came round more than once to keep her company. She insisted on taking Val away from the house for a long, exhausting walk, then cooking for them both. One afternoon she was especially energised. She had news, she had texted ahead. It was about Ledru. Now she sat Val down with a glass of Fleurie, assumed her most serious face and, without wishing to upset her, told her that both Clément and she – and they had come to this conclusion quite separately – had reason to suspect that the policeman was married: *spoken for, Val, has a wife, for Christ's sake!*

Val laughed with relief. She knew already. It was old news. He had told her as much.

"It's no secret, Gret. And they split up years ago."

"Oh. Right." Well, she was very glad it hadn't been a dreadful surprise. There was still a little wind in her sails, however. Clarisse, she was called. Val knew that already too. Greta knew the woman who had sold her her wedding dress. A friend in the business with shops in Orléans and Blois. They had suppliers in common.

"I can get an address for you, if you want, Val," she said, raising her eyebrows.

This was typical of Greta. Was client confidentiality a thing in France?

"But why should I want to speak with his ex-wife, his wife, whatever she is?"

Greta drew breath and swallowed a mouthful of wine.

"Listen, dearie," she continued, enlightening Val as to the digging that Barachet had done on her behalf since he had met Ledru for the first time in those early hours after the break-in. Marius had a reputation as a chancer, she said: he cut corners, he was unreliable, he let colleagues down at the drop of a hat.

"Did you know his transfer from Orléans to Blois was really no more than a disguised demotion, a disciplinary issue? Barachet has spoken to civil lawyers, police prosecutors and others who knew him there."

Val insisted that he had recently been given a promotion for his work in Blois. Greta could not contradict her but left her with a warning, take it or leave it:

"Be careful, dearie. Clément has that sense of smell, you know. And he reckons your Ledru is a wrong 'un."

Ever since her "fumble" with Florian, Val had been questioning her judgement. Part of her clung to the belief that, his infidelities aside, Bobby was fundamentally a decent man, not the kind of man whose love for her could turn to hate at the flick of a switch, who could target her vulnerability so callously. Had she got him so wrong? And Marius, her lovable garden gnome, her teddy bear? Barachet was putting two and two together and coming up with 'dishonest'. Unreliable? Putting a few colleagues' noses out of joint? Was that dishonest? Was it even worth her worrying about?

On cue she heard a car arrive on the drive. Four new tyres already covered in dust. It was Marius, straightening his tie as was his habit, who came striding towards her door with a spring in his step.

"I think we've made a breakthrough, Val!" he called to her even before he pecked her cheek.

She sat him down in the lounge before he was allowed to continue.

"Bobby has been seen in the area," he announced. "More than just seen. He was spoken to."

"When?"

"A week ago. Before the break-in here. A lady in Mauzé-le-Vieux. Out on the route de Romarantin."

Val nodded. She knew the place.

"She spotted him in his van," Ledru went on. "Sadly she couldn't give us any vehicle details, beyond the colour and how dirty it was. Anyway, she flagged him down. Actually stopped him in his tracks. Asked him if he could do a little job for her. She was one of his old customers, you see. He'd put a shed up for her years ago and the door hinges needed replacing. At first he wasn't having any of it, she said. He seemed bad-tempered. He wasn't doing that kind of work anymore, he told her. But she gave him the helpless old lady routine. He did have some tools with him, he said, he'd have a look. If it was a small job, maybe he'd have time to do it there and then, that afternoon."

He has a soft heart, Val said to herself. Bobby could never deny a poor old damsel in distress.

"You got all this directly from her, did you, Marius?"

"I did. Not just one of the team. Me. When the call came in, I thought, *this one's mine*. And what's more," he said, his eyes twinkling in excitement, "we have got more than just a witness. We have evidence."

"What do you mean?"

"He left something behind. The lady found it after he'd gone. He must have been in a rush. He left a Swiss Army knife on the floor in the shed."

Val's cheeks coloured the instant she heard the three words. She could think of nothing beyond the shaded interior of Amanda Ringer's pale blue tent, the fug of body odour, the rucksacks, the sleeping bags, her furtive rooting among their belongings.

"A knife? That's interesting. Have you examined it?"

"Of course. That's what I'm here to tell you, Val. The lab have had it checked for prints. It's covered in his. In Bobby's."

"Bobby didn't have one of those knives, Marius. Not since we've lived here."

"Well, he has now. Or at least he did until he forgot to take it with him."

"Do you have a photo of it?"

Ledru scrolled through the gallery on his phone.

"I have several."

Val knew that Swiss Army knives came in a range of shapes and sizes, colours and designs. Suddenly she was looking at the image of a bulky red one, exactly the same model as the one she had found in Dean Buckle's rucksack. It could be one of thousands but she swallowed hard. Even if it were Dean's no-one knew she had seen it before. If Marius pushed her she would have to admit to stealing into the tent. She let him slide one picture after another into view: a variety of angles and close-ups.

"Does it have any significant characteristics?" she asked.

"Significant?"

"I don't know, like a scratched blade or a wobbly cork-screw?"

Marius pulled his phone away.

"The corkscrew is very loose," he said, "as a matter of fact."

"I'd like you to do me a favour," she said finally.

"What's that?"

"Send me those photos to my phone. And check the thing for my DNA."

"Yours?"

"Get them to swab the saw blade, Marius. The jagged one. I cut my finger on it. It'll still have traces of me on. I'm certain of it."

"I was wondering about that," he said after a moment.

"About what?"

"I did have my suspicions that you were the woman who shopped the British teacher last summer. You say 'shopped', is that the word?"

She nodded, said nothing, let him reel her in.

"I didn't push it. There was a Swiss Army knife found in the boy's bag, wasn't there? You're too modest, Val. You did the police a big favour. I was just waiting for you to tell me one of these days."

CHAPTER 9

CLARISSE LEDRU

Her bed, once *their* bed, was both a blessing and a curse. Alone in its wide, luxurious spaces Val could stretch her limbs and still her toes and her fingertips would never reach the mattress' edge. She could roll over twice and still be sure of its comforting support. She was a sole survivor and this was her private desert island. Most nights she slept well, she slept the sleep of the just. Other times she fretted at the cold vacancy beyond the tight knot of her body. The bed could be as hard, as vast and as unforgiving as a deserted tennis court where she played alone, hitting ball after ball over a net to a long absent opponent who would never return a single one of them.

One night, at the darkest point of its span, when her bedroom was shrouded in a velvet blackness that dissolved all shapes and shadows, Val was roused from her sleep by the pitiless cry of a strangled animal. At first all she recognised was the shrill sound of pain. Disorientated, she had no inkling of its provenance. She guessed a fox, wounded in a fight, dying at the edge of the woods. Then suddenly she heard it again: louder, clearer, a shriek, not from the wild, but surely from within. Within the walls of her house. On the ground floor.

She sits up in bed, her heart pounding, tries to gather her thoughts. She finds her phone, touches it on and the small oblong of light pierces the darkness around her. She notices it is ten minutes past one, but the time means nothing. Covering herself in her dressing gown, she creeps out of the room and slowly, silently begins to follow the staircase down into the lounge. Here too the darkness is absolute, there is no hint of light infiltrating through the gap in the curtains. The animal sound has long ceased. All she can hear is the soft touch of her feet on the polished oak floor and the blood pulsing at her temples. Then a flickering, pinkish glow sends the shadows dancing around her: a flame ignited from the kitchen, beckoning her towards it.

She pauses, takes a breath, but says nothing. No cry or warning. No bluffer's bravado. No empty threat. The candlelight, for now she can see a single candle set in a small vase of pink glass in the middle of a wooden table, draws her towards it hypnotically. Its shimmering casts a cloak of shadows over the kitchen which has become a space that Val does not recognise. She is standing in her own home yet in a room from another time. The wall cupboards, what she can make of them, are sparse and wooden, a pair of ancient taps serve a metal sink that is on the wrong side of the room. Curtains hang limply where her blinds should be. She stands in the doorway transfixed, then aghast as a human shape appears in the gloom behind the candle, raising itself to its full height: a young woman, monochrome, staring back at her with an expression of deep sorrow in her liquid eyes. It cannot be, but it is. It is Rosette, from her photograph, *in* her photograph: Rosette at eighteen in her cotton summer dress, her dark hair falling to her shoulders, its sheen catching the light.

"Rosette," Val begins to say, as if to comfort her, but her voice fails her. In its place she hears the girl gently sobbing, sees her shoulders quivering, her left hand lifted to her face to wipe away the tears.

Slowly Val approaches her, eyes drawn towards her colourless form. She notices hanging limply from her right hand a long, curved object: the candlelight picks it out, glinting off the blade of a machete – two foot long, whetted to razor sharp – with blood dripping from its tip on to the stone floor.

"Rosette," she says again, and this time the echoey sound makes the girl look away. "*Qu'as-tu fait, toi?* What have you done?"

She is pointing to the floor to her left side where shadows shift-shape. Trembling, Val takes another step closer. She reaches the table as Rosette backs away into the black recesses.

"What have you done?" Val repeats, the solidity of her words giving her the courage to push the vase carefully to the edge of the table where the flame can cast its jittery glow on the silhouette of an open sack, weighed down by an amorphous entity, lifeless yet emanating warmth. The invisible Rosette gasps as Val pulls away the loose neck of the bag and lifts out the mutilated body of a dark-coloured kitten. Its fur is matted and gluey, blood spills on to her hands and down her wrists, running sepia over the sleeves of her dressing gown. The wretched creature is decapitated.

"Where's its head?" Val cries out in horror. "Rosette! Where's its head? Rosette!"

But the girl has vanished, the candle has gone out and Val is thrashing around in her bed with a pillow tight between her fists. It is the violence of the movement which wakes her, which shakes her back to the reality of her bedroom, the cold sweat at her neck, the shuddering of her heart, her breathlessness.

And, as if to confirm the truth of her existence, she let the pillow drop and leaned over to pick up her phone. She drew her tousled hair away from her eyes. It was there where she had left it, cold, solid, where it should be. All was well, and the time it showed was ten minutes past one.

Much later that morning, in a modern kitchen filled with sunlight, Val was reminded of her dream by the sight of a carving knife lying on the chopping board. She had used it the previous evening to trim a line of fat from a strip of sirloin. She had left it out – an oversight – its blade still tacky and smudged. She placed it in the dishwasher with her breakfast things and tried to think no more about it.

Bobby sat in his draughty office, staring out of the window beyond the line of caravans towards the raised lip of coast-line where, in the distance, the volunteers stood leaning on their spades, drinking tea from a thermos, watching the gulls dipping down to a sea streaked with glacier blue. It was a decent day: dry and breezy with shafts of late September sunshine breaking through a flat bank of clouds. He would go out and give them a hand later on. There was less to do on the site now that autumn was approaching. Most of the caravans were empty for a start. Before the worst of the weather set in, groups of sure-footed members of the South West Coast Path Association had been repairing sections of the ramblers' way: for the past fortnight a three-mile stretch which included the fraying ribbon along the high end of Smugglers Top. The degradation of the path here was as bad as anywhere. Once-firm areas of rock had worn to treacherous sloping shelves of loose grit, below which, in certain places, a drop of a hundred feet or so took the eye directly to a stony shoreline battered by endless waves. Here on the bluff the team were repairing the path or closing off sections of it with temporary stakes and plastic tape, plotting instead a new route ten yards inland through the tufty, windswept grasses. Bobby was anxious that any secondary path should not impinge on the space in front of the caravans. He had volunteered to help with the digging, even to refresh the thermos from time to time, but he had also taken the chance to speak with the group leader and put in his two penn'orth.

Sitting in the office, waiting for his computer to boot up, watching as the men – and a doughty old woman, he noticed – resumed their work, he wondered why on earth he had bothered to express an opinion. It was no real concern of his. Smugglers Top was not his business, it was just a short-term job, mildly fulfilling, a way of marking time. It had its compensations, notably the number of young women on the site minimally dressed for the summer. Campers were the best, often in pairs, often foreign students walking the coastal path for whom a night in his bed was far more appealing than another spent in a saggy tent on a useless roll mat.

Once back in Dorset, Bobby had tried to import his Sologne business plan – if this didn't sound too grand for a relaxed arrangement of picking up odd building work or mechanics' jobs here and there – but he had found the market more or less saturated. As expected he had received little support, either moral or financial, from his parents. It was his uncle, a younger and more sympathetic version of his father, who had found him this job managing the site. It was owned by a friend of his, a Dorset man but one who kept an eye on a portfolio of property from a base in London or, more often than not, at arm's length from a villa on the Costa del Sol.

Bobby still thought of himself as a young man. His good looks were wearing well and he was proud of them. Both at work and at play he had always been physically active and there was little chance of him putting on weight and turning to fat, at least not until middle age and, in his head, he was a very long way off that. Which is where he parted company with Val, both metaphorically and literally.

Even in their frostier moments he had never been vicious enough to tell her to her face that she was looking her age, but, sadly, it was the truth. He had never lost any of his affection for her, but that age gap had become more pronounced with every passing week. Apart from him, all of her friends were pushing fifty or worse. His friends, especially the footballers and their girls, were of a younger generation entirely, and one he instinctively felt more comfortable with. And as for women, it was quite natural for him to fancy twenty-year-olds more than someone whose best years, frankly, were behind her, wasn't it? No-one could blame him for that.

Val might not see it quite as clearly as he did, but then she often ran with her blinkers on. After so many years, Bobby knew better than anyone what she was like. She was constant, stubborn, hard to budge. Call it loyalty, call it laziness – part of her makeup informed her way of re-treading familiar pathways in her life. Perhaps it was a fear of change. If it were not for him she would still be living in that gloomy university city in the north of England. She drove a Renault back then – how many times he had washed that battered cream-coloured Supercinq for her – and she still drove a Renault today. He wasn't the first blond-haired man she'd gone for; she had talked of other boyfriends, including the creepy toff, Zachary – all Nordic types. Her taste in music hadn't altered much since she was a girl. No matter how much he had encouraged her to listen to stuff from years more recent than the eighties, she stuck with her favourites, never straying too far from her default options of Phil

Collins and Annie Lennox and, God help us, Kate Bush. She was cringingly brand-loyal when it came to her fridge, her television, mobile, computer, even her kettle. She wore Adidas trainers and only Adidas trainers. She had done business with the same insurance company for decades: car, house, life, travel. Switching was anathema. And as far as he knew she had been a customer of the same bank forever. Bobby would be astonished if she ever changed any of her ways. Or if she ever changed any of her online passwords.

A jaunty run of half a dozen musical notes alerted him that the office computer was ready and able. Emails could wait. First he would check the business account, just as he did at the start of most weeks.

Penetrating Val's bank accounts, both private and business, was like shelling peas. He knew the convoluted spelling of her mother's maiden name, her memorable address, the town of her birth and her favourite meal. He knew the make of her first car (Renault 5 TL), her favourite artist (Gauguin) and both of her passwords. Yes, she had two: one for each account. Now and then – and this was the extent of her security awareness – she might alternate them. Quite why she was obsessed with the novel *Le Grand Meaulnes*, Bobby could not understand. It was a book she had read at school, she had told him, an A Level text, a French classic and so much more significant now that they were actually living in the Sologne! She'd made him start it, in translation of course, but he'd got no further than page ten. And so, passwords 'FrantzdeG' and 'YvonnedeG', brother and sister de Galais, pivotal characters in the novel. Apparently.

A moment or two later Bobby had already reached the final stage of entry. YvonnedeG did not work today. He tried brother Frantz. He was surprised that his name was also rejected by the bank's security software. No matter. The o in

Yvonne had been a zero before, a clever, if uncharacteristic disguise on Val's part. He gave it a try but, zero for o, access remained blocked. What else? No other letter could be given as a substitute character. Bobby pondered, becoming ever more fidgety. The z of Frantz as the number 2? He tried it, without success. Now he was starting to worry. This had never happened before. Password subterfuge was as alien to her as drinking beer straight from the bottle. He needed to be able to get into the business account. His whole strategy, flimsy though it might be, depended on it. For he knew that he'd never be given half of the business, half of the property – his solicitor had spelled that out to him quite bluntly – but if she sold it, *when* she sold it, when she put the money from the sale into this account – even if it was just temporarily before she bought some other place – in those few weeks, maybe months, then Bobby simply had to be able to find a way into that account and make his glorious, fully merited withdrawal.

So, not Frantz with a 2. He hears a shout from the cliff edge. It's one of the volunteers cracking a joke or catching the toe of his boot with a spade. Bobby looks back at his keyboard, tries to concentrate. He has to imagine Val sitting at her own computer, plotting her crafty legerdemain. Her hands hovering over the keyboard. Within easy reach of her right hand very likely a glass of wine, probably Beaujolais or a white Vouvray – wine, another thing that once she found a type she liked she stuck with it. Val's desk was never a clutter, never a shambles of bits and pieces like his toolbox or worse, the back of his van. There was a photo, wasn't there? One of the pair of them smiling somewhere sunny. Or was he imagining that detail? And her desk calendar, that was a fixture: that cherrywood thing she was attached to, the one that held those little marble tablets with numbers on. It comes to him from out of the blue: those little marble tablets. She's being clever. She's using Roman numerals. He re-reads the passwords and finds it immediately: types in a number 5 for the v in Yvonne and, abracadabra, he's in and the first page of figures is his to gaze at.

Without a moment to savour his own cleverness he is trying to digest what he sees: a balance in the account almost sixty thousand euros higher than it was the last time he checked. Sixty thousand? Has she won the lottery? Is it worth taking a share of the business right now? Help himself while the safe is wide open and forget about any house sale?

Val had already agreed to let Marius park his tax rebate and bonuses in her business account before Greta had turned up at *Les Genêts* playing Cassandra. Of course she had tormented herself, worried, wondered, wobbled. But, she told herself, Greta had been wrong before and she suspected that Barachet's sense of smell also let him down from time to time. She even wondered if Greta was a little jealous of her relationship with the detective inspector.

The bank transfer was completed in the privacy of Ledru's apartment in the Frileuse district of Blois, by means of his own computer, the morning after a romantic night in the city. She had visited his place before but had never previously spent the night in his bed. It was a spartan set of rooms he rented, devoid of any feminine touch. It appeared that when his wife had disappeared from his life she had taken every last vestige of her spirit with her. There were no pictures, few books and certainly no flowers. The furnishings were as functional and unadorned as the crockery he had used when he presented her with breakfast, yet he swore that *oui, c'est ici qu'on a vécu ensemble*, once upon a time it had indeed been a shared nest.

She may have long since departed from Blois but the woman lived on in the memory banks of his computer. For just as he was shutting it down, her face popped up in the rolling sequence of random saved pictures that featured on his desktop. It was a brown face, mixed race, sharing the tiny square with her husband's, staring lovingly into his eyes, the background indistinct.

"Who's that?" asked Val impulsively.

"That? That's Clarisse."

"Sorry. I shouldn't have asked like that."

"It's not a problem, Val. It's Clarisse, my wife. I haven't purged her from my photos."

"You look happy."

"Do we? I suppose we do. That photo was taken a very long time ago. Look at my hair, my face – the features of a much younger man!"

He laughed to himself as the computer screen silently turned to black.

"Where is she now?" Val persisted. "You said she'd left Blois."

"She's moved south. To Marseille. It's a long way from here to the Mediterranean. Marseille is where she has a sister. Thank you again, by the way."

He leaned over and kissed her.

"For what?"

"For sheltering the money. Sheltering it from her. From Clarisse."

The result of the DNA test on the little saw blade came as no surprise to Val. Marius telephoned her as soon as he was given the report: there was a positive match between traces on the blade and the controlled sample of her DNA. When she asked the inspector what he made of that, he turned the question back on her. She was the one who had asked for the comparison to be made; surely she must have her own suspicions about the significance of the result?

And, of course, she had. She'd had them from the moment Marius had mentioned the discovery of the Swiss Army knife. In her mind it wasn't so much a question of what Bobby was up to repairing a shed door in Mauzé-le-Vieux as what on earth he had been doing carrying around a knife that belonged to Dean Buckle.

What was it about Marius Ledru and his estranged wife with her Afro-Caribbean heritage, living on her sister's doorstep in the port city of Marseille? For days the rolling desktop photo turned over and over in her mind's eye. What was it about them that made Val keep on scratching the itch?

Once they were satisfied that the psychological scars caused by the break-in were healing, Greta and Clément Barachet had stepped back and given her space. Val saw neither of them for ten days, and then it was she who made the first move. It was a short telephone call, a plea for help.

"Has Clément told you all he knows about Marius, Gret?"

"Everything."

"So there's nothing more?"

"Nothing, dearie."

"Nothing more than rumour and gossip?"

"Well, rumour and gossip have to start somewhere."

A silence while Val gathered her thoughts.

"Val? You still there?"

"I need to be sure, Gret. Before I do anything daft."

"Daft? What, like telling him you're in love with him?"

"I think I already did that."

"You did?"

"Not in so many words."

Another silence, shorter than before.

"You said you could get me an address."

"Whose address, dearie?"

"Clarisse Ledru's"

"You seemed set against it."

"I've changed my mind."

"You want to speak to her?"

"No. Not necessarily. I just want to know where she lives."

"Give me a day or two, Val. I'll ask around. Unless she's moved away I'll get her address for you, if that's what you want."

Knowing Greta's relentlessness, not to mention her formidable networks, Val was not surprised that by the early evening she already had her answer.

"I couldn't get a home address for her, dearie," said her friend, but with such cheer in her voice that Val knew that she had not drawn a complete blank.

"I'm sorry about that. All I could find from my expert team of operatives" – she loved to ham this stuff up to the maximum – "was a place of work. That okay?"

"Go on."

"Clarisse Ledru, and it looks like she's kept her name – fair enough, she's still married – she works in a nursing home in Orléans."

"Orléans?"

"Yes, Orléans. That's not so surprising, is it? She's lived there before. You got a pen and paper, Val? You still listening, Val? Here's the address. I guess she'll be there most days. It's a place called *Le Bosquet*, Orléans Nord."

There was no opportunity for Val to leave Saint-Benoît for several days after the call. She had an electrician in, along with a pair of Tunisian brothers camped in the studio who were stretching out the joinery and painting work required after the break-in. Thankfully the visitors' season was over and the gîte was empty of guests. Meanwhile her enthusiasm for promoting next year's rental opportunities at *Les Petits Genêts* was miserably low. Her determination to have words with Clarisse Ledru, however, remained absolute.

She googled *Le Bosquet*, Orléans Nord. Situated in a modest residential quarter, it was a small state-run care home specialising in dementia patients: a two-storey building at the end of a cul-de-sac, surrounded by a garden of mature trees and partly hidden from the road by a long conifer hedge.

Val was by no means familiar with the streets of the city but once she had driven over the Pont Joffre on to the Loire's right bank, the main D road took her on through the commercial heart of the central district, past the snarl of side roads by the railway station and then breezily towards her destination. The streets in the northern quarter were busier than she had expected: buses ran this way and that, full of shoppers and schoolchildren. Mothers with prams waited to cross at traffic lights, young moped riders buzzed around corners, pedestrians strolled and strutted and scurried left and right. Cars like hers rolled forwards in low gear, unreasonably close to each other, horns on a hair trigger. It was a featureless Tuesday afternoon; the air was mild and damp, the sky as flat as an empty canvas. She had no idea if her quarry would be on duty that day, nor if she would be free or even willing to talk to her. She located the address, pulled into a wide car park and backed into a space with a clear view of the residence's main entrance.

She clicked through a security door and took in the heavy scent of industrial air freshener. She was in a reception area, faced with a small plastic sofa and an empty low table, a pair of closed, unmarked doors and, to her left, an unguarded office space, partitioned behind a large sliding window. From somewhere in the building drifted the muted sound of classical music. Val pressed a button by the counter and a harsh bell rang, making her jump. She had waited almost five minutes before a young Arab man appeared. He wore a navy blue uniform, looked to be no more than eighteen years old and was out of breath.

"*Je m'excuse*," he said with a shy smile. "*Un temps d'agitation.*"

She took his words to mean that there had been some kind of emergency and the place was understaffed.

"*Vous rendez visite à quelqu'un?*" the young man asked, taking a seat behind a computer terminal.

"Not a resident," she explained. "I'm looking for a member of staff. Clarisse Ledru. Is she working here today?"

Yes, she was, but she was up on the first floor, would be busy till six. No breaks allowed this afternoon.

Val sighed. Okay, she'd wait. Or come back later.

She went for a walk around the block. It was an unpretentious neighbourhood, mainly of apartment buildings several storeys tall, divided by wide strips of grass dotted with young trees whose trampled leaves had collected in drifts at the kerbsides. Some of the buildings housed various small businesses on the ground floor, which on this corner and that formed clusters of shops and services. The smell of the air was quite different here, she thought, quite different from the earthy freshness of the land around her home. It wasn't really a smell you would notice if you were used to it, just a hint of a smell, or rather a series of hints: exhaust fumes, tobacco, warm food, people living their lives on top of each other.

She went into a *pharmacie* and bought some expensive moisturiser that she didn't really need; she had a bathroom shelf crowded with tubes of the stuff. She picked up a copy of the local newspaper from the *tabac* next door. She found a café and ordered a *grand crème* and a *tartelette aux fraises* to pass the time. From her seat in the corner she watched the charming interaction between a mother and her daughter: they were teasing each other, sharing a joke, playing with words. The girl looked to be about twelve years old. She had soft features, bright eyes, unblemished cheeks and there was no doubt whose child she was. Her mother had met her straight from school, Val guessed, was treating her to a *diabolo* and a pastry after, what, an appointment at the dentist's, a visit to the library, with a spot of shopping together afterwards? A pang struck Val somewhere below the heart. It was a pain she had felt before, a dull ache of emptiness like an unsatisfied hunger. No matter how hard she tried to distract herself, no matter how much alcohol she drank, there were times when the torment of childlessness would not go away. How she envied this mother her sweet daughter. How she would love to take a child of hers to a library, to the shops, even to sit with her own girl or boy, holding hands in a gloomy dentist's waiting room! One of the hardest things to forgive Bobby for, sometimes even more than his philandering, was his refusal to give her a child. He would never see it as a deliberate act of cruelty and in a way she understood that. He wasn't a heartless man, but he had little imagination and suffered from a chronic lack of empathy.

Presently she headed back to the nursing home. She sat in her car listening to the radio, reading her newspaper, checking her phone, daydreaming as the daylight began to fade. She lifted her eyes and watched the sun drop behind the stark silhouette of an apartment building. She thought of her father. One day before too long maybe he would end up in a home like this. Even if dementia didn't claim him, frailty certainly would. And it would come to her too, eventually, she supposed, but she could never imagine dying in a bed other than her own. Never in a place like this one, never living like a prisoner in a cheap hotel, becoming more and more infirm by the day, comforted by overworked carers on a minimum wage, drifting from hour to hour, visited, if you were lucky, by friends and family whose names you had long forgotten. The past fading from view, the future a wall of fog. And the present: a song on the radio, a fractured conversation, another cup of weak tea.

She looked up and was glad to see a pair of young women arriving at the front door: reinforcements, part of the evening shift. Other cars came and went around her. At a quarter past six a slim woman with curly, greying hair and caramel-coloured skin emerged, zipping a padded jacket up to her chin and looking up and down the car park. She slung a small backpack over her shoulder and stepped away from the door. Val got out of her car and walked over to greet her.

"Madame Ledru?"

The woman looked startled.

"I'm sorry," said Val with less composure than she had planned. The woman was exhausted and wanted to go home. Ambushing her like this was thoughtless and, frankly, embarrassing.

"I'm really sorry," she ploughed on regardless. "*Madame, on peut se parler un moment?* Please, may I speak with you for a couple of minutes? *C'est important.*"

She took it as a good sign that the woman looked more puzzled than angry.

"*Qui êtes-vous, madame?* Who are you? What do you want?"

"My name is Val. I'm a friend of Marius, your husband."

"A friend? What, a girlfriend? His latest?"

"I'm his girlfriend, yes."

There was a commotion behind her and suddenly Clarisse Ledru was paying her no attention. An older woman had appeared from the far end of the car park where a streetlight had just flickered into life, casting its pale glow over the perimeter hedge.

"*Maman!*" said Clarisse to her. "*Désolée que je suis en retard.*"

Val turned to watch the pair briefly embrace. The mother was quite short, dark-skinned, and was standing over a child's pushchair.

"*Il dort, le petit?*" Clarisse asked. Her mother nodded.

It took Val a moment to understand what it was she was seeing. Almost buried beneath a little crocheted blanket a baby boy was sleeping; the older woman was both a mother and a grandmother.

"He is your son?" she asked, interrupting the family reunion.

"This is Benny," replied Clarisse proudly. "*Mon petit ange.*"

"But I thought…"

Val's brain was processing the confusion, was about to shape an expression of bemusement but happily her mouth remained shut.

"*Il est adorable,*" she said finally, peering into his carriage. "*Il a quel âge?*"

"*Chut!*" whispered the grandmother, a finger to her lips.

"My mother, Apolline," explained the daughter with a tired smile.

The older woman nodded cursorily and busied herself with the baby's blanket.

"I'm sorry," said Val softly. "You'll be wanting to get home."

"You have a question about Marius?" Clarisse insisted, taking Val lightly by the forearm and stepping away from the pushchair. "Is he ill?"

"No. No, he's fine. It doesn't matter."

She looked back at the sleeping baby.

"I think I already have my answer."

"Is it about money? Does he need money?"

Val hesitated, looked into the face of the wife once more. She had eyes the colour of chestnuts; even after a long day's work they shone with a rare purity. They were eyes which said *you can trust me.*

"Is he asking me to bail him out?"

"No. No, it's nothing like that. It's the opposite. He's got plenty of money."

"Well, that's alright then," she said with a throwaway laugh. "Get him to spend some of it on you, *ma chère!*"

"But…"

"*On va aux magasins ou non?* Are we going to the shops?" It was the grandmother, getting impatient. "Otherwise I'll put Benny back in the car."

"*Un moment, maman,*" said her daughter, and then back to Val: "But? But what?"

"Never mind. I'll leave you."

"But what?"

"Marius told me … Marius told me you'd be after his money. I suppose you're more entitled to it than I am. You're still his wife, after all."

"Hey, I've moved on. What did you say your name was? Val? I don't want his money, Val. I don't need it. I've moved on. He's all yours if you want him. I'm happy here. I don't need Marius anymore. All that's over."

"Does he know you have a son?"

"I haven't told him. I haven't spoken to him for two years. You can tell him for me, Val. Pass on my good news. Tell him my baby is doing fine. Benny's ten months old and he's doing absolutely fine. Tell him we're both doing absolutely fine."

It had been a warm morning for the time of the year and while the Tunisians were inside on their last day of decorating – *C'est une promesse, Madame Val!* – she had taken herself into the garden to dig over the vegetable plot. The autumn had yielded a disappointing crop but she knew she'd been apathetic and there was nobody else to blame.

And now her heart wasn't in these exhausting labours. There was no-one in the gîte to give her the excuse of stopping for a chat, and on the other side of the line of laurel was an example of even greater neglect: the fallen fruit left like litter to rot, the house was still, its curtains drawn shut and she'd neither seen nor heard Madame Motta for weeks. She wasn't so neglectful a neighbour that she hadn't knocked on her door but it was clear that, whatever the reason, the place had been abandoned.

By lunchtime Val was thoroughly bored with spadework. She couldn't clear her head of thoughts of Bobby. Fifteen months ago – yes, it was that long – he would have been here to give her a hand. She had convinced herself that he was responsible for the break-in; a conviction that had allowed her to dismiss any fanciful involvement of phantoms and hauntings. Even so, she wondered why he would chose such a crude way of punishing her , of frightening her. And the link between him and Dean Buckle continued to torment her.

Meanwhile the meeting with Clarisse Ledru had left a more immediately troubling impression. To clear her head, she decided she would drive out to the forest, tramp over to the Etang de Broussaille, take some late afternoon photographs. The air temperature would drop fast and there would be mist on the waters. She rang Greta to invite her for a short hike – she would mention the baby boy and they could toss around a few hypotheticals – but there was no answer. No matter, and no need to leave a message.

The Tunisians packed up, took her compliments with good grace and told her they would email an invoice overnight. They had done a tidy job. Val was reorganising her equipment when her mobile rang: it was Marius. He had the afternoon off and wanted to spend it with her. He felt she left him last time with a cloud hanging over them. Didn't she have the same impression? No. No, she didn't feel that way. She told him her plans for a walk, neglected to tell him that she wanted to be alone, and crumbled when he invited himself to join her.

"It's a great idea, Val. Some fresh air. I've been in the office all morning. Paperwork. I'll drive us. I can be over there in twenty minutes, okay?"

Her impatience was curdling to anger when his Audi pulled into the drive over an hour later. The best of the light had already gone. She noticed a bouquet of lilies lying on the backseat as soon as he opened the passenger door, along with their heady perfume.

"They're for you," said Marius with a penitent smile.

"For me? What have I done to deserve flowers?"

"Well, I think you probably deserve an apology."

He turned the car into the lane and they headed out of Saint-Benoît. She lifted her camera bag on to her lap.

"An apology?"

"Well, apart from being late. I'm sorry you had to see that photo of Clarisse."

"You don't need to apologise for that, Marius. It was just a random photo. I didn't take offence. I don't expect you to scrub away your past for me."

"Well, that's very noble of you. But I think it embarrassed you in some way. It was clumsy of me."

"I think you're making too much of it. But if it makes you feel better, I will forgive you. And thanks for the flowers."

Ledru drove fast. The car radio offered unobtrusive music from a local station. They had left the town behind them and were following a succession of *voies communales*, empty unmarked roads crossing the woods.

She saw him smile to himself, felt him pat her on the knee like he might do an obedient lapdog. She swallowed. Took a breath and swallowed again.

"There is something else on my mind, Marius."

"Something else I need to apologise for?" he said, taking his eyes off the windscreen for a second to offer an ironic smile.

"It's the money," said Val, eyes not meeting his, fixed on a point thirty metres ahead in the middle of the road.

"The money? The money we put in your account?"

"*You* put in my account."

Semantics. He turned off the music. It was giving him a headache anyway.

"I put, we put, whatever. What about the money? Are you planning on spending some of it? Seen something nice?"

"I want you to take it back, Marius."

He was approaching a bend in the forest road and found himself in the wrong gear, revving hopelessly as the car lost speed.

"I don't feel comfortable with all that money in my account," she added.

"Comfortable? You felt perfectly comfortable with it not so long ago."

"Well, I don't anymore."

He said nothing, overtook a cyclist and picked up speed.

"So," she went on, "when we get back…"

"It's better where it is," he interrupted.

"No, something doesn't feel right, Marius."

In the distance a thin mist was rising from the tree roots on both sides of the road. They were on a stretch with a narrow gravel verge. Suddenly Ledru pulled over and, kicking up dust, brought the car crunching to an abrupt halt.

"Doesn't feel right?" he repeated, eyes forward, fingers tapping out a rhythm on the steering wheel.

Val was still winded by the unexpected tug on her seat belt.

"Okay," he continued. "It doesn't feel right. So? So what? Put it back in my account? Let the taxman find it? Let my wife's accountant find it? Let Clarisse have it? Let her spend my money on all her friends in Marseille?"

"She doesn't want your money, Marius," said Val softly.

"She doesn't... What do you mean?"

"I've met her. I've spoken to Clarisse. Yesterday, in fact."

"You can't have. She's in..."

"She's not. She's not in Marseille, Marius. You were wrong, or you were lying. Were you lying? She lives in Orléans. She works at a care home. I spoke to her."

Ledru unbuckled his seat belt, gave himself a second or two to reset, then turned to face her. She was fiddling with the strap on her camera bag.

"Well, if you say so, Val. Really? Orléans? I must have been mistaken. I'm pretty sure I wasn't lying to you. How is she? What did you two have to say to each other, if I may ask?"

"She's fine. She wants you to know that she's moved on."

"Moved on!" he sniggered.

"And I met her mother too. You remember Apolline?"

"*Oh, mon Dieu! Quelle hypocrite!*"

"And her lovely son."

"Her son?"

"Benny. He's nearly a year old."

Suddenly Ledru had no words.

"He's gorgeous, Marius, he really is. She's done very well, Clarisse – for a woman who is incapable of conceiving."

She turned to meet his studied look of disbelief.

"Another lie, Marius. How many more? I thought I could trust you."

"Don't talk to me about trust!" he shouted back at her. "*I* trusted *you*! I thought we were close. I trusted you and yet you go behind my back, stalking my wife, upsetting my mother-in-law…"

Val unclipped her seat-belt, made to open the door.

"I'll walk from here, thanks," she said.

"Wait," he insisted. His voice was calm again. "Wait. Listen, it's complicated. Don't do anything rash. Just put the money back into my account if you have to and let's just leave it like that. Okay? You have my details, right?"

She nodded, gave him space to go on.

"Just a straight reverse transfer. And I'm trusting you to keep it to yourself. Don't go causing a stir, Val. Don't go poking around in a hornet's nest. For both our sakes. You understand? If there's a stink about this with the tax people you'll be implicated too. You're an accessory."

He was overplaying his hand, Val thought. Had he anything else to add, any other threat? Apparently not.

"I think you should put a different officer on my case," she said, her voice as emotionless as she could make it sound.

"That's if you're still investigating it."

"Of course. If that's what you want. Mind you, with another detective it'll go to the back of a long queue. I hope you're prepared for that."

Val had opened the door and was already standing on the gravel.

"I don't really care, Marius, to be honest."

"Really?"

"I think I can take care of it myself from this point."

Only the soft idling of the engine sliced into the silence of the woods. He was leaning out of his seat towards her door, a hint of desperation in his grey eyes.

"So, is this it?" he asked after a moment.

"It?"

"The end. Goodbye. *Adieu*. 'Enjoy the rest of your life.'"

"Yeah," she said with a sigh. "I suppose it is."

"It's all very sudden."

"As sudden as the moment I realised you were lying to me."

He looked out to the featureless road ahead. It was a hollow moment. She waited, uncertain for what. Then he turned his face to hers once more.

"You might as well take the lilies."

"Keep them."

"I hate them. And that's not a lie, Val. Something about the scent. Please, help yourself."

He leaned over to pick the bouquet from the backseat and handed it to her. Now that she knew him better it was hard to tell if the regretful smile on his face was sincere or simply a mask.

In spite of herself, a tear ran down her cheek as she stood watching his car pick up speed and disappear with the curve of the road. A few seconds later its sound faded away and he was gone. She wiped away the dampness with her sleeve. She'd only just got over the loss of one man; she wasn't going to let herself melt over another.

She realised with a start that she was still several kilometres from the lake. The idea of a hike had lost its appeal and it was closer to walk back home. She needed a drink: water, wine, anything. Above her a clamour of rooks were heading for their nesting sites. She turned around to get her bearings. Ledru had taken a road she rarely used. All around her stood armies of trees, mainly stiff-backed pines, shadowy dark green and black, row after row stranded in dampness, towering towards the empty sky, whose fragile blue was deepening in the east. Was that right? The lighter sky to the west? Which would mean if she retraced their route she'd be heading south, when surely Saint-Benoît was to the north.

Around the feet of the trees the mist was wrapping its floating tentacles. She tugged the zip of her parka up to her throat and hauled the camera bag over a shoulder, then turned to stride out back the way they had driven. Sooner or later she would see something she recognised or she'd hitch a lift with a passing vehicle. The bouquet of flowers in their cellophane felt ridiculous in her hand but she decided against flinging them into the woods.

Nobody passed her for half an hour. The only signs she saw were for single-track side roads leading to hamlets she had never heard of. With little confidence in her sense of direction, with wisps of moisture snaking around her ankles, she felt vulnerable and terribly alone. Eventually she flagged down a motorcyclist who confirmed that she was on the road to the Quatre-Routes, though she was approaching it from an unfamiliar bearing. On foot she was still an hour from Saint-Benoît, she was told, but she allowed herself to breathe a sigh of relief. The mist was thickening with each passing minute but there was still enough daylight to guide her home.

Her feet were getting sore by the time Val arrived at the crossroads. She picked out the shrine to the Madonna and finally recognised where she was. A few paces away stood the war memorial. She approached it and solemnly stooped to place the lilies against its plinth. Surrounded in mist, the cottage across the road was barely visible save for a light in a downstairs window. She thought of Florian arriving here in the springtime on his moped, Florian mowing the grass with his earphones in, Florian making love to her in the garden room amidst the potted plants. She wondered if anyone was sitting on that sofa right now, squashing its corduroy, idly flicking through the glossy pages of a book about Jeanne Moreau or Belmondo or Fernandel. She stepped a little closer to the hedge and the shape of a board nailed to a post came into focus. *A Vendre*. The old cottage, once the home of the young laundrywoman who had exposed the betrayal of Widow Merel, was up for sale.

Clément Barachet was most interested in what Val could tell him about Marius Ledru. She told herself that what she was doing was not an act of betrayal. No, indeed, it was the inspector who had betrayed her trust: he had played her, hadn't he? Had there ever really been a spark of love glinting between them or was it just a trick of the light?

The money trail led to an obscure bank in Basle, Switzerland, Barachet reported a day or two later. He would tell her more as soon as the investigation team allowed him sight of its findings.

*

It was more than the sign outside the cottage at the Qua-tre-Routes that convinced Val to contact an estate agent in Saint-Benoît. In her heart she knew that she had been ready to sell *Les Genêts* months ago. Almost from the moment that she admitted to herself that Bobby wasn't going to come back and share it with her. Since then she had been doing no more than going through the motions, marking time. What she would do next, where she would go, she had only the vaguest of plans, but there was no reason to delay the inevitable.

She had several conversations on these lines with her friend Greta Barachet, who was distraught at the prospect of losing her.

"But you love the Sologne, Val! You don't truly want to leave it, to leave us, do you?"

"I might not move very far away," Val had said, "but then again, it might be time for me to make a fresh start."

"A fresh start? At your age, dearie?"

"But first," continued Val, ignoring the sarcasm, "I want you to do me a favour. I've got something else to do before I ever start packing my trunk and leaving this place for good."

And so, armed with a friend's promise, a few assorted items bought at the local Brico-Jacques and the outline of a plan, Val made her arrangements. She would sail to England early the following week on the overnight car ferry from the port of Caen-Ouistreham.

On the morning of her departure she was interrupted at breakfast by a telephone call from Barachet. *Bon voyage and all that, Valérie, but before you go I thought you'd like to know.* The man kept his voice as neutral as he could: professional mode, no hint of personal vanity on show so early in the morning. He could have crowed but it really wasn't his style. Not today at least. He had been given notice of the Ledru case. *Yes, I know, first thing this morning. I'm still sitting here in my dressing gown!* Val took it all in as her coffee slowly went cold.

Marius Ledru had been arrested the previous evening. He was as much a wrong 'un as could be. He had blackmailed a number of corrupt local politicians. He had turned a blind eye to certain drug dealers, taking a percentage for his troubles. Not to mention the blackmailing of the boss of an office-cleaning company employing scores of illegals. Most, if not all of this happened during his time in Orléans. Certain evidence pointed to his involvement in similar, more recent scams in operation in Blois. Something along the same lines at a string of budget hotels.

"He was setting your business up to launder money, Valérie. I'm sure you can see that now. We call it *le blanchiment* – you know that word? You had a lucky escape. You will be required to ratify your statement at some stage. You'll be in England for how long? A week at the most? That won't be a problem here. No, you have a good time. A short holiday, is it? Oh, and Greta says make sure you change all your passwords on your computer, if you haven't already. But I'm sure you don't need to be told that, now, do you?"

CHAPTER 10

DEAN BUCKLE

The only bits of the county of Northamptonshire that Val had ever seen before were the forgettable stretches glimpsed at seventy miles an hour from the asphalt corridor of the M1 motorway. She had certainly never stopped and tasted the air in this, the so-called Rose of the Shires, nor had she explored any of the county's varied landmarks. And quite unfamiliar to her were the narrow residential streets of this town: Dean Buckle's home, the town that formed a part of the address she had read once and remembered from the inside back page of the teenager's passport. Emergency contact, written in black ink in the self-conscious hand of a schoolboy: Mr and Mrs H Buckle, 8 Swann Street.

The only reason it had stuck in her mind was because of the swans nesting by the Liselle that summer, the pair she had disturbed when she made her inelegant escape from inside Amanda Ringer's tent. Number eight? The memory of the house number was not so clear but Swann Street was a short side street, something of a rat run, she guessed, linking two busy arterial roads. Pressed beneath brooding afternoon cloud, a terrace of a dozen or so decent-sized houses with tiny front gardens – most given up for parking spaces – followed the line of the street along one side only. The other was fronted by some kind of low-rise factory space, then open ground and finally a large, ugly church built of dark brick over a hundred years ago.

If not number eight, Val was sure the neighbours would know where the Buckles lived, especially with the family being in the news so much last year and all. As it happened the frosted glass door of number eight was opened to her by a woman in a cardigan whose face she recognised. Mrs Buckle was shorter than Val had remembered from her fleeting appearances on television, plumper too, but then she had usually been addressing the screen from a sitting position, flanked, in Val's recollection, on one side by a solemn-faced police officer and on the other by her dead-eyed husband.

A dog had started barking from behind a door, closed to the narrow hallway at the woman's back. It was a deep-throated bark, more in greeting than in threat, Val thought: some big protector dog, maybe an Alsatian.

"Yeah?" Mrs Buckle was looking up at her, wiping her hands on a tea towel.

"Hello, Mrs Buckle," said Val with a polished smile to go with her well-rehearsed opening lines:

"My name is Liz Jones. I'm a social liaison officer attached to your son's school."

"Which one?" the woman interrupted. "His new one?"

"His new one?"

"He left Nene Bank after all the trouble. So, you're from the college?"

"No. No, I'm not," said Val, already knocked out of her stride. "I'm representing Nene Bank. Sorry, I am new to the authority."

She had no idea that he had left the school. The woman continued to wipe her hands, waiting for her to say more.

"Is Dean at home?" Val asked. "Would you mind if I had

a word? Just five minutes? I know it's a pain. It's to follow up on the events of last summer. On behalf of the authority I need to set everything we've learned in stone, as it were."

"You have a card or something?" asked the woman, dead-pan. "Proof of ID?"

"Of course. Yes, forgive me. I should have…"

Val fished out a laminated card, produced two days earlier in her redecorated photography studio, and handed it to Mrs Buckle for her cursory inspection.

"As long as you're not from the papers."

"No, I can assure you I'm not."

"They're still bothering us even now. They're a bloody nuisance."

"I'm sorry to hear that. They can be pests, I know, from personal experience. May I come in?"

"Watch that carpet," said the woman, ushering her through the door. "It's loose."

The corridor harboured a smell of warm tomato soup.

"There, go into the front room," she continued. "You don't want the dog bothering you. I'll put the fire on." And then, shouting up the stairs, "Dean! Dean, you've got a visitor!"

The room was cold and dark. Since the clocks had gone back, evenings came gloomily early on days like this, with its overcast sky and rain showers. Val had chosen to arrive in the late afternoon in the hope of catching the boy after school.

"Have a seat. Yes, there on the settee. You can shift that magazine. Dean! Come downstairs!"

Val parked herself on the edge of the leatherette cushions, placed her briefcase between her feet and waited.

"You need me too?" asked Mrs Buckle.

"No. Just Dean will be fine."

"He's eighteen soon. He can answer for himself. I've got things to do, and I've had it up to here filling forms in. I was just putting tea on when you knocked and then I'm off out to work."

"Oh, where's that? In town?"

"The new Lidl's"

"Right. And Mr Buckle?"

"He don't live here no more. I'm surprised they didn't tell you."

"Sorry," said Val, patting her briefcase. "It'll be in the paperwork here somewhere. They've given me quite a case-load since I moved down here."

The woman turned again to call up the stairs.

"Dean!" and then to Val, "He'll be on his computer. He'll have his headphones on."

She waddled out of the room and Val heard her tread as she padded up the staircase. In the next room the dog had stopped its noise. That Mrs Buckle had volunteered to withdraw to her kitchen was a bonus. She needed to speak to Dean on his own and no tactic she had thought of to distract his mother had much merit.

The sitting room was tiny. A sofa, a matching armchair, a standard lamp, a set of shelves and an old-fashioned music centre sitting on a nest of melamine tables filled it completely. She rubbed her hands together for warmth. Mrs Buckle had forgotten to switch on the electric fire. Val stood up and peered through the window into the street where the traffic was picking up. Then Dean entered the room.

"Hello there, Dean," she said, turning to greet him with a smile and an open hand.

"Alright," replied the boy, taking it sheepishly. It was a lifeless handshake; clearly he was still unused to shaking the hands of unfamiliar adults.

He leaned over to turn on the lamp, filling a corner of the room with a sickly, yellow light. Then he pulled the curtains roughly together. They sat and he watched wordlessly as she plucked out a random folder from the briefcase and opened it at a page of typed notes. She faced him and smiled again. His dark, curly hair had grown long and he was trying to produce an adolescent beard. The suntan she remembered had long since faded to an English pallor. The slim, powerful physique remained, however: he was wearing a pair of sweatpants and a long-sleeved tee-shirt which clung to his shoulders, his upper arms and moulded itself to his chest. Val had never forgotten her first sight of this Adonis stepping away from the shower at the campsite pool in his pale yellow trunks. If he steered clear of junk food and lager, by twenty-five he could be more beautiful than even Bobby was at that age.

"You still swimming, Dean?"

"Yeah. I still do a bit."

"Listen, Dean. Don't be alarmed but I'm not actually from school."

He continued to watch her, his expression unchanged.

"You've absolutely nothing to worry about," she went on, "but I have to ask you a couple of questions."

"Who are you?"

"You don't need to know my name, Dean."

The boy made to get up.

"No, don't, Dean, please. Don't call your mum. Just hear me out. You can call me Liz if you want to. Two minutes and I'm gone, trust me. It's about the campsite."

"The campsite?"

"The site in France. In Saint-Benoît. By the river. Where the police caught up with you. With you and Miss Ringer."

Dean shuffled on to the edge of his seat, intensifying his clear-eyed gaze.

"I know you," he said, in little more than a whisper. "I've seen your face before."

"Yes, you're right, Dean. You have. I bumped into you on that campsite. You were making tea together, weren't you? I disturbed you looking for my dog."

The boy looked out through the gap in the curtains. Into the fading light of the street where a pair of motorbikes were tearing past, one chasing the other, contemptuous of the speed restrictions.

"Mandy didn't believe you," he said suddenly, cocking his head back to catch her eyes.

"Really?"

"She said you were, like, snooping around. Was she right?"

"No, I wasn't snooping," Val replied with a short, nervous laugh. "I was looking for my dog."

"I remember you saying that. I understood your French."

"I was. He's always running off."

"Were you the one that gave us up? Was it you that called the cops? A couple of hours after you showed up at our tent the place was, like, swarming with police."

To avoid his stare she closed the file and made a fuss of replacing it in her briefcase.

"It was you," he said, more to himself than to her, and sat back in the armchair with a look of triumph on his face.

"Listen, Dean," she countered, "I was doing you a favour. Doing both of you a favour. You know that, don't you? Especially now, over a year later: college, A Levels, your life's back on track."

"What do you know about my life?" he sneered. "I'm not even doing A Levels."

"Sorry," she answered, raising her palms to him. "Of course, you're right. I know nothing about your life. But if you have put all that behind you and you have rediscovered what fun it can be to be a teenager and to hang out with other teenagers, then I am happy for you. Genuinely, I am."

Dean scowled, shuffled in his seat, ran a hand through his hair, took a moment to reorder his thoughts.

"What do you want, anyway?" he said finally. "You said two minutes."

"I want to ask you about a knife," said Val, over the hurdle, regaining her composure.

"A knife?"

"A red Swiss Army knife."

Opening the photo gallery in her phone she let him see the screen.

"This one."

"Yeah. A Swiss Army knife. What about it?"

"It's yours, isn't it?"

"No."

"It *is*."

"It *isn't*."

"It *is*. It has a loose corkscrew. It was in your ruck…"

"What?"

"No, sorry. What am I saying? I'm getting mixed up. This knife was found very recently near Saint-Benoît. When I saw it at the police station I thought I recognised it from somewhere. At the time of your arrest there was a report with details of everything the police found in your tent. In your rucksacks. In both of your rucksacks."

Her hands were cold but she could feel her face was flushed. And she was talking too much. She drew breath.

"You live in France?" he asked. "I know you can speak French."

"I do. I've lived in Saint-Benoît for fifteen years. That campsite is only a mile from where I live. And I do know people in the local police force. I was told about the discoveries in your tent. Including a knife like this. Exactly like this. Like yours."

"It's not mine, I told you. Even if it's the same knife, it's not mine!"

"What do you mean?"

"It's not my knife. It's Mandy's."

"Mandy's? Miss Ringer's?"

"Yeah. She took it to France with her. I was with her when she bought it. At St Pancras station."

Val looked again at the image of the chunky red object, its range of tools and blades neatly tucked away inside itself.

"Why is it so important?" Dean asked.

"Never mind. If it's not your knife, Dean, then it doesn't concern you. But I do need to find Miss Ringer. Do you know where she is?"

"I've no idea."

"Is she still living around here?"

"God, no. Course she's not. I've not seen her since France."

"Where would you guess she might be?"

"Why do you need to know?"

"Don't worry, Dean. She's not in any trouble, trust me. I'm not with the newspapers and I'm not with the police. It's just to help me find a friend. A missing friend. Someone very dear to me."

The big dog in the back room suddenly began to bark again. Mrs Buckle must have disturbed it. Yes, Val could hear her voice through the wall. Dean's gaze had settled on the briefcase; he might have already realised that it was full of bogus paperwork.

"She might be living with her parents," he said. "She talked about them, like, a lot. She was pretty close to her dad."

"Her parents. Right. Thanks, that's helpful."

"Or she might be on the other side of the world."

"That's less helpful." A cautious smile. "Where do her parents live? Any idea?"

"Somewhere down south."

"The south of England?"

"Like, near the sea. She'd done a bit of sailing."

"Dorset?"

"She never mentioned Dorset."

"Devon?"

A shake of the head.

"Cornwall?"

A shrug of the shoulders.

"Hampshire?"

"Hampshire."

"Hampshire?"

"Yeah."

"You're sure?"

"Yeah. I used to swim for Northants. County schools. She talked about, like, trials she'd had once for her county. Cross-country running. She'd had trials for Hampshire."

"Any particular town?"

"No. She'd been to uni in London."

"London, okay, but what about her parents' home? No place ring a bell?"

"No."

"Southampton?"

"Dunno."

Val was closing down her phone.

"You've had your two minutes," he said, suddenly springing to his feet.

"I have. And you've been very helpful, Dean. I'm sorry if all this brought back bad memories."

"Not really. I had a great time in France with Mandy. Like, not many lads can say they got off with the fittest teacher in their school!"

It was the first time that afternoon she'd seen him smile. It was a beautiful, bewitching smile, lit up by a twinkle in his bright brown eyes.

Internet search engines. Val could remember a time before them, of course she could: a time of tramping into libraries and council offices and making expensive telephone calls to utilities and travel agents. Footslogging, burrowing in dusty archives, waiting in queues. With its telephone boxes and its typewriters and its endless shelves of curling paper, along with its carbon copies and its magnetic tape and its Polaroid processing, the twentieth century had already receded into something of an alien dimension. Admittedly for the modern magic to work, a half-decent network delivery depended on a reliable signal; mercifully she had found in this part of rural Hampshire, if not perhaps in the entire county, that all was well.

After a leisurely breakfast – she had not enjoyed a full English fry-up for years – she had spent an hour on her phone: investigating, making notes, adding new information to her memory bank. It was common knowledge that Amanda Ringer's mother was a primary school headmistress; she had said as much in the magazine interview. Val discovered the name of her place of work by searching through a Wiki-list of Hampshire schools until she found her name on a "who's who" staffing page. Julie. Mrs Julie Ringer. There were no photographs on the site apart from ones of the facilities. It looked like the sort of homely primary school Val would have wanted her own children to go to. The autumn term's calendar was especially helpful, a mine of information: dates of trips and rehearsals and fundraisers and training days. The following evening there was to be a Parent Teacher Association meeting starting at seven o'clock. Julie would be there for sure. And for Val's purposes it would be much better to have her out of the way.

Next she visited BT's Phone Book website. Mr and Mrs Ringer were of such an age and a disposition – she guessed

– that a domestic landline would not yet have been replaced entirely by a mobile, and for whom the telephone directory was probably still valid. There was a chance that the negativity provoked by their daughter's misadventures had obliged them to remove themselves from the public list but Val crossed her fingers and carefully typed the family name and town into the spaces. She had to assume that their home address was not too far from Julie's school. She was rewarded with two Ringers: a Mrs Sheila and a plain S. Stephen? Sam? Solomon? However he was christened, S had to be Julie's husband. In the same neat frame appeared a telephone number and more importantly an address with postcode.

As a precaution, and not trusting her sense of direction in unfamiliar surroundings after dark, Val had already driven down this twisty lane earlier in the day. She was on the edge of the South Downs, in an unchanging rural England of soft, sloping meadows and ancient woodlands, of footpaths and farms and narrow, muddy roads. There were no suburbs here: once you left the town you were slap in the countryside, sharing the carriageway with tractors and horse riders. She had been delighted to discover that the Ringers' place was somewhat isolated and had a roof of plump thatch. She had never been inside a thatched cottage before.

As the sun dropped, so had the temperature. The moon's slim white curve was hanging in a cold, inky sky already filling with stars. The time was just after six thirty. Val steered the Mégane into the wide gravel drive and parked behind another, smaller hatchback. The moment she switched off her headlights the cottage and its surrounding bushes were transformed into a shadowy space that reminded her of the set of a television thriller. As if to complete the scene an owl or some similar night bird hooted from the depths of the woods. A pale glow peeped from behind the curtains of a ground-floor window. She skirted the lawn and was approaching the door when a bright floodlight suddenly offered her the clear sight of a pair of large stone slabs set as steps. Directly in front of her face was a heavy door knocker which she rapped three times.

It took Mr Ringer a moment or two to reach the door, unbolt it and open it to the unexpected visitor. Standing in a dimly lit vestibule, he was a tall man with a slight stoop and his hair, thin and grey, was in need of a trim, she thought. His narrow face was dominated by a heavy pair of spectacles.

"Mr Ringer?" she said cheerfully, offering him a hand to shake.

"That's right," the man replied, his own hands clasped rigidly together over his middle.

"I'm terribly sorry to disturb you, sir," continued Val, peering past his head into the hallway from where a faint smell of woodsmoke reached her. "I was hoping to catch Amanda. Is she in?"

"Amanda? No. No, she doesn't really live here. Not permanently."

"Oh. I was told she had moved back in with you and your wife. Back into the bosom of the family, as it were. Mind you, when I didn't spot her old Fiesta outside I guessed I'd made a wasted journey."

There was no reaction from Mr Ringer beyond a raised eyebrow.

"Sorry," she went on, "let me introduce myself. My name is Liz. Liz Jones. I was a colleague of Amanda's at Nene Bank."

"Really?" he asked, pausing to run the name through his memory. "Liz Jones? I can't say I recognise the name."

"It's a large school, Mr Ringer. Amanda had lots of friends

on the staff. I could have phoned, I suppose, but I did want to return a book," and here she patted her handbag. "I borrowed it from her over a year ago, just before she went on her … jaunt."

She threw in a theatrical frown which the man ignored.

"May I…?"

"Come in? Yes, of course. It must be chilly standing out there. Come in for a minute, Miss Jones."

"Call me Liz, please. No, a friend did say that Amanda was back here. I imagined, you know, recharge her batteries, get her head together, focus on the future now that she's out of prison."

"She told me she had done all of those things while she was *in* prison," he declared as he led Val past a staircase into a low-ceilinged sitting room illuminated by the flames of an open fire.

"It's Simon, by the way," he added with the faintest of smiles. "You've missed Amanda's mother, too, I'm afraid. My wife's at a meeting. Sit down, please. Yes, take that armchair by the fire."

The man spoke slowly, measuring his words, choosing and then delivering them gently and with great care.

"I'm sorry to bother you. You weren't eating, were you?" said Val.

"No, we had an early meal."

"She's a teacher too, isn't she? Your wife?"

"Yes. Yes, she is. The meeting is school business. I don't expect her to stick at it for much longer. It's changed, hasn't it, teaching? So she says. Well, you'll know all about it, Liz. She's head at the local first school, which means she hardly teaches a lesson these days. It's all financial controls and filling out forms and writing reports. And meetings. So she says. She's talking about retiring next year."

"I know what she means," nodded Val empathetically.

Simon Ringer was making himself comfortable on the near corner of the sofa.

"Are you still at Nene Bank, Liz?"

"No. I left last summer. My husband's job took us north. I'm still looking for a new post."

"You taught French with Amanda, did you?"

"No, I'm an art teacher. But I do speak a bit of French as it happens. That's one of the reasons she invited me along on the last of her Normandy trips. You know, I could be more useful than just another chaperone. That's when we really got to know each other."

"I see."

The conversation had arrived at a natural pause. On the top of a cabinet in the corner of the room a framed picture of Ringer caught her eye. It was a large graduation photo: mortar board, black gown, hood edged with russet brown and she was smiling the smile of the sainted. She had a cherubic face, not quite yet the face of an adult, glossy hair, bright hazel eyes, that pretty nose. She was the apple of her father's eye, the only child, loved to death. How he would have wished she could stay like that, if not for ever, at least for a few more years. For a moment Val felt her presence in the room. The young woman's stare pierced the polished glass, *she* was spying on *her*, waiting for her to trip up over her own cleverness.

"Do you teach, Simon?" Val asked abruptly.

"No, no. That's not for me."

He had stalled again. She looked up at him inquisitively.

"No. I worked at the OS."

"OS?"

"The Ordnance Survey. You know, mapping work. Mostly GPS these days."

"Maps!" she exclaimed. "I never could read a map properly!"

"Then I dare say you can't have been taught properly."

"I'm sure I wasn't taught at all."

"Well, you've made my point for me. It's like reading anything else: words, music. And maps. It's a skill that needs to be learned."

Val nodded in appreciation.

"Would you like a drink, perhaps, Liz?"

She thought he was never going to ask.

"Tea? Coffee?"

"A cup of tea would be lovely, thanks."

"Milk?"

"Milk, no sugar, thanks. I'll fish out Amanda's book."

"I'm retired, actually," he said suddenly. "I had a problem with my eyesight. Bit of a health issue generally. We think it was related in one way or another to stress. You know, with Amanda's sentencing."

It occurred to her to ask him how he felt about his daughter's reinvention, what he thought of Mandy Roundtree and her decision to jettison the family name, but she held back. It would be too cheap a shot, too cruel.

Mr Ringer rose from his chair and as he disappeared

from the room, Val took from her bag not only the copy of a novel she had picked up earlier in the day from a charity shop but also her phone. Nimbly she opens it, dispatches the briefest of text messages: *2 mins*.

"Could I quickly use your loo?" she calls into the kitchen, and before the man has finished telling her there's one in the hall, right where she came in, she is already at the top of the staircase on a wide landing lit by a chintzy table lamp.

She pushes open a bedroom door but it is Mother and Father's. Along the landing she needs look no further: there's a door with a ceramic letter A hooked on it, painted with little red apples. She is swiftly inside, closing the curtains before putting on the light. It is a small space: single bed, neatly made, wardrobe, cupboards and bookcase in matching pinewood, all as she would expect. It has to be a rudimentary search but Greta will give her a little more time. On cue, as she is rustling through drawers of clothes, she hears the house phone ringing downstairs. Her heart is beating rapidly, her eyes flit from this to that and back to this again, her fingers working faster than a lacemaker's. Clothes offer no clues, shoes likewise. She doesn't really know what she's looking for, but she will know when she finds it. She flicks in between books on the upper shelves, fashion magazines on the lower. Finally a bedside table with a small drawer. And here she strikes what could be gold: a mobile phone with a cracked screen. No longer in use but not thrown away. She slips it into her hip pocket.

She is about to leave the room when her eyes are drawn to the wall behind her. To the left, preserved by nostalgia, is a large poster of a boy band from the turn of the century. To the right, in a deep red frame, a grey and white photograph of a young girl in a summer dress caressing a kitten. Val cannot believe her eyes. She leans in for a closer look but there is no doubt in her mind. It is her picture of Rosette, stolen from her house: her sad-faced Rosette hanging on a bedroom wall in a thatched cottage in Hampshire. She lifts it off its nail, a nail hammered into the plaster by Amanda the thief. But she cannot walk downstairs with it under her arm like a bailiff. She opens the door, pokes out her head. It sounds like Simon the mapmaker is still talking. On the back of the door she spots a flurry of scarves on a coat hook. She takes a couple of chiffons, the longest, knots them together and ties one end to the wire behind the photo frame. She darts to the window, opens it as quietly as she can, and threading the scarves carefully through her fingers lowers the treasure gently to the ground. It feels like it's landing in a bush. She lets the scarves fall into the darkness, closes the window and heads out of the bedroom and back down the staircase.

Mr Ringer was sitting in the lounge, holding a mug of milky tea for her.

"Sorry it took me so long," said Val sheepishly. "I had a bit of a dizzy turn up there."

"Did you?" he asked. "Are you sure you're alright?"

"I'm fine now. I have been on the go all day. Haven't eaten since breakfast."

"Really? Would you like me to make you a slice of toast and marmalade?"

"No, thanks. That's kind but I'll get off and find something in town."

"You tea is getting cold, I'm afraid."

She took it from him, drank a long slurp and put the mug on the table.

"I don't normally give those calls the time of day," the man was saying. "Cold callers. But I've just had a lovely chat with a young Scottish lady. She was selling home insurance specifically for thatched properties. I didn't take her up on it but she knew this part of Hampshire. She'd lived in Winchester for ten years, apparently. A lovely, warm Scottish accent. Edinburgh, she said. I think she quite appreciated the chat, actually. It must be terribly dull sitting in a call centre all day, don't you think, flogging insurance?"

"It must," agreed Val.

She looked again at the mug, decided to ignore it. Instead she picked up her bag.

"I'll be going, Simon," she said, buttoning up her coat.

"You left the book, then?"

"Yes, it's there where I was sitting."

Fifty pence from a charity shop and she hadn't even registered the title.

"I'll see she gets it," said Mr Ringer, getting to his feet. "It was nice to meet you, Liz."

"And you. Thanks for the tea. Give my regards to your wife, won't you? I'll probably give Amanda a ring later in the week. Have a bit of a catch-up."

Val was sitting in her car in a dark passing place by a narrow bridge, a quarter of a mile from Simon and Julie's. In her hand, the target of her concentration, was a mobile phone with a cracked screen, battery level at ten per cent.

On bidding poor Mr Ringer goodnight, she had waited until he had settled down for the evening before doubling back and, cautious not to activate the floodlight sensor, had kept to the edge of the garden on her way towards the shrubs that decorated the front of the cottage. Catching a glint of moonlight was a flimsy strip of silk. The picture appeared undamaged. Having wrapped it in the scarves, she crept across the lawn with it and then back into the shadows of the lane.

The car was cold. Val shivered, rubbed her hands together, pulled Ringer's discarded phone out of her pocket. She switched it on; it was unlocked. It appeared to be light on apps and empty of photos. She scrolled through her contacts, names that meant nothing. No contact with Dean Buckle. No Bobby listed, but there was a Bob, on a number she didn't recognise. Bob also had a landline number, area code unfamiliar. She opened up the chats with Bob and found texts that ran on and on. Five threads in all, the words blurring in front of her. She could pick out incriminating phrases but couldn't be sure what they meant, her eyes were racing ahead of her brain. She was starting to panic, stopped herself from being mesmerized by the hieroglyphics, took a deep breath and looked away from the tiny screen. She faced into the darkness of the bushes, saw her ghostly reflection in the side window.

The battery was down to eight per cent. She opened up the camera on her own phone and prepared to record the texts one screen at a time before the power died.

And so for a third time, more composed now, she was reading the exchanges. It was the chill making her tremble but still the blood thudded hot at her temples.

The first, from the middle of July:

B: *You coming over this week, babe?*

M: *Friday OK? Early pm to beat the traffic.*

B: *Can't wait! Xxx*

M: *Me too xxx*

Then a week later:

M: *You heard from V?*

B: *No.*

M: *She doesn't suspect anything?*

B: *No I was dead careful*

M: *Will she sell up?*

B: *Must have Xed her mind. Dead scared.*

M: *Luv you xxx*

B: *Luv you too (heart emoji)*

It was beyond denial. Much loved Bob was Bobby. Much loved Mandy was a conniving bitch. Unsuspecting V was her.

The following week, something more prosaic:

B: *Can you pick up a decent red on your way over?*

M: *None in your shop?*

B: *Nothing good enough for us!*

M: *Rubbish campsite! Are we celebrating?*

B: *When are we not, babe?*

M: *Love you Bob x*

Campsite?

In early August came a fourth dialogue:

M: *Is your passport in date?*

B: *Yeah. 2 more years on it. Remind me what time the ferry leaves.*

M: *Ferry sails at 22.45. See you at P'mouth at 21.00*

B: *Booked a cosy cabin, did you?*

M: *Bunk beds!*

B: *Dead cosy x*

Plans for a trip to France. Val cast her mind back to the date of her studio being ransacked.

A fifth and final thread, a couple of weeks after the fourth:

M: *Don't forget your kit bag*

B: *Everything I need will be in the van.*

M: *Got your keys?*

B: *At Seba's.*

M: *We'll put the fear of god up her*

B: *Can't go wrong, Manz. She'll be a gibbering wreck.*

        See you at 9 x

M: *(Kissing face emoji and French flag)*

A conspiracy captured. Banged to rights, "Manz". And Sébastien Albiero was a damned liar.

Car headlights danced and flickered in the distance, approaching her down the wooded lane, rising to take in the little bridge, blinding her for a second. Then the vehicle, an estate, cruised past, taking the bend and dissolving into the night. Julie, escaping the PTA meeting earlier than expected.

She genuinely was hungry and was more than ready to turn on the car's engine but there was one more thing she wanted to do before she fled the scene: check kit bag Bob's landline number. Val's quick fingers searched out the BT area code finder. In an instant her suspicions were confirmed: Bobby, aka Bob the cosy cabin-boy, was obtainable at the end of a telephone line registered in south Dorset, just over an hour's drive away.

CHAPTER 11

BOBBY AND VAL

Val shook the metal gate on its hinges, checked for a final time that the heavy duty padlock was secure and that the barrier was fastened shut. Flanked by a narrow wooden stile for walkers, the gate was a five-bar, farmyard type, guarding the entrance to the caravan park. She had bought the padlock – industrial grade, four digit code security – from a hardware store in Brockenhurst. In the privacy of her bolt-hole in the New Forest she had familiarised herself with its workings, clicking and re-clicking the spinning number wheels, channelling her nervous energy, selecting a code: 7373, predictably, the date of her birth.

This kind of undercover activity was not really in her nature, although so far she had been behaving like a pro, even if she said so herself. Moreover, she had checked into the B&B under a second false name; Liz Jones was already history. She had kept away from the other guests – there were secondary reasons for this in most cases – and for her own amusement she had studied the behaviour of her hosts from a safe distance. Short, middle-aged, as English as buttered scones, they were an odd couple. Mr was superficially charming but beneath the veneer Val sensed a barely controlled exasperation towards every aspect of his life. Mrs was mostly invisible; she lurked, was a quietly embittered presence and smelled constantly of fried bacon.

To kill time Val had dozed, rehearsed her moves, watched

daytime television. She listened to radio talk shows, surfed social media and read the news from a variety of sources. Lately the country had got itself into a bind, if that wasn't an understatement. She had the impression of a troubled population being pushed and pulled through a forest of brambles, not by the cleverest amongst them but by those with the loudest voices. And being led, it seemed to her, fractious and scarred, towards a future coloured by nationalism and hubris.

A day earlier, from a public call box, she had rung Bob's – Bobby's – landline number retrieved from Ringer's phone. She had been prepared to put on a fake voice – after listening to Greta Barachet for so many years she could do a passable Scot – but he had answered on the second ring: *Smugglers Top, hello.* She had said nothing, let the sound of Bobby's voice fill her ears, just those three words in a voice she had not heard for over a year, before abruptly ending the call. She had been prepared to say something opaque and subtly threatening too, something to disquiet him, put the willies up him, but that wasn't really her style.

Smugglers Top. Within a minute she had found the address of the caravan park. She had studied its website, viewed its aerial mapping and had seen how it was perched on a point on the Dorset coast. She'd picked out a cluster of buildings, the green canopy of woodland, even the five-bar gate. As she'd done with the Ringers' cottage, she felt the need for daylight reconnaissance. She considered it worth the risk to drive on to the site, even in the Mégane with its French plates, in order to get a better sense of the property. She had breached the open gateway, followed a lane sloping uphill through the small wood, then emerged between terraces of caravans left and right which finally gave way to public areas: toilet blocks, play park, reception, shop, what looked like communal rooms or a bar. And set back a little, at the top of the slope, allowing ample parking space, stood a kind of lodge: a small house, bedecked on its ground floor in darkened half-cut timber to give a log-cabin effect. Beyond the house stretched a field lined with more empty caravans: two rows, the furthest of which had the most splendid prospect of the sea. The whole area appeared to be deserted, although from somewhere she could hear the faint buzz of a chainsaw.

There was a ramblers' right-of-way through the site which led to a junction with the coastal path. The metalled lane petered out beyond more trees and fed into a public car park. Four other vehicles had arrived there before her. Reluctant to step out, she had pulled up the hood of her jacket and wound down the window. Even so close to the sea the air was still, and warmer than she had expected. Her attention was attracted by voices: about fifty metres up ahead she had noticed the heads of men walking, or were they working, just out of sight, on path repairs? Maybe Bobby was with them; she was in no hurry to find out. She had turned the car round and steered back down the hill, past the lodge, and there she had seen him, or someone who looked very much like him: Bobby with his back to her, walking into the campsite shop with a roll of tarpaulin tucked under one arm and the other wrapped in a sling.

The shiny new padlock reflected the soft light of the waxing moon. Posted against the hedges stood the sign: *Welcome to Smugglers Top Campsite & Caravan Park. Closed till Easter*, harder to read now without a torch. Val looked back towards her car, hidden in the shadows on the outer side of the gate. She looked beyond it, further back up the lane to the kink before it joined the road. She had waited for Ringer but there had been no sign of her. Not a soul had visited the site since she had arrived to sit here in the dark almost two hours earlier. The air was still mild, unseasonably so for November; she unfastened her jacket, slipped over the stile and headed up the hill, a cloth bag over her shoulder and in her right hand a small, recently purchased lump hammer.

During the day she hadn't noticed the kerb lamps dotted at intervals up the driveway. Their dim lights helped guide her through the gloom and past the ghostly caravans, ranked like shipping containers, rigid in the rising tide of mist rolling down the bank. Finally she arrived at the lodge, already a little out of breath. Here too a mist was creeping over the verge, spilling in off the sea.

The cabin building stands in near darkness. Val ignores the door, darts across to a window offering a finger of light. A gap in the curtains allows her a peep into a living room where she sees a leg clad in denim and an arm in a plaster cast. Also beer cans on the edge of a low table, and the corner of a television screen, the source of faint music.

Bobby cannot get comfortable and he has just realised that, half an hour in, he's seen this film before. His forearm is itching like crazy but he's been told that this is a good sign. The plaster will come off next week, all being well. It has been a proper test of his patience, this lay-off. *Partial* lay-off. He can still do bits and pieces, paperwork which he hates, phone calls, answering emails, restocking the shop, cooking a meal when Mandy comes over. But he's behind with the heavy stuff, the lifting and carrying, all the bending and stretching. He's only part way through thinning the trees for a start; it was overreaching with a saw that had him falling ten feet and breaking his wrist.

He leans forward in his chair to pick up his beer with his

good hand. As he is draining the can he hears a rattling at the back of the house. There it is again, someone at the kitchen door. He pulls himself to his feet and staggers out of the room. Before he has time to switch on the kitchen light he is dazzled by a dancing glint of pink torchlight beaming through the window, sending shadows jerking in all directions.

"Mandy?" he shouts across the room. "Is that you?"

The pink light vanishes, he has reached the door, he pushes it open.

"Mandy?" he calls again but realises he is talking to nobody.

He snaps on an outside light. Peers this way and that, sees nothing but the empty back yard and beyond it a line of pine trees with their trunks half-covered in a fog. Suddenly there is a great crashing sound from behind him, somewhere in the house, the shattering of glass. He runs inside, his heart thumping, adrenalin fighting the alcohol in his veins. Back in the living room the window pane has been shattered from the outside, splinters of glass cover the carpet, and into the fug of the room the night air gently drifts between the torn curtains that hang limply like flags of the defeated on a battlefield. Meanwhile the actors in the TV film continue playing their parts, reciting their lines as the music ebbs and flows behind them.

He has no time to react before there is more banging, more smashing of glass, now at the back of the house once again. The outside lamp has been destroyed. He finds the kitchen window in pieces, shards in the sink, over the floor. And somewhere in the pines, hanging in the darkness is the same pink glow. Bobby cannot believe what he is seeing. Finally words trip out of his mouth like they are tied together:

"Is that you, Mandy? What the fuck? What you think you're doing, you madwoman?"

There is no answer from behind the torchlight.

"Mandy!" he yells in desperation.

Silence save for his own heaving breath.

Then the torchlight goes out. Bobby retreats and fumbles for the kitchen light switch. By the time he has found it a figure has advanced from the trees and now stands directly in the square of light thrown into the yard.

"Val!" he gasps. "What the fuck are you doing here?"

She is breathing heavily but manages to reply in a measured tone:

"I am here to ask you the exact same question," she says, lowering her hood.

"You've gone crazy, you mad bitch!" he shouts. "What's all this about?"

She steps towards him, he spots the hammer swinging from her hand and rushes at her before she thinks to strike him. She backs away, surprised to be assaulted, but he's on to her, grabbing her wrist with his good firm hand, forcing her to the ground by his sheer weight. He slaps her face, strikes the side of her head and, grunting like a hog, turns her over, pins her down and then suddenly stops. She is squealing, gasping for breath. She is not fighting back. She might be no threat to him after all.

The first thing Val notices as she wakes up is the taste of blood. Then a stinging sensation in her ear. Then the light searing into her eyes. And the smell of roast chicken reaching her nostrils. She realises she is sitting on a hard wooden chair and her hands are not only bound together behind her back but they are also tied to the seat with what feels like plastic rope. Her wider surroundings come into focus little by little. Her bag slouches by her ankles. She is positioned just a couple of feet from a kitchen table. On it, directly ahead of her, sits an open laptop. Behind its screen she can make out the shapes of the lump hammer and her torch. To the right of the computer, perched on the table with his legs dangling to the ground, is Bobby. He looks shaken. She has seen him like this before. The room is cramped, quiet, the whole house is quiet. Down the hallway the television is now sleeping.

She cannot guess at how effective the torchlight was but she was still pleased with the idea. She had found it at Brico-Jacques: a basic torch with a set of transparent coloured lenses you could screw on over the glass. It was the same principle as with the filters she used with her cameras. The blue one produced a light that was cold and otherworldly, the orange one made everything look warmer but sickly, like a tropical disease. The pink one? Well, that was just perfect: it was the blush of betrayal.

"So, you found me."

It was a voice she doesn't recognise. Until she does.

"I said, well done for finding me."

She doesn't feel much like replying.

"Clever old you," he goes on. "*Old* being the operative word."

"Have you been rehearsing that line?" she sighs, for a moment not even recognising her own voice.

"What are you here for, Val? What do you want?"

"That's another one of *my* questions."

The words on the computer screen are coming into focus: a familiar logo, a familiar font.

"Is this what it's all been about?" she asks.

His eyes follow hers to the home page of her bank's website.

"I'm only after what I'm owed."

"You're not owed a penny."

He shrugs. She can talk but she's in no position to deny him.

"It was my capital," she says, "and you know damn well it was."

He is about to say something but she cuts him off:

"Maybe you should have married me after all, when you had the chance."

He stands up from the table, chooses to move behind it, directly behind the laptop. The table divides them like a barrier should she make him lose his temper.

"I built that business with you. You know I did."

"And then you let me down. You betrayed me, Bobby. More than once."

"So, what, you track me down, come round here and break up the place? That's your idea of revenge?"

"Just paying you back."

She cannot tell if his look is one of regret or contempt. On a series of hooks beneath a shelf behind him a line of mugs has come into focus. One has the Aston Martin badge on it. It's the one he left behind. No, it's a different colour. He has bought himself a replacement.

"Was it you with all the others in town?" she picks up.

"The others?"

"The other acts of vandalism? You were haunting other innocent people, not just me? Spray painting that Porsche – that really was low. And poor Madame Motta?"

Another shrug.

"They were distractors, of course they were. You were the only one that counted for anything."

"So, you creep back to France and try to unsettle me. Scare me half to death. Until I work out it's not some zombie criminal, it's the man I shared a bed with for nearly twenty years!"

"I wanted you to sell up. Spook you into it. I could get my hands on the money that way."

She shakes her head and sighs.

"It was you with the dead bird, yeah? And the black hood? You knew Barachet's story as well as I did. You even tried to read his book, didn't you? Did you ever get past page one, Bobby?"

His eyes harden.

"You're not in a position to make jokes, Val. You'll not be joking when Mandy gets here."

"Ah, Mandy. Or is it Manz? That her smoochie name, is it, Manz?"

He looks away. The broken window catches his eye, the splinters poking out from the smashed frame like a cartoon explosion. She knows how to use a lump hammer, he'll give her that. And she is still speaking:

"It didn't work, though, did it?"

"Did what?"

"You couldn't make it work, not on your own. I didn't

226

budge. Not even the second time, when you got Ringer involved."

"*She* came to *me*," he says, turning to face her again. "She has her own agenda. She has her own reasons for hating you."

"So, what, this time *she* was Merel? And you didn't just move Rosette off the wall, this time you stole her. You actually stole her. She put a bit more lead in your pencil, did she, Mandy? You've always needed a woman to tell you what to do, Bobby, haven't you? It's Bob now, right? Mandy and Bob. Isn't she a bit old for you? The attraction of seventeen-year-olds wearing thin?"

The yellow light of the single bulb does him no favours, highlighting wrinkles, casting shadows below his brow, over his flushed cheekbones, his jaw. His lovely hair is starting to recede.

"I like an experienced woman," he retorts. "I fell for you, didn't I?"

Val's mask offers a smile. She shuffles on her seat, the rope chafing her wrists, the muscles across her shoulders starting to burn.

"What's her agenda?" she persists. "She wants to pay me back, does she? She thinks that I put her inside? Did she tell you about me stalking her and that schoolboy? And, what, you said great, you'd help her stalk me back? Was that how it was? And what is it now? Is she happy with theft or does she want to do me real harm? Injure me, Bobby? Or something worse?"

"You can ask her yourself. But go easy on the jokes. She has a nasty side to her," he says, raising his wounded arm.

"She did that?"

"That's my joke," he laughs.

He is walking round to her side of the table. He taps on the computer.

"You can make it easy for yourself if you open up your account for us. I see you've finally changed your password. Lifetime habits broken, Val? You really must be cracking up."

He is crouching behind her, his mouth inches from her ear.

"We'll take that sixty grand for starters," he whispers. His breath smells of beer and salted peanuts.

"You're too late," she says. "It's gone."

"Gone?"

"Gone. I transferred it."

"You're bluffing."

"Try me."

Bobby stands back a moment.

"Open it up."

"I'll need my phone. My files. For the security. I don't remember the new codes."

He has retreated further into the shadows.

"Mandy will be here soon. I'll wait."

"Wait? What for? Her permission? Be a big boy, Bobby. Take the initiative for once. Won't it look good if you're in control of the situation when she rocks up? Won't she be impressed?"

He steps closer again, unable to stop himself raising his voice:

"You can't help yourself, can you? Can you? You've belittled me ever since I've known you. That's why I love Mandy. She's not like that. She's not like you, Val."

"You love her? You've only known her five minutes."

"Six months. We've been together six months."

Val digests this detail, eyes fixed on the web page, moving words floating in its margins advertising loans and mortgage offers.

"Listen," she says, "are we going to do this thing? You can undo this bloody rope for a start. We're not in some gangster movie."

She's right. The bondage thing was a bit over the top. He unties her and, alert to any unwise actions, watches her touch the dried blood around her lip, then fish around in her bag for her mobile phone. It takes her longer than it should to find it, then she deliberately struggles to open the thing.

"Sorry, you're making me nervous."

Eventually she finds the secure file where her passwords are kept. She hesitates. When he sees that she isn't kidding, that the account really has been emptied, he's going to explode. The phone screen goes blank. Bobby is standing over her. She sighs loudly.

"Sorry. It does that. I think it's the battery."

Suddenly another phone rings and he looks past her into the hallway. It's the house landline ringing loud and true. This is her chance.

In the glare of her car headlights at the bottom of the hill Amanda Ringer is standing by the five-bar gate, banging the padlock against the catch. In frustration she is shouting into her phone:

"Bob? Bob, it's me! What have you put a bloody lock on the gate for?"

"A lock? I haven't even been down there. The gate should be open."

"Well, somebody's put a padlock on it. I can't get the car through. You got some bolt cutters up there?"

"Somewhere I do. Can't remember exactly where, anyway, I can't leave the lodge, I can't leave her up here on her own, Mandy, she's here, we've got a visitor…"

"What? Bob, you're gabbling. Slow down."

"I said she's here, she was smashing the place up…"

"*Who's* there?"

"Val, who do you think?"

"Val? So, the bitch has found us? Saves us looking for her."

"I've got her on the laptop opening the account."

"No, don't do anything yet. Wait for me. I'll have to walk up. I'll be up in a sec."

"Mind how you go. It's got misty up here."

"Has it? It's clear down this side. Hang on, two minutes, okay?"

"She's on her way."

Bobby has reappeared in the kitchen.

"On foot. Your padlock, yeah?"

Val has nothing to say. She heard his half of the conversation. From the gate to the house is a brisk walk of one and a half minutes.

"She's in a foul mood," he is saying. "The only thing to pacify her is transferring that money. Here's where to."

He slips a piece of paper showing groups of numbers on to the table. She has restarted her phone and reluctantly shuffles forward to access the account.

"Sorry about the mess in your living room," she says.

As he looks back in that direction she lifts up the laptop and hurls it at his head, grabs her bag, the torch off the table and bolts for the door. Bobby is knocked off balance, he curses, feels blood trickle from behind his ear. He turns to see her dashing out of his kitchen into the mist.

"Come back, you fuck!"

She hears his screams, then his footsteps behind her but she knows she's already out of sight. She is running in a blind panic, left then right, through lines of caravans, now dark, heavy shapes like great coffins floating on a sea of fog. She slows, turns her head to look back: the lights of the house are already invisible. She needs to find a way back down the hill but the lane is somewhere back behind the house. If she can find some trees she will trace a path back through the woods.

She has stopped running, out of breath. Surely the caravans were lined up at a different angle this morning? She presses on. She's on the flat crest of the hill, the gradient offers no clue as to which way is down. And the more ground she covers the mistier it gets. She switches on her torch and its pink light, instead of piercing the fog with a sharp beam, is diffused uselessly into a flat rosy glow. All she knows for certain is that the caravans have disappeared and, with sweat dripping into her eyes, she is walking on a path of grit and sand.

*

The anxiety that Amanda Ringer is harbouring as she follows the kerb lights up the slope is multiplied as the shattered windows at the front of the lodge come into view. She peeps in through the curtains, sees the beer cans surrounded by shards of glass.

"Bob?" she calls out, bursting in through the front door. "Where are you? Where is she?"

Her questions are left unanswered. The staircase is in darkness. She heads into the kitchen where she comes across the smell of roasted chicken and a scene of some confusion: a broken computer lies on the floor, there is a tipped-up chair bound with plastic rope, a shattered window frame and sitting alone at the centre of the table is a wooden-handled lump hammer that she has never seen before.

"Bob? Bob!" she cries again.

He's lost her. He's lost control. She told him to do nothing and to wait for her. Now he's out there like an idiot in the fog trying to reel her back in. Ringer takes a torch from her backpack and heads outside, up towards the car park, listening for voices. The fog is thicker up here, the air hangs heavy and still. A few minutes later she hears footsteps on gravel and then Bob's despairing voice: *Val! Come back inside!* She veers in the direction of the sounds but will make no noise of her own. She will catch the bitch by stealth.

Bobby has headed through the caravans, guided by the scuff of footsteps and the fuzzy pink ball of light which disappears then reappears.

"Val! Come back inside!" he yells through the mist.

He knows better than she does that she is heading towards the coast path. The pink light has gone again.

"Val!" he screams. "Come back here! Follow my voice! Don't go near the cliff edge! Val! The path is dangerous!"

Val hears his shouts. If he is on the coast path warning her off, then the opposite direction will surely take her back towards the caravans. She finds herself stepping into damp, tufty grass. She flicks her torch back on.

Bobby is at his wits' end. Why doesn't she answer him? He knows exactly where he is. It's the spot where the abandoned path runs out and falls away ninety feet down broken ledges to the beach. There are marker posts somewhere that the volunteers put up.

"Val!" he calls out again.

And then suddenly there are two pink lights in the mist, one to his right, the other, much closer, to his left. Two lights but only one set of footsteps scuffing the stones. A post looms up at him and he grabs it with his good hand. A moment later he spots her outline staggering towards him.

"Come away from the edge! Grab me!" he shouts, leaning towards her. It is a fateful move. She is knocked off balance, loses her footing and frantically reaches out to claw at his plaster arm.

"Bob! What you doing?" screams Mandy. "What the hell, I'm falling!"

"Mandy? Grab hold of my arm!"

He twists away from the stake.

"No, this one! Mandy! My hand!"

"Help me!" she cries.

He leans towards her, over the rim, sees the terror in her eyes, hears the scraping as the loose rock gives way, her fingertips twitching helplessly, too far from his own.

"Bob! No!"

Her cries fade as her body slips and falls, followed by invisible stones and clumps of chalky earth, catching a shallow ledge, dropping again and again as a tiny pink flare burns out and is lost in the fog.

Val had heard his warnings, then the woman's shrieks ripping through the cloud, she had seen the fading firefly. She headed towards the noise and before long she stumbled across what looked like the shape of a child. She discovered Bobby crouching, squatting on the damp shale, clasping the wooden post to his chest as if it were a holy relic. He was trembling, muttering to himself, maybe he was sobbing, she could not tell. Her torch bathed him in an infernal haze.

She switched it off, stood over him, placed a hand on his shoulder. It took him a moment to acknowledge her.

"It was an accident," he said softly. "It was an accident."

"Of course it was."

"You don't know that!" he shouted, suddenly angry, as if she'd intruded into his private grief. "You weren't here. You couldn't have seen."

Without warning he was on his feet, walking towards the edge.

"She might be alive down there." He was talking to himself.

"Not with that drop," said Val, but he wasn't listening.

"I'm going down. She needs me."

"Leave it, Bobby."

"I'm going down!"

"You'll kill yourself. Come away. Bobby, please."

"I'm going down."

"Bobby!"

She pulled on his sleeve. Wordlessly, still looking out to the invisible sea, he let her slowly guide him on to the grass.

"Let the police deal with it."

"The police? They might say I pushed her," he said, facing her with anguish in his eyes.

"It was a terrible accident," Val insisted. "It's obvious."

"They might, they might say I pushed her."

"You wouldn't do that, Bobby."

"They might *say* I did."

"They might say *I* did. I had more of a motive than you."

Bobby had sat down again by the marker post, facing the void, looking out into the floating fog, out towards to cliff.

"She'll have plaster under her nails. She was scratching at my arm. Oh, Val. What have we done?"

He stared across at her, still shaking, holding his injured arm tight to his chest.

"I would never do that," he said.

"Do what?"

"Lie, lie that it was you who pushed her. I would never do that, Val."

"No. I know you wouldn't."

"I never hated you, Val."

He took a deep, tormented breath.

"The only person I hated was myself."

Val took a step away. Surrounded by the clouds of mist, they were in a bubble of their own, isolated and invisible and had been for too long. There was no sound beyond their breathing, not even a murmur from the sea. She picked out her phone, made the call to the emergency services, gave the police the padlock code.

"Your birthday," said Bobby, listening in.

"Not very original. One I've used before."

He was on his feet now, and took her hand in his.

"I'm sorry I made your lip bleed."

She smiled. She had forgotten it was ever bleeding.

"Come on, Bobby, let's get inside. You're shivering."

A minute later they were walking on concrete, skirting the top car park; their hands had fallen apart.

"The saddest part …" he said, suddenly stopping in his tracks. She noticed the tears welling in his eyes, heard the pain in his crackling voice as he stammered out the rest:

"The worst of it, really the saddest part is that she was expecting our baby. It's true, Val. She was, she was expecting our little baby."

CHAPTER 12

RUNAWAY

SIX MOIS PLUS TARD / *SIX MONTHS LATER*

It was not so strange, during Val's final evening in Saint-Benoît-en-Sologne, that she found out the truth about her neighbour from somebody who lived on the other side of town. In the spirit of enduring friendship Greta Barachet had invited her for a sentimental last supper, accompanied, as it turned out, by two of her husband's very best bottles of Nuits-Saint-Georges. Clément had insisted that he was delighted to select a couple of his finest in her honour.

"Sylvie Motta?" Greta had said, as the future of *Les Genêts* was raised. "I'm not surprised you haven't seen her, dearie. She's been in and out of hospital for the best part of a year."

The Scotswoman explained that she knew the woman's sister-in-law through a regular customer in the dress shop.

"She's had breast cancer. With complications, sadly. She had chemo on and off for months. Anyway, no, it's good news, we think. She's come through it, is on the mend, touch wood, and has been recuperating since around Easter with her daughter in Paris."

"I didn't know she had a daughter."

"She left the area years ago when she got married."

Val felt guilty that she had made such little effort to talk to Madame Motta, especially after her husband had passed on, but the truth was that the woman had become a cantankerous widow of very few words. Her illness would only have made her more dispirited. It was partly to make herself feel better that Val had written her neighbour a card and posted it through her letterbox first thing that morning. It was most unlikely that she would ever see her again but she was keen to leave a warm message and write a proper farewell.

So, as far as Val was concerned, she had said her final goodbyes to Greta and Clément at their house the night before. Yet here they were again, their oversized car blocking her drive, walking towards her hand in hand with smiles on their faces. Ominously, Greta was carrying a compact cool box; a little self-conscious, she looked like she was transporting an emergency supply of rare blood.

"One for the road, dearie?" she called, shielding her eyes from the sun.

"What are *you* doing back in my life already?" grinned Val.

"We couldn't let you go without one more hug," replied her friend.

"My wife is hoping you might relent and take her with you," said Barachet, deadpan.

"Give you some peace, you mean?" quipped Greta, setting the box on the ground and opening it to reveal a bottle of champagne, three crystal flutes and several large slices of fruit cake.

"Dundee," she confirmed. "Home-made, of course. I think I baked one for you before, Val, years ago. My grandmother's recipe."

"Well, thanks, but you needn't have done this. I'm glad

you brought your own glasses. Everything's packed up, or already gone."

"We knew that. You can eat the cake out of your hands."

"*Eh bien, Valérie*," said Barachet, walking around the loaded Mégane and its little trailer attached, "You look like you're ready to go."

"Another hour and you'd have missed me."

The champagne popped open and half a dozen birds flew up into the sky from their morning roosts.

"That's the sound we like to hear!" said Greta, filling the glasses.

"Just half a glass for me, thanks," warned Val. "I've got a long drive ahead of me."

Everything had fallen into place since the start of the year. Without any thought to the consequences, her artist friend Rosée had mentioned that her father, a photographer of renown and something of a mentor to Val in the days when they had first arrived in Brittany, was retiring. It took only two or three days for her to turn this piece of news into a plan for the next stage in her life. There was still paperwork to be signed and processed, but the top and bottom of it was that Val was buying his business: a shop, studio and first-floor apartment in the medieval heart of Quimper. All being well she would be able to afford a modest place on the coast as well. A view of the Atlantic but nothing too fancy, just room for one. Maybe a second bedroom for guests.

"You'll visit, won't you, Gret, come and see Finistère?"

They had talked about it last night.

"If I do it'll be on my own, dearie," had come the reply. "Clément won't come, will you, *chéri*?"

A shake of the head from her husband.

"He's not keen on the coast. Any coast. He gets vertigo or

agoraphobia or seasickness or even a combination of the three."

Val was just as excited about it all as she had been fifteen years earlier when she had moved to the Sologne with her young lover. That part of her life was over now. The charm of the forests and lakes, the secret stillness, the sun's rays filtering through the trees, burning away the mists, all that had worn off. She had enough photographs of this mysterious part of the country to fill a dozen books.

She had always been happy in Brittany. Rosée was thrilled that she was returning, *coming home*, she had said. And Val was looking forward to nothing with more pleasure than spending time with her godson, Val, rarely Valentin. *He's dying to meet you, Val!* She was one for exaggeration, was Rosée. *He's already loving his paints. You know, getting his little hands in all the colours. I can see his talent already!*

She helped herself to a slice of cake, caught Barachet's eye and chinked glasses. What a treasure he had been. The man had proved a beacon of moral support around the time of the harrowing inquest into Mandy Roundtree's fatal tumble. Greta, too, it went without saying.

Bobby and Val had been interviewed independently and at length by the police. Open wounds on both their parts were prodded and probed, statements corroborated by the *commissariat* in Blois. Mercifully the investigators concluded there was no evidence of foul play in the death of the woman discovered at the foot of the cliffs and neither was charged. Later Val had given evidence at the hearings at the end of which the coroner recorded a verdict of accidental death. Bobby was obliged to speak too, of course, suddenly ten years older, hollowed out by his own testimony. Even more than his unflinchingly sombre expression, what had left the most pitiful impression on her was the face of

Simon Ringer, as wan as the December sky, a father broken under the tension between grief and disbelief. Across the courtroom she had seen lemon-juice tears behind his thick-rimmed glasses. In a heavy, dark suit, white collar and tightly knotted bottle green tie, he listened in distraction to the witness statements, the summaries and finally the verdict. Val knew it was cowardly but she had avoided eye contact. The last thing the poor man needed was consolation from a woman with two names who had deceived him in his own home just forty-eight hours before his daughter's death. He had thought she was a friend returning a book. He had offered to make her a slice of toast and marmalade. His wife Julie sat next to him, as stiff as a mannequin, clasping a handbag on her lap like life support, complexion like chalk.

Bobby and Val came to a mutual agreement over the damages caused and they were both willing to draw a line. They had shaken hands like a couple of mismatched politicians going through the diplomatic motions, both fully aware of the significance of that line. It was an end to hostilities, an end to a long partnership, and it was the very end of their journey.

Val and Bobby, Bobby and Val: the end.

Secondly there was the matter of the tarnished international uncoupling. *The shift in your country's arrangements with continental Europe will have no bearing on your right to continue to live in France*, Barachet had advised her. He was both sad and incredulous at the outcome. *Not sad for Britain, nor particularly even for France*, he had said, *but sad for Europe*. All Val understood was that half of the country had voted for something else. Meanwhile he had pointed her in the direction of the *carte de séjour*, helped her fill in the application and put her mind at rest.

Finally the house sale, where his expertise and local contacts had made the process much less fraught than she had expected. Only a handful of prospective buyers had visited *Les Genêts* in the early months of the year but they were all genuinely interested. At the end of March, Henning and Laurent had pounced on it and they had been a pleasure to do business with.

"Henning!" Val called over the oleander. "Come and join us in a glass of champagne."

Henning and Laurent had been living in the gîte for the past week – a temporary arrangement while Val tied up all her loose ends. They told her they had met on a hospitality management course in Switzerland. Henning from Denmark, Laurent from a wealthy family in Blois, this was to be their first business venture together. They were brimming with excitement, so many plans. *We like how you have the gîte, Val, but we have so many plans!* And one very major plan to get married next summer. So wise, thought Val, but she had kept her comment to herself. She'd wished them good luck with everything, assured them that her regulars were bound to keep coming. She felt confident that she was leaving the place in safe hands. Both were personable, engaging and, in their different ways, attractive. Especially Henning, with his sun-kissed skin, his Baltic blue eyes and the shapeliest of backsides, but who was clearly a lost cause. A Dane and a Frenchman, the one blond the other dark-haired, a Viking and a Gaul, a lovely pair of boys with eyes only for each other. Boys? They shared an energetic youthfulness but were probably both touching thirty. Val had sighed at the thought.

"Have some cake too," insisted Greta. "Where's your friend?"

"Laurent is in Blois this morning," said Henning, helping himself from the cool box.

"Oh, Val," he went on, turning to her. "Did I tell you about our latest idea?"

"What's that?"

"We're going to put a swimming pool over there in the garden."

They both looked over to the middle of the lawn, neglected like the rest of the outdoor space. Once she knew she was selling up, Val's heart had no longer been in it. She knew exactly where Henning had in mind: the scrubby patch where the chicken run had stood. A swimming pool. Val raised her eyebrows in surprise but she could remember a time when she and Bobby had themselves talked about the exact same project. It had never got much beyond talk, though, as they never quite had the money for it. She wondered what Rosette would have thought, having a large tiled basin sunk into the ground where the chickens once strutted and clucked and scratched at breadcrumbs. And Widow Merel too. Could she ever have imagined English families frolicking in a pool on that spot, splashing and squealing and tossing about gaudily coloured inflatables imported from China?

Suddenly a bird flew down and landed precisely where her gaze had fallen. A blackbird. It seemed to be looking up at her, inquisitive, judgmental, just for a second or two, before it took off and disappeared over the golden froth of the broom.

"*Une idée formidable!*" declared Barachet, offering a top-up of champagne which Henning did not refuse.

"We think we have found a contractor," he said, "who can start digging the hole for us early next month."

*

It was already midday. There had been the theatrics of the final hugs – *no tears, please, today* – and Val stood alone looking at the house that had been her home – *their* home – for so many years. The car was full, the trailer stuffed with odd-shaped boxes tied as securely as possible with a length of old plastic rope that Bobby had left behind. It was fraying in more than one place and she did not trust it to last the five hundred kilometres to Quimper. Before she got properly on her way she had two stops to make. Firstly at Maxi-marché for a tankful of petrol. And secondly at Brico-Jacques, the emporium of everything. She would buy a tarpaulin to keep her life's possessions dry – showers were forecast further west – and some bungee cords to keep them contained. Dear Barachet had been happy to provide the French words: what she needed was a multipack of heavy-duty elasticated restrainers, or *tendeurs élastiques*.

And if in the course of her five minutes in and out of the largest shop in Saint-Benoît she bumps into her former employee Florian (which she will), if he still works there (which he does), she will be no more or less embarrassed than him.

The young man will look up from his task, smile and fix her with his clear blue eyes. He will run his hands through his wild thatch of hair and open his mouth to speak.

"It's water under the bridge," he will remark sagely, "you and me, Madame Val."

And he will add, with an unaffected grin of pride, that he has a new girlfriend these days. They've been together for nearly a year. She's called Amira and she works in a supermarket. A girl his own age. Her birthday's the day after his. There's just twelve months between them.

AUTHOR'S NOTES

Inappropriate Behaviour is my fifth novel and the first to have a female character at its heart. My other books all feature strong and significant women, notably Erika Fleet, Geena Dale, Columbine Snow, Amande Puybonieux and Mally Shore but each of them is to some extent presented as a foil for the words and deeds of a male protagonist. Finally, perhaps belatedly, I offer the reader a woman to follow, to support, sympathise with, worry about, get angry with and maybe forgive.

Val first appeared eight years ago, in a short story I wrote about an English teacher travelling to France with a teen-age pupil and a British expat who recognises them, spies on them and is torn about whether or not to report them to the authorities. The story was called *Runaways* and was reworked with very little change as the opening chapter of this novel. I based it on the well-publicised news story of a thirty-year-old English maths teacher, Jeremy Forrest, who in September 2012 took a fifteen-year-old schoolgirl to France and who was arrested in Bordeaux after eight days on the run. I twisted the male-female roles, slightly altered the age difference and had them marking time and hiding in plain sight on a campsite in the Sologne at the height of the summer season. I leave the reader to infer to what degree sexual politics have a role in the story. As a former teacher I was more curious to consider the mind-set of someone who must know that their actions will jeopardise or more likely destroy a career that presumably was dear to them, not to mention the effect on the child.

Nevertheless, having set up this scenario I quickly realised that it was in fact the character of the witness, the spy, that interested me the most. Val took over the story and yet at the end of *Runaways* she was still only partly developed. One of the reasons I returned to her was to give her a fully-fledged central role in a novel, along with her long-time partner Bobby, and to expand the themes thrown up in *Runaways* of trust and betrayal. The format of a novel also gave me the chance to explore in more depth the teacher's motivation and how she might react to having, in her mind at least, a single person to blame for her arrest.

Although all my stories are very different, the one from the other, *Inappropriate Behaviour* is closest in spirit to *An English Impressionist* in its dual setting, in each case primarily in a part of rural France. I enjoyed writing the tale of Trevor John Penny's life in the Dordogne so much and wanted to recreate that sense of an English character living abroad, giving the reader something familiar yet foreign, something slightly exotic. In *Inappropriate Behaviour* the Sologne provides a rarely visited backdrop. More or less an extensive triangle of flat land unfolding south of the Loire between the towns of Orléans and Blois and descending to a point at Bourges, it is a quiet area of lakes and forests dotted with isolated villages. A town the size of the fictional Saint-Benoît does not really exist in its heart; I transposed a version of the real town of Lamotte-Beuvron, home of the famous Tarte Tatin and situated on the north-south axis D2020 (quite appropriate for the year of publication), about thirty kilometres further west into the middle of the vast woodlands.

The preference in France for renovation rather than demolition and rebuilding makes it easier to imagine life in rural villages as it was eighty years ago. As with *An English Impressionist*, I wanted to give Val's surroundings their particular sense of history and in this case the reference point was the German occupation and the activities of the local members of the Résistance in the year 1942. The story of Widow Merel allowed me to give historical depth to the novel, to introduce the imperative of history repeating itself and, just as importantly, to heighten its dramatic potential. Principally, however, this is a modern novel and for its finale I brought the story much closer to home, namely to an England on the cusp of leaving the European Union and specifically to the Dorset coast whose breath-taking section of the South West path I have often walked.

I completed the book with the help of the same team that has guided me through previous projects, and so in conclusion I wish to express my gratitude once again for advice, suggestions and good humour in both the editing process and publication to Warren Shore and, at Honeybee Books, Chella Adgopul.

Brent Shore

September 2020

ABOUT THE AUTHOR

Brent Shore grew up in Hyde, a small town on the eastern edges of Manchester. He studied Modern Languages at the University of Nottingham, where he also trained as a teacher. Following a varied career which took him via North Yorkshire and Bermuda finally to Dorset, he now channels much of his energy into writing fiction, both contemporary and historical.

He has published five novels:

Shillingstone Station (2015)

Bailing Out (2016)

An English Impressionist (2018)

Blessèd are the Meek (2019)

Inappropriate Behaviour (2020)

Visit: www.brentshore.co.uk

Contact: stories@brentshore.co.uk

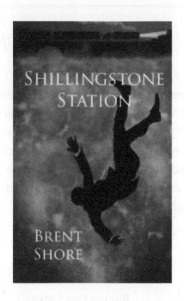

Andris Fleet's life has been damned by self-doubt and insecurity ever since he was left lame by a mother who had no inclination to care for him and fatherless by a conspiracy to murder in the interests of national security. As his mother admits: *Little Andris, poor lamb, he was born into a cess pool of deceit.*

Less of a spy story than one of the *generational consequences* of spying (and lying), **Shillingstone Station** gives the reader a mystery to solve, the coat-tails of a blighted biography to hang on to, and, in the end, a very human tale of resilience, warmth and forgiveness.

From the author of *SHILLINGSTONE STATION*

BAILING OUT

BRENT SHORE

Retirement from the police force and the accidental death of his wife have conspired to turn Don Percey's world upside down; he finds himself at the most isolated, loneliest point in his life and yet, bizarrely, also at his wealthiest. Resolved to do something genuinely noble, he becomes involved in the lives of a poor Dorset family from a run-down pocket of social housing – with brutal consequences.

Elements of a whodunnit, a fragile romance and a family tragedy create the fabric of **Bailing Out**, a story of generosity and judgement, of compassion and of risk.

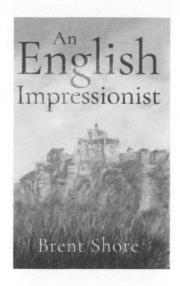

Following a series of misdemeanours, Trevor John Penny, working class boy reinvented as an Oxford-educated lecturer, has had his ambitions thwarted. He fetches up in an academic backwater in the Dordogne where he finds a little-known cultural treasure chest and an enchanting American student, and both can change his fortunes for the better. The discovery of five sublime yet mysterious paintings in a Somerset barn raises the stakes and Penny must decide what is truly important in his life.

An English Impressionist is a moving novel about literature, art and family secrets, and – just below the surface – vanity, deception and revenge.

Blessèd are the Meek

Brent Shore

The Plug Riots of the 1840s: violent, significant steps on working people's long road towards justice and equality.

Based on historical truth, *Blessèd are the Meek* reflects on the life of a man who lived through these times: James Shore, a machine mender in the cotton mills of Hyde, seven miles to the east of Manchester. Politicised by poverty and injustice, he became a Chartist, a rioter and a convict but his story amounts to far more than that of a lengthy prison sentence. A son, a husband and a father, he was a man who sacrificed his freedom for the prize of equality, who glimpsed its light in the distance, but who was born too early to bask in its glow.

All titles are available at the Shop at

www.brentshore.co.uk

BV - #0069 - 301120 - C0 - 203/127/15 - PB - 9781913675066